A Brother's Oath
A Warlord's Bargain
A King's Legacy

The Rebel and the Runaway

*Novellas*
The Visitor at Anningley Hall (a prequel to M. R.
James's 'The Mezzotint')

www.christhorndycroft.wordpress.com

## *As P. J. Thorndyke*

*The Lazarus Longman Chronicles*
On Rails of Gold – A Prequel to Golden Heart
Golden Heart
Silver Tomb
Onyx Town

www.pjthorndyke.wordpress.com

# A WARLORD'S BARGAIN

## CHRIS THORNDYCROFT

A Warlord's Bargain
By Chris Thorndycroft

2015 by Copyright © Chris Thorndycroft

www.christhorndycroft.wordpress.com

*For Maia for her constant encouragement and my parents for their unwavering support*

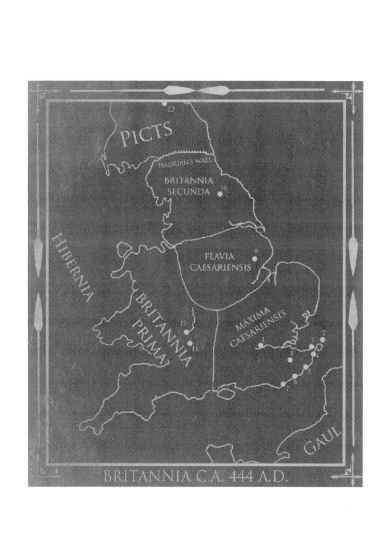

PICTS

HADRIAN'S WALL

BRITANNIA
SECUNDA

HIBERNIA

FLAVIA
CAESARIENSIS

BRITANNIA
PRIMA

MAXIMA
CAESARIENSIS

GAUL

BRITANNIA C.A. 444 A.D.

# Place names

| | Latin | British | Anglo Saxon | Modern English |
|---|---|---|---|---|
| | Britannia | Albion | Britta | Britain |
| | Hibernia | Eire | | Ireland |
| | Cantium | Ceint | Cent | Kent |
| 1 | Londinium | | Lundenwic | London |
| 2 | Tanatus | | Thanet | Thanet |
| 3 | Regulbium | | Raculf | Reculver |
| 4 | Rutupiae | | | Richborough |
| 5 | Dubris | | Dofras | Dover |
| 6 | Lemanis | | | Lympne |
| 7 | Anderitum | | Anderida | Pevensey |
| 8 | Durovernum Cantiacorum | | Cantwareburh | Canterbury |
| 9 | Lindum | | | Lincoln |
| 10 | Eboracum | Cair Ebruac | Eoforwic | York |
| 11 | Corinium Dobunnorum | | | Cirencester |
| 12 | Glevum | Cair Gloui | | Gloucester |
| 13 | | Din Eidyn | | Edinburgh |

*"This year Marcian and Valentinian assumed the empire, and reigned seven winters. In their days Hengest and Horsa, invited by Wurtgern, king of the Britons to his assistance, landed in Britain in a place that is called Ipwinesfleet; first of all to support the Britons, but they afterwards fought against them. The king directed them to fight against the Picts; and they did so; and obtained the victory wheresoever they came"* - The Anglo Saxon Chronicle

# PART I

*(Đorn) "Đorn byþ ðearle scearp; ðegna gehwylcum anfeng ys yfyl, ungemetum reþe manna gehwelcum, ðe him mid resteð."*

(Thorn) "The thorn is exceedingly sharp, an evil thing for any knight to touch, uncommonly severe on all who sit among them."

South East Britain, 447 A.D.

# Horsa

The white caps heaved and belched spume as the *Bloodkeel* cut through the water. The distant island of Thanet drifted nearer like a grey hump rising from the waves. Horsa the Jute, exiled son of an ealdorman, barked orders and his men heaved on the oars with all the power in their arms. He gripped the bulwarks, his heart pounding to the drumbeat of the coxswain. His nostrils flared, drinking in the salty spray and the cold wind; the thrill of the chase beating its barbaric rhythm deep within him.

The little trader, not more than a league ahead, struggled to outrun its pursuer and make for the island where its crew hoped to skirt the coastline and lose it. The merchant vessel was fast, accustomed to the constant threat of raiders in this stretch of water; being the narrowest trade route between Britta and Gaul. But it could never hope to outrun the tightly disciplined and well experienced raiders that chased it.

Following close behind the *Bloodkeel* was the *Raven*, matching the speed of its companion ship stroke for stroke. At its stern stood Hengest, brother to Horsa, his flaxen hair billowing about in the wind. Horsa grinned. He could almost see the queasy look on his brother's face across the water. Hengest was no seaman and the constant rising and falling of the deck beneath his feet always made him feel sick, despite the sea having largely been their home for the past two years.

Thanet drifted closer and Horsa bellowed an order to increase speed. His men were tired, but they could not lose their prey now. Beyond the island lay Horsa's third ship; the *Fafnir*, which he had won after killing its captain. Under the command of his good friend Asse, the *Fafnir's* crew had pledged loyalty to Horsa and his brother in return for pardon in their part in the kidnapping of Hengest's wife and children.

But that was ancient history. The *Fafnir's* crew had proven their worth a dozen times over in the two years of raiding that had followed. Hidden from view, the forty-manned vessel would emerge just as the trader tried to round the tip of the island, blocking its path and forcing it to tack. That would give the *Bloodkeel* and the *Raven* enough time to catch up with it and board it before it passed Thanet.

"Keep her steady!" Horsa shouted to Beorn, his first mate. "Keep on the headland!"

The trader was almost rounding the tip now and Horsa could see the men aboard it, scurrying back and forth, tossing items overboard to lighten the load. It would be no use, no matter how much they were able to increase their speed. The trap was set. There was no escape.

The dragon prow of a ship appeared around the headland. Its carven grimace leered like some nightmarish creature. The merchant vessel quickly tacked, its sail tilted to direct the craft as the new ship soared towards them, threatening to slam into their side.

*Too soon!* Horsa gritted his teeth. *Blast that Asse!*

But as he watched, he realised that the new ship was not the *Fafnir*. It was some other vessel outfitted for raiding.

"Who, by all the souls in Waelheall...?" he exclaimed.

And then he recognised that carven figurehead. He had encountered it many times since he and his brother had arrived on the shores of Britta. It was the figurehead of their biggest rival.

"Ceolwulf!" spat Horsa as if it were an oath. "What the blazes is he doing here? And where is the *Fafnir*?"

He watched in dismay as his rival drifted into the path of the trader. Cries of alarm floated to him across the water, mingled with the cheers and shouts of the raiders as their vessel crunched into the side of the trader, splintering timbers and shattering the bulwarks. The crew of the raider latched on grappling hooks and stormed the smaller vessel, swinging blades and cutting the traders down with all the savagery pirates were known for.

"Ship oars!" Horsa called to his crew. "Someone's beaten us to it. Beorn! Drift alongside!"

Beorn the Bald, first mate of the *Bloodkeel* - a massive Angle with a single blond plait of hair hanging down from his otherwise bald head - scrambled to his captain's side. "Who is it?" he asked.

"Ceolwulf."

"But what is he doing this far south? His territory is north of Thanet."

"My thoughts exactly," replied Horsa, his voice sour.

The sheer volume of raiders that plagued the south eastern waters of Britta meant that an agreement was necessary regarding territories. Dictated by the various men of power in the coastal towns and ports who creamed the profits from piracy, each raiding crew was assigned its own area. Transgressions always resulted in bloodshed.

"Your brother hails us," said Beorn.

The *Raven* crept close to the *Bloodkeel* and drifted alongside. Hengest called out; "What's going on?"

"Ceolwulf," Horsa shouted back across the small stretch of water between the two vessels.

"Shall we take him?"

Horsa considered this. The *Fafnir* had still not shown itself and that boded ill. Even with one ship down they still commanded nearly sixty men, but Ceolwulf also had a large force. A sea battle now would be bloody and long with much lost on both sides.

Horsa shook his head at his brother. "Too costly. We'll take this up with Eldred when we get back to port. Coxswain, forward! Beorn, bring us alongside the merchant. Pass him close and quick! We'll at least give that bastard a fright."

The two ships ploughed onwards towards the trader where the fight was still underway. As they drifted closer they could see the bilge of the trader awash with blood. The crew of Ceolwulf spotted them and let out jeers and provocations.

Horsa's men gripped their oars tightly and glared at them, their hands itching for their swords and axes that would bring death to their rivals. But their captain stood, unwavering, his steely eyes cast upon the helmed head of Ceolwulf who laughed and waved his bloody sword in the air, watching them pass. The fallen trader drifted out of view as the *Bloodkeel* and the *Raven* rounded the furthermost edge of Thanet.

6

"It churns in my gut to let those bastards get away with plundering our prize," said Beorn, his hand resting upon the head of his large battleaxe.

"You're not alone in that, old friend," Horsa replied. "But it would be too costly to fight them now when we are one ship down. Let us find Asse and then we can plan our vengeance with clear heads."

Beorn grinned at him. "You get more and more like your brother every day. Back home you would have been the first to jump into battle whatever the odds."

Horsa frowned and turned towards the prow.

"Look!" he cried, flinging out a pointed finger. "There's the *Fafnir*!"

In a small inlet lay the third of Hengest and Horsa's raiding vessels. Its sail was down and several of its oars lay floating in the water nearby. There was no activity onboard.

Horsa had the *Bloodkeel* directed alongside it and stepped aboard, carefully treading between the ugly wreckage. The deck was littered with bodies and blood ran freely in the bilge. The *Raven* dropped anchor at the stern of the ship and Hengest joined him.

"I'm going to gut that Ceolwulf from belly to throat" he said.

Horsa didn't reply. He squatted down by the body of Asse and checked his pulse. He was dead. He sighed heavily. Asse had been a good friend to him. They all had been. He had infiltrated this very crew in order to track down his brother's kidnapped family. They were a rough lot, but he had eventually been accepted by them and had been proud to count himself amongst their number. Now they were all dead.

"Why was he here, Hengest?" Horsa asked. "What business did he have this far south?"

"I don't know," the older brother replied. "Just plain greed, I expect. But by the gods, we shall take this up with Eldred. He can't get away with this."

Horsa nodded. "Take their bodies aboard the *Bloodkeel*," he said to his men. "We'll give them the funerals they deserve when we reach port. Beorn, take ten men and crew the *Fafnir*. We'll head back to Rutupiae and count our losses."

# Hengest

The settlements of the south east coast were dominated by the towering walls of the massive shore forts that had been built by the Romans during their final days. These rectangular outposts with their rounded towers had been something of a last ditch attempt to protect the island against the tide of Germanic raiders that had broken upon it when Roman control over Britta had been in its death throes.

With the legions now gone, the very people the forts had been built to repulse were free to live within the frowning shadows of their walls, and they did so, mocking the British authorities like errant children might misbehave under the stern eyes of a bedridden parent. Once they had been bitter enemies, but now Briton lived side by side with Saxon, Jute and Angle.

The town of Rutupiae had once been the main port of the province and the gateway to Britta itself. Much of the old settlement had been demolished to build the fortress walls that now surrounded it. The stones of the triumphal arch that had straddled the main road to Londinium and the bricks that had made up the old amphitheatre were now part of the deep walls of the fortress that overlooked the shabby town.

Rutupiae was now a mixture of styles both Roman and Germanic. The plaster walls and red tiled roofs of the late empire survived beneath a veneer of timber and thatch constructed by the settlers from across the sea. The muddy cobbles of the streets rang with a myriad of tongues and accents. In addition to the Latin speech of the merchants and clergy, there was the Celtic language of the native Britons, and the air had a distinct Germanic flavour in the form of Frisian, Angle, Jutish, Saxon and even Danish tongues, all squabbling for dominance in the crowded marketplaces where bread, meats, fruits and fish lined the stalls. Oysters, for which the town was famously credited by the Roman poet Luvenalis, were hauled in everyday and sold by the wagon full.

Wine shops, ale houses and brothels were wedged between ramshackle buildings that festered amongst the heaps of refuse and human waste that even the heavy autumn rains could never fully dissipate. Whores sold themselves in broad daylight and crippled beggars lay slumped in the gutters whilst scrawny, feral children played and fought in the streets. Temples and altars reflecting a myriad of gods and religions were scattered throughout the settlement. Most of the British population was Christian and their priests could often be seen standing on street corners, waving their crucifixes about and shouting themselves hoarse, commanding the Germanic portion of the townsfolk to repent their evil pagan ways, and convert to the worship of the Christ-messiah.

The lack of any sort of official governing body in the wake of the Roman withdrawal over twenty years previously only added to the chaos. The old Roman mansio which had been the main administrative building in days gone by had fallen into ruin and was inhabited only by rats and beggars. The military fortifications were abandoned and anything representing law and justice was absent.

That just left Eldred.

Eldred was an Angle whose family had settled in Britta during the early days of the Roman withdrawal. A shrewd business man and slippery as an eel, Eldred began by setting up his own gold lending business, progressing to extortion and murder in record time and, before he was forty, he had the entire town in the palm of his hand. There was a similar story in every town in that part of the land. Without any form of law and the remnants of the Romano-British ruling class cowering in their villas further west, it fell to the various criminal gangs to orchestrate order on the east coast.

But Eldred's influence extended beyond the straggling outskirts of Rutupiae. Once he had bullied and extorted the fishing trade into his control, he set his sights upon the various raiders who operated throughout the waters between Britta and Gaul. Building a power base of tough rogues and bloodthirsty profiteers, Eldred had set about organising the pirates and distributing territory to various captains whilst creaming the profits from their activities. The criminal rulers of the other towns looked to Eldred as something of a leader and it was to him that all disputes concerning territory were put.

Eldred operated out of an old bakery in the town. It was a large building that had once provided bread for most of the town's populace. Now it had been converted into something of a tavern with its great stone ovens housing barrels of Gaulish wine looted from merchant vessels and kegs of mead and ale. A wooden stairway led to an upper floor which was an extension in the Germanic style of timbers and thatch. It was here that Eldred conducted business.

Several faces turned to look at Hengest and Horsa as they stepped into the old bakery. The two Jutes were recognisable to many in the town, particularly the younger brother who had a reputation for drinking and fighting.

"Business or pleasure, Horsa?" asked a whore who had sauntered over to them, her hair bound high up on her head and her tunic parted to reveal her ample breasts. She slid her arm around Horsa's neck and stroked his shoulder length, chestnut hair.

He shoved her away and followed Hengest who was already making for the stairs. Neither of them was in the mood for fun. The woman frowned and muttered some derisive comment before moving on to other potential customers.

A burly man blocked the stairs, his massive arms folded across his chest. This was one of Eldred's cheap security measures. His blond locks had been shaved from his forehead in the Saxon style which made his face seem larger and more intimidating.

"The chief in?" Hengest asked.

"Busy," replied the guard. "Have a few drinks down here, then maybe he'll see you."

"Piss off, Octa," snapped Horsa. "He'll see us now. Unless you'd rather take a wager as to whose saex can gut the other first."

The Saxon's eyes followed Horsa's hand to his belt where the long-bladed knife of the Germanic peoples hung in its seal skin sheath. He stood aside and said nothing.

"Gutless Saxon mercenaries," muttered Horsa under his breath to his brother as they climbed the stairs. "Couldn't keep a pig out of a shit pile."

Eldred was indeed busy when the two brothers entered his office. Hengest recognised the whore who was bent over his desk, her dress up around her middle and her face looking thoroughly bored by her employer's energetic thrusting.

"Thunor's cock, can't a man be left in peace?" Eldred exclaimed, looking up at the two Jutes who stood on the other side of the desk. "I'm going to hang that Saxon up by his balls!"

Hengest and Horsa waited patiently for him to complete his task. It took about a minute. The whore got up and rearranged her tunic. She winked at Horsa before sauntering out of the room. Eldred buckled his breeches and slumped down into his chair before pouring himself a cup of wine. He offered some to his visitors. Hengest shook his head.

"Suit yourself. It's good stuff," said Eldred. "Newly liberated from a trader last week. From Sicily I believe. Wherever the fuck that is."

"And in whose waters was it taken?" asked Hengest. "Or does the treaty no longer apply?"

Eldred glanced at him. "What can I do for you boys?"

"You can start by telling us what in the blazes of Waelheall Ceolwulf and his sea rats were doing in our waters!" said Hengest.

"Ceolwulf?" asked Eldred suspiciously. "His territory is north of Thanet."

"Well perhaps somebody should remind him of that. Or maybe he got lost. Either way he cost us a trader yesterday and butchered an entire crew of ours!"

Eldred sighed and sipped his wine. "What would you have me do? There are too many pirates in these waters. The treaty has done its best to organise things but sometimes lines on a map get blurred in people's heads. Let it go."

"Let it go?" said Horsa. "That's all you have to say on the matter?"

"If I start making threats and putting pressure on Ceolwulf, he might just say that it was you who was in his waters. And then where would we be? Who am I to trust?"

"Ceolwulf is a sneaky bastard," said Horsa. "He knew what he was doing. He slaughtered our men and left one of my ships riding free. I want him dead!"

"Forget it!" replied Eldred. "Ceolwulf brings in too much profit for me to have him killed. Who would take his place? You two?"

"Think we can't handle the extra territory?" asked Hengest.

"As you just said, you are one ship down," Eldred answered with a smile.

Hengest felt his brother stiffen at his side and placed a restraining arm across his chest to prevent him from lunging forward and dragging Eldred across the desk by the throat.

"Listen," Eldred continued, seemingly oblivious to the present threat to his life. "I feel bad. You two have brought me plenty of profit over the past year, so I'll throw something your way. Word has reached me of a trader loaded with grain which is due to put out from Dubris within the week."

"Grain?" asked Hengest. "We're not bakers."

"It is what is hidden within the grain that interests me. Forty of the sacks contain a single bar of gold each. Forty bars of gold, boys. Some British nobleman is fleeing to Gaul and wants to take his wealth with him. That good enough for you?"

"And what will your cut be?" asked Horsa.

"My usual twenty percent. The rest is yours. Now that's a good deal for good friends. Can't say fairer than that."

"And you're sure about this information?"

Eldred frowned. "When have my agents ever failed me?"

# Horsa

The two ships followed the coast, cutting south-westward beneath scudding clouds. Hengest and Horsa stood at the stern of the *Bloodkeel* whilst the *Raven* rode under the command of Guthlaf, the senior of Hengest's two Danish thegns who had proven his most loyal followers since the disaster in Frisia. When they were within two leagues of the port of Dubris, they would cut southward and intercept the trader with its sacks of grain and forty bars of gold.

"Do you think Eldred has any suspicions about the last lot of gold we hauled?" Horsa asked his brother.

Hengest shook his head. "I don't believe so. If he did he wouldn't have just let us continue about our business. Although what he could have done about it, I can't imagine. He may have once been a powerful man, but his influence has waned. We raiders are just getting too powerful for him to control. You saw how unprepared he was do anything about Ceolwulf."

It was a dangerous game to play, but they had been cheating Eldred for nearly a year. With his family still in Angle-land, Hengest was desperate to raise enough funds to buy a sizeable homestead on Thanet or in the farmlands surrounding Rutupiae. Only then, when he was strong and wealthy enough to be sure of their security, would he have his wife Halfritha and his son Aesc and daughter Hronwena come to join them in Britta. Until that day came, they would remain with Beorn's family on his farm across the sea. There they were safe but Horsa knew there wasn't a day that went by that his brother did not miss them terribly.

And so, little by little, in small amounts so that nobody would suspect, they had been putting gold and silver aside in addition to their regular profits, the majority of which went towards the upkeep of Horsa's three ships and their crews. If Eldred found out that profits were being kept from him, things would go badly for Hengest and Horsa.

"If the old bastard truly is weakening," said Horsa, "then the time will soon come for him to be replaced. And he has no sons."

Hengest nodded. "There is a lot of power sitting there in Rutupiae under Eldred's fat arse. The one who rules Rutupiae, rules the coast."

There were five settlements on that part of the coast, each with its own Roman fort. Rutupiae was the senior amoung them and the best situated. Control of that entire corner of Britta that the Romans had called Cantium could be gained by controlling Rutupiae.

It was mid afternoon when the trader was spotted; a wide-keel riding low in the water. Horsa gave the signal to the *Raven* to move ahead and pass across the smaller ship's bow whilst the *Bloodkeel* hung back to bring up the rear. The trader continued on its path seemingly oblivious to the threat that drifted in its wake.

Hengest snorted. "You'd think they would have a stern lookout in these waters."

Horsa shrugged. He was rarely talkative when the scent of prey was in his nostrils, but something about this was too easy.

The *Raven* drifted into sight of the trader's bow and shipped oars. The men under Guthlaf's command armed themselves, ready to storm the trader.

And then something unexpected happened.

The men from the trader – and there seemed to be an awful lot of them – leaped up to meet the raiders with axes, swords and knives. Sometimes crewmembers on traders armed themselves, especially in these waters, but these men looked far too professional for Hengest's liking.

"They're ready for us," said Hengest.

"And they don't look like traders to me," said Horsa.

"Captain!" shouted Beorn. "Ship off the *baecbord* bow!"

They turned and stared. Coming towards them at a furious pace was the dragon-prowed ship of Ceolwulf.

"This whole thing was a trap to begin with," cursed Horsa. "I'm betting that those men on the trader are Ceolwulf's. Now he's trying to come upon the *Raven* and cut them to ribbons before turning on us. If he does that then we're finished. Row men! Row like you've never rowed before!"

"What are you planning?" Hengest asked, donning his iron helm and tucking his long flaxen hair up under it.

"If we can intercept Ceolwulf then we may have a chance to save the *Raven*. And escape with our lives."

"But he's too far! We'll never reach him before he joins the battle!"

Horsa looked to the men on the *Raven*. "I'll not lose another ship to that pig-spawn! Row men! The lives of our comrades hang in the balance!"

Horsa's men rowed. Their muscles heaved and their backs sweated as they dug and tugged, powering the craft onwards with brutal strength. Perspiration stood out on brows and breaths came out of bodies in pained grunts. Few captains could ask so much from their men and receive it. But Horsa was a well-loved leader. He never asked something of his men that he could not give himself. If there had been an extra oar and a space to sit he would have joined them at the benches

"If you push them too hard, they'll have no energy for the fight ahead," Hengest warned.

Horsa waved aside his fears. "My men will fight like Woden's hounds until the very last drop of strength in their bodies fail them. You'll see. We don't leave our own men to be butchered."

But the men were tiring. The distance between Ceolwulf and the *Raven* was painfully close and the distance between the *Bloodkeel* from both of those two ships was agonisingly far. Yet still they rowed. Horsa gripped the bulwarks until his knuckles glowed white, his teeth grinding in his skull.

The great sweeping side of Ceolwulf's ship drifted nearer and finally Horsa deemed them close enough to ship oars. The order was given and as the *Bloodkeel* glided onwards, the crew began arming themselves for combat.

There was a great shudder as the two boats crunched together and the crew held fast as the prow splintered through the bulwarks of the enemy.

"Bring them death!" cried Horsa and his men began to storm the other raider, eager for bloodshed.

Bringing up the rear, Hengest and Horsa let out howls of war and charged. Hengest's sword, *Hildeleoma*, which his brother had taken from a buried hoard of treasure in Dane-land, swung through the air and parted mail and flesh with slithering strokes. Horsa's men, tired though they were from their punishing chase, revelled in their victorious slaughter of their rivals. They had beaten Ceolwulf to the *Raven* which was still engaged in battle with the trader far out on the water.

Horsa fought his way towards Ceolwulf, battering aside friend and foe as he strode the deck. Ship captains were something of a speciality for him, having killed the captains of both the *Bloodkeel* and the *Fafnir* to gain control of them.

The battle slowed around them as all began to watch the two captains fight. Horsa's advantage in experience showed through and it was not long before Ceolwulf fell to the deck of his own ship with his throat opened and his blood pumping freely. The fight went out of the enemy by that point. They were already outnumbered by the crew of the *Bloodkeel* and many threw down their weapons in surrender. Across the water the fight was also drawing to a close on board the trader. Having not received the reinforcements that had been intercepted by the *Bloodkeel*, Ceolwulf's ambushers found themselves at the mercy of the *Raven's* crew.

None were left alive.

# Hengest

Eldred sat at his desk fumbling through papers and checking profits. It was an arduous task, keeping track of the money coming in and the expenditures going out. He was still in the gold lending business and that was enough to keep any thriving businessman on his toes. His extortion rackets also increased the amount of paperwork that lay piled up on his desk in untidy heaps.

But Eldred was merely a cog in the poorly oiled and clapped out machine that was fifth century Britta. Whilst he ruled Rutupiae with an iron fist and creamed the profits in the form of bribes, tribute and extorted payments, he in turn had to pay tribute to a more powerful chieftain in one of the larger towns further inland. Every month men from the west would come to Rutupiae and Eldred would hand over a hefty sum of gold and silver so that his position at the head of the town would remain concrete and unthreatened. It was a miserable state of things that any of his substantial profits should go to a pocket other than his own, but such was the way of things.

The door swung open, propelled by a huge amount of force and slammed against the wall. Eldred looked up, irritated at such a disrespectful and noisy intrusion. His face froze.

"Didn't expect to see us again, eh?" asked Hengest, his face livid and stained with smears of dried blood.

"Come in boys," said Eldred, his face paling.

The two men strode into the room. Horsa closed the door behind them.

"Wine?"

The question went unanswered.

"You betrayed us," said Hengest, his voice raspy with cold anger.

"Now, boys," began Eldred. "I don't know what this is about. Did you find the trader?"

"We found it alright, only there was no gold aboard. No grain either. Only Ceolwulf's men! You sold us out, you traitorous son of a whore!"

"I'm insulted," said Horsa stepping up to the desk and planting his fists upon its paper-strewn surface. "Did you really think that Ceolwulf's sea rats were a match for my men? They're all dead. Looks like you backed the wrong man, eh Eldred?"

In a sudden and impressive display of backbone, Eldred managed to draw himself up before the two Jutes. "Don't you speak to me of betrayal!" he spat. "I'm wise to the fact that you've been keeping profits from me. I've had men killed for that before, and don't think I won't have the same done to you!"

"But you already tried," said Hengest. "Isn't that right? You thought you could do away with us by sending us into a trap and then have Ceolwulf take over our territory. Well, Ceolwulf is at the bottom of the sea. I suppose that leaves all the more territory for us."

"You little pig-spawns!" said Eldred, spitting flecks of phlegm. "You were nothing when you came to these shores! Who set you up? Who showed you the ways of the land and handed you territory? I did! And you dare to betray me! Without me you'd still be the stinking sea rats that you were a year ago. Two rotten exiles with three old tubs to your name!"

Horsa shouted a curse and drew his saex. With a sudden thrust forward, he sunk the long blade deep into Eldred's throat, pinning him to the back of his chair. The two Jutes watched as their employer writhed and squirmed in his seat, clutching at his neck. Blood ran from the corners of his mouth as he choked and thrashed about, but the blade was fixed too deeply into the wood for him free himself.

It took several minutes for him to choke to death on his own blood. When he was completely still, Horsa reached across the desk and wrenched his saex free. Eldred's corpse slumped forward over his desk, his papers gradually becoming saturated by the blood that pumped across the surface.

Downstairs, Octa the Saxon observed a dice game between two Angles. The stakes were high and a large crowd had gathered around the table to watch. Octa frowned. He didn't like Eldred, that was true, but he liked being pushed around by those two Jutes even less. But he didn't get paid enough to tangle with them. Especially when they stormed in with smears of blood on their faces and angry fire in their eyes. So he had stood aside as before and let them up to see his employer. Whatever their beef was, they could argue it out up there.

One of the dice players let out a yell of triumph when the small cubes of whale bone favoured him. His celebration was cut short by the fall of a heavy body which seemed to tumble out of nowhere and land in the centre of the table, splintering it and scattering horns of mead and dice in all directions. Men fell away from the wreckage with cries of alarm. The corpse was

Eldred, his chest red with blood which still seeped from an ugly opening in his throat. His eyes were open and he gazed through them, frozen with the terror he had felt in his final moments. As one, all heads in the old bakery turned upwards to see from where the body had fallen.

The faces of Hengest and Horsa peered down at them from the opening to the late Eldred's office, the wooden banister smeared with his blood. Octa drew his saex and whistled to two of his men who loitered by the door to the bakery. The crowd parted as the guards charged in, their spears held low.

"Drop your weapons, boys," called out Horsa to them from the top of the stairs. "My men are in the street outside. If anything happens to us, they'll be in here wreaking a bloody slaughter on my orders."

Octa and his two men halted at the foot of the stairs, considering this.

"I don't imagine Eldred paid you much," said Hengest. "And now he's dead, so I would think that you can consider yourselves free from his service. Unless of course you feel some need to avenge the greasy old drunk in the name of honour. In which case, come up here and we'll send you to Woden's hall with all the honour you'll ever need." He drew that impressive rune-etched blade of his slowly and deliberately. The spears of the two guards clattered to the stone floor. Octa's saex quickly joined them.

"Well, Octa?" said Hengest, sheathing his blade. "Care to come up and drink some mead with your new employers?"

# Hronwena

Hronwena frowned at the waves that sloshed and splashed their way past the hull as the *Raven* made its way towards Britta, it's sail bulging. Her mother stood with Aesc at the prow, telling him stories she had heard about the strange land they were soon to call home and the people who dwelled there. Eormenhild - Beorn's wife - was tending to their large hound that was tied up beneath the canvas canopy at the stern. The theows that had accompanied them from Angle-land milled about, some of them helping the crew and others merely sitting on their haunches looking homesick. Hronwena knew how they felt.

She had mixed feelings about coming to Britta. She had not seen her father in two years. Although she had missed him dearly in the beginning, she had been a child when they had last met. Now she was a woman and those two years felt like an age. She couldn't remember his face when she tried to picture him and that worried her.

Leaving Beorn's homestead had been hard on her. After the traumatic events that had dominated the year preceding her father's journey to Britta, it had taken her some time to settle back down to farm life and feel secure once more. Eormenhild and her children were more than welcoming and did their best to make her and Aesc feel like part of the family. The homestead was a happy one but Hronwena could never free her mind of the memories of the farm of Brand and the fire and slaughter that had consumed it when the raiders of Halga Eadwulfson had come to take them away.

The horrors of the slave camp stayed with her as did the memories of the terrifying crossing in Halga's ship where he had raped her mother night after night while Hronwena lay awake wondering when her turn would come. The nightmares had persisted for many months and she had often awoken in a cold sweat, certain that bloodthirsty raiders were hammering on the door to the hall to drag her and her family away. She had remained wary of men and whenever she was in the village she did her best to avoid the large males with their booming voices and the stink of mead on their breaths. They made her feel small and vulnerable and she hated their coarse mouths and terrifying size.

After a while the nightmares ceased but it was many months until she stopped jumping at shadows and crossing the street to avoid men. Aesc seemed to cope with things better. But boys knew how to hide their emotions and he had no knowledge of their mother's dreadful secret. Only Hronwena knew that her mother's ravaging had resulted in a child; a child which Halfritha had been forced to kill in the womb so that it would not know a life of slavery. It was the memory and knowledge of her mother's sacrifice for them which hurt Hronwena the most.

After a time, and despite her universal distrust of men and their violent ways, Hronwena had fallen in love. A local potter's son called Thrydwulf had taken her fancy. He was of the same age as her and nothing like the rough, coarse men with vulgar tongues and powerful, frightening bodies. Thrydwulf was shy and thoughtful and spoke with such a soft voice that he was often mocked by his male peers. He was beautiful too.

High cheek bones and pale skin free of blemishes or stubble gave him an Aelfin appearance only increased by his soft, blond hair that was somehow always clean and silky. There were some who said that he must have Aelfin blood in him, probably on his mother's side for his father was a dark, heavy set man.

But kind and thoughtful though he was, Thrydwulf never paid Hronwena a second glance. She made every excuse to ensure that their paths crossed and he was always pleasant to her, without committing himself with any kind of flattery or preferential treatment over the other girls in the village. So Hronwena had resorted to rune lore.

There was an old woman in the area who was known as a wicce. Hronwena often went to buy herbs and beeswax from her and sometimes stayed to talk with the old woman. She told her about the runes. Hronwena was fascinated and began to practice on her own, carving the little symbols on sticks and marking them on stone with burnt wood. The old woman helped her and soon she knew all the runes by rote and their little gnomic verses which described their uses.

There were many ways in which the runic symbols could be used. Simply carving them upon small tablets of wood or bone and studying their fall pattern after casting them upon the ground could give an idea of important events likely to occur in the future. Carving certain runes upon weapons or armour could give those objects special properties that would aid their owner in battle and Hronwena remembered that her father's sword had such runes on its long blade. Curses could be cast by giving the offending individual an item which was marked in a concealed place by a particular rune. The results could be anything from hair loss and mild illness to infection and even death. But such practices were frowned upon in their society and were never admitted to.

But in the matter of love, as they say, all is fair just as it is in war. Runespells could be used for love much in the same way as they were used for curses. Hronwena and her mother spent most days mending clothes for the villagers who paid in food and other goods. Hronwena was provided with the perfect opportunity to weave her magic when Thrydwulf brought an apron for repair. Within its stitching, she hid a small splinter of wood carven with her spell; so small that it would never be detected through the tough leather.

It took several days before any sign of success was noticeable. First came the shy smiles whenever the two of them passed, but little by little, Hronwena could notice Thrydwulf warming to her and within a month they were talking like old friends. Within two months they were sneaking away together to hold and kiss each other. The magic had worked and for the first time in her life, Hronwena felt the joy of love and warmth within the embrace of a man's arms.

But that was all over now. Her father had sent word that they were to join him in Britta where their new life awaited. Hronwena had wept bitterly at this news for she knew that her time with Thrydwulf was at an end and she would likely never see him again. Her mother knew her pain and tried to comfort her by telling her of all the fine things they would enjoy in their new life across the sea.

*The sea.*

Hronwena hated it almost as much as her father did. Although she did not suffer from the terrible sickness that plagued him, to her the sea was a frightening void; a border between worlds and a gateway to strange and unfamiliar settings. And no settings were as unfamiliar to her as the port town of Rutupiae.

As soon as she stepped onto the wharf she knew that she had entered a new world, the like of which she had not known had existed. Beyond the wooden docks and warehouses she could see the rooftops of buildings fashioned from stone; monolithic constructions with open windows, balconies, tiled roofs and walkways. She had not known that men could build such things.

Her father and her uncle Horsa stood waiting for them on the dock along with Beorn, eager to see his wife. Her mother, tears of joy in her eyes, fell into her father's arms and he kissed her again and again. When he was done he turned his eyes upon her and Aesc who waited in nervous silence. He looked older than Hronwena remembered, but his face seemed to slot perfectly into her memory, filling the gap there and she wondered how she could have ever forgotten what he looked like.

"My children," he said, walking over to them, his arms open. "Aesc, my boy, you are twice the man since I last saw you."

It was true, Aesc had grown and developed more than Hronwena had. He was tall, eleven years old, lean and hard. Two years was a long time for a boy to be without his father but that did not stop him from rushing forward into his father's embrace.

His father laughed. "Have you been training hard?" he asked.

"Very," replied Aesc. "No man can beat me in swordplay back home. And I can ride well too."

"Good! I may have need of your skills and courage in the days to come. You shall soon take your place in my war band, son."

Aesc beamed at this. He was nearly considered a man and to fight alongside his father in battle had been his dream since he had been able to walk.

And then, their father turned his attention on Hronwena. "Well, daughter?" he asked. "Do you have a hug and a kiss for your father?"

She could not hang back anymore. Nervous though she was, she wanted to do her duty and show her father her love for him. She had loved him once, an age ago, it seemed. Now he was all but a stranger to her. Could she love him again? She would try. She reached up and kissed her father on the cheek and he hugged her tightly.

"Come, my family," he said at last, drawing them all closer to him. "Come and see the home Horsa and I have made for you."

They turned and made their way along the wharf. Hronwena felt her uncle's hand on her shoulder.

"Cheer up," Horsa said to her. "Britta isn't all that bad. Not half as bad as it was, now that we're in charge of this place." He winked at her.

"Yes, uncle," she replied quietly.

Reddasporth back home was the largest settlement Hronwena had ever seen, but she had never been in a town before. All around them was activity. Men carried sacks of provisions and goods to and from the warehouses as the various ships docked there were unloaded and loaded again. They passed the *Bloodkeel* which was moored in the choicest spot in the harbour. The *Fafnir* was nearby too, under repair. Hronwena shivered at the sight of it for this had been the ship of Halga Eadwulfson which had carried her and her mother and brother to the slave camp. She looked around nervously, seeing if any of those same men were about for she knew that her father had pardoned them and taken them into his war band; an act Hronwena did not understand much less like.

They passed into the town itself. The streets were paved with stone and grooves had been cut along the sides for rainwater and refuse to pass along. Hronwena was surprised at the laziness of the people who milled about in the streets. In the settlements she was used to, people were relatively clean and hardworking, always busy with their trade or in the upkeep of the buildings. Here, the people seemed dirty and idle. There were beggars lying in the filth by the side of the street and some brightly coloured women who just stood about calling to men. Hronwena had a good idea what their trade was.

The buildings, although impressive in their construction, were filthy and in poor repair. It was strange to her that in a town that was, at first glance, so advanced and superior to the settlements of her homeland should be in such a sorry state. It was as if the gods had built a palace and then left it open to rats and stray dogs.

They rounded a corner and faced a large stone building with a wooden extension that formed a second floor. It had a yard and an iron gate where two men with spears stood guard. Within came the sounds of boisterous laughter.

Hengest turned to them. "Welcome home!" he said with a broad smile. "It's not much but it's a temporary measure until I pick out a nice spot of land to build something new."

They were silent as they looked up at the shabby brickwork and bits of cloth that were hung out to dry from various windows. There seemed to be a good deal of people within and the lyrics of a lewd Jutish song carried out to them on the smell of wood smoke and roasting meat.

"It's very nice dear," said her mother, dutifully. "But what is it?"

"It used to be a bakery," Hengest replied. "Now it is our headquarters and home rolled into one. There are rooms upstairs where we shall all sleep. Come, let me show you!"

The interior of the strange building hit Hronwena like a powerful stench. Stone steps led down to a cavernous room which was filled with Saxons, Jutes, Angles, Danes, Friesians and Britons. The smells of cooking food, stale mead and sweat rose up to collect in the rafters. A few faces looked up at them as they descended the steps. A couple of loosely clothed women were serving drink and they glanced up at her father and uncle with smiles. Hronwena looked at her mother and saw her face was rigid.

They ascended a flight of wooden steps to the upper floor where Hengest showed them their rooms. One belonged to Horsa and another was Hengest's office, where a large table was strewn with parchments and empty ale cups. A room adjoining the office was Hengest's sleeping quarters; the largest in the whole building.

"I'll have the theows bring your things up," he said to her mother. "You'll be settled in in no time. Aesc, Hronwena, you are next door. I know it's all a bit cramped, but as I said, it's only temporary. Soon we will have a huge hall to call our own. You will both be wanting to take spouses soon, I expect." He winked at this.

Hronwena quickly looked out of the window, her heart suddenly yearning for Thrydwulf.

"Oh, that's not a problem," she heard her mother say. "We all shared a room back on Beorn's farm. And my babies are not quite yet ready to take partners just yet."

Aesc rolled his eyes at this and began inspecting a breastplate and helmet which stood on a stand in the corner.

The room they were to share was not too bad. Straw beds lay on one side and there was a table next to a window where enough light came in to make the place seem welcoming. A leather curtain could be pulled across when the sun or stench of the street outside became too strong.

Her mother placed a hand on her shoulder. "Once your things are put in place, this will feel like home in no time, you'll see."

Hronwena nodded in silence.

# Aesc

The following week was spent settling in. Hronwena and Halfritha did their best to make their quarters feel more homely. They spent most of their time upstairs, reluctant to mingle with the rough types whose raucous drinking kept them awake at night. Aesc on the other hand, revelled in the new company and spent more time in the yard than upstairs.

Octa the Saxon - one of his father's warriors - had been instructed to continue his training. They trained hard with sword and spear and soon Aesc had made quite a name for himself, taking on all comers from his father's men. In the evenings he enjoyed sitting with the men in the old bakery and, although he was careful not to drink too much for his father would not have approved, much less his mother, he thrilled to the stories, jests and songs of the warriors.

Some had been born here and knew all about the history of Britta and its battles against the Romans and their own Germanic tribes. A group of Alemanni - a tribe from the northern Rhine river - told him of how their grandfathers had come to Britta as auxiliary troops for the General Theodosius in order to crush the Great Conspiracy.

This was the term used for an alliance in 368 between the Saxons and the tribes of northern Britta and Hibernia; an island in the west almost the same size as Britta where the people spoke a similar Celtic tongue to the Britons. This confederation had attacked Britta and Gaul and brought the island to its knees. The cunning General Theodosius had suppressed the attack and the Alemanni auxiliary troops had stayed put and raised their families on this south-eastern corner of Britta.

One morning a group of warriors came to the bakery. Aesc was training in the yard and was the first to see them. He instantly smelt trouble. They were Britons; that much was clear from their clothes and thick accents. There was nothing unusual in that, for British warriors were often seen in the town, some wearing swords they had inherited from their fathers. But the way the six of them strolled together with an arrogant swagger, their hands resting on their sword hilts made everybody in the yard stiffen and pay close attention to them.

Aesc ran inside to tell his father.

"Stay here," Hengest said, strapping *Hildeleoma* around his waist.

"But I want to confront them with you," Aesc pleaded. "You said that I could be a part of your war band."

"And you shall be," his father replied. "But let's see what they want first. No good ever came of attacking people who came in peace."

Most of the men loyal to Hengest and Horsa were down at the docks or slumbering in the local taverns and brothels, but there were enough, Beorn included, to show a decent display of force to the newcomers. Aesc disobeyed his father and followed them out.

"What do you want?" asked Hengest, striding out into the yard to meet the strangers.

The leader of the men, a burly, scarred Briton who wore two daggers at his belt said something in his own

Celtic language. Although Aesc had begun lessons in British he had only been in Britta a week and understood the bare minimum.

"If you wish to speak with me then you must use my tongue," his father said to the Briton.

The Briton shrugged and spoke the dialect of the Angles with a strong accent. "Last month's payment never arrived. What happened to Eldred?" he asked before spitting on the ground as if the Germanic language was offensive to his tongue.

"He has been replaced," his father replied. "Who are you?"

"Such an action was not authorised."

"We require no authority to replace a backstabbing little maggot like Eldred. But this is not your concern. I ask again; who are you?"

"I think you will find that it is our concern, *Saeson*," the Briton replied, using a term unfamiliar to Aesc, "for we are the men of Gwrangon."

"Never heard of him."

"Perhaps you should educate yourself. He is the ruling power in these parts. He had an agreement with Eldred. Twenty one sacks of grain per month and five percent of all gold taken in these waters. It is an agreement he expects to continue."

"Tell him to whistle for it," Hengest said with a scowl. "We are no man's errand boys."

Tension grew in the yard so that the air was thick with it. The two groups of men drew themselves up and faced each other off.

"Take care, *Sais*," said the Briton, "you are out of your depth here. This is Albion, not Germania. Here we have different customs."

Hengest raised an eyebrow. "Looks to me like there are more of us than of you, Briton. This whole town is ours. Now get lost and take your flea-ridden wolves with you!"

The man spat on the ground once more and muttered some curse in British before turning on his heel, his followers behind him.

"What did he call you, father?" Aesc asked once the Britons had disappeared into the crowded street.

"*Sais*," said his father. "It's what the Britons call us. Means Saxon."

"Saxon!" exclaimed Aesc. "Why did he mistake you for one of those dogs? No offence, Octa."

"None taken, boy," Octa replied. "It's their term for all of us. The Saxons have been settling here since way back. The Britons apply the term to Jutes, Saxons and Angles these days, it makes no difference to them. They can't tell the differences in our languages. To them we're all of the same cursed stock."

# Hengest

The following night a fire broke out in one of Hengest and Horsa's warehouses which nearly set the whole town ablaze. Huge amounts of grain which had been stored for the winter were destroyed. On top of that a group of Hengest's tribute collectors were set upon by unknown assailants and beaten to a pulp. Their payment was stolen and one of the men died with a distinctly British knife lodged in his ribs. Hengest was furious.

"Who is this Gwrangon man?" he demanded of Octa.

"Local British chieftain," the Saxon replied. "Lives over towards Durovernum. Eldred was his lackey. He has a finger in every port town along the south east coast and they all pay him tribute which he then passes on to his own masters, whoever they are."

"Well, he's not getting tribute from us. No matter how hard he tries to sabotage our operations here. Rutupiae is ours!"

"It might not be that simple," Octa said. "Gwrangon is a powerful man. He won't let a couple of Jutes take one of his towns from him unpunished. If he did then he would lose all of them."

"What do you suggest then?" asked Hengest. "That we bow down to this bully?"

Octa was silent.

"We must fight him, else we will lose all that we have fought for," said Hengest. "I don't care how powerful he is. I have just brought my family to these shores thinking them safe. I will not let this Briton destroy my plans for their future. What's this place of his like?"

"Some sort of house in the Roman style. I've never been there myself but men tell me that it is out in the countryside. Isolated."

"Ha! And he thinks he can hold a place like that against our men?" exclaimed Hengest.

"I don't know how many men he commands," said Octa. "He may have a good sized army encamped there. But I do not think it is wise to take him on, Hengest. He has powerful friends further west."

"Octa may be right," said Horsa. "As much as I hate to admit it, even if we defeat Gwrangon, there is no telling how many chieftains and petty governors will come asking for tribute in his place. We are still foreigners in this land. We don't want to bite off more than we can chew."

"Have the whores of this town sucked all your iron spirit and self respect from you, brother?" Hengest demanded. "I came to this land to carve a kingdom for ourselves. I will not be pushed around by a money-grubbing little whelp like this Gwrangon. Enough talk. We go to war!"

There had not been so much activity seen in Rutupiae since the withdrawal of the Roman legions. Hengest and Horsa already commanded a massive force of raiders hailing from all corners of the Germanic world and the promise of loot and bloodshed attracted a good deal more willing fighters from the town and surrounding countryside.

The preparations for war consumed the town like a frenzy. Food was stockpiled and loaded into wagons, blacksmiths hammered out weapons and repaired bits of armour like never before, scarcely believing their luck at seeing so much business. Hopeful men flocked to the old bakery, camping out in its yard and filling its interior, keen to prove themselves and win a spot in the Jutish brothers' army.

Aesc was distraught to learn that he would be left behind with the women whilst his father and uncle and all the other men would march off to war without him.

"Patience, my boy," Hengest told him. "Your time for battle will come. But this enemy, this Briton, we do not know how he fights nor how strong his army is. It would give my heart great comfort to know that you are here protecting your mother and sister. And I promise, when I know our enemy a little better, you shall join us in the fight against him."

"If there's any fighting left to be done," Aesc grumbled as he walked away.

"He reminds me of you at his age," Hengest said to Horsa. "Always wanting to throw himself into the fight."

"He'll learn," said Horsa. "Just as I did. When killing becomes the same as any job, there's precious little glory in it."

The banner of the dual horses that had been stitched by Halfritha and Hronwena was brought from the *Bloodkeel* and given to Guthlaf whom Hengest had made his standard bearer. Hengest kissed his wife and children goodbye and rode off with Horsa to the head of the army. With a great cheering and bellowing of horns, they set out.

41

A long road, straight as an arrow, led from Rutupiae all the way across Britta. Built by the Romans it was a testament to their iron-hard organisation. Paved with cobbles and lined by drainage ditches, the road led all the way to the town of Londinium, passing first through Durovernum Cantiacorum. Hengest and Horsa had seen little of the land they now called home having spent most of their first two years in Britta at sea. What they now saw was lush green pastures and thick forests cut by streams and hills.

"This is fine farmland, Horsa," said Hengest, marvelling at the stark contrast to the dirty, disease-ridden coastal towns that they were used to. "Good, dark earth for crops and wide open stretches of pasture for grazing livestock. Why don't the Britons make better use of it?"

"They're all too busy cowering in their huts!" said Horsa. "When they're not stealing each other's cattle, they're being robbed by Saxons, Jutes and Angles."

It was true; every hamlet or village they passed seemed deserted. Doors were bolted and cattle penned up while their owners hid indoors, never having seen such military might stomping across the land.

They camped the first night and helped themselves to cattle and swine from nearby farms whose owners put up no protest. Hengest sent scouts out to find Gwrangon's villa which was believed to be nearby. They returned as daylight was breaking and described a large area of farmland that surrounded a complex of buildings and a Roman villa.

"Is there any wall defending the settlement?" Hengest asked his scout.

"None, lord. Just farmhouses and granaries. There is a wooden fence that surrounds the villa proper."

"A wooden fence?" said Hengest incredulously. "I thought this man was the most powerful ruler in these parts. But he defends his home with nothing but a fence?"

"This just doesn't feel right," said Horsa. "Why isn't he living in a fortress or something?"

"Things are obviously done differently here ," Hengest replied. "Perhaps he relies on the protection of his Christ-messiah. Whatever his defences are, we shall crush them more easily than I thought."

# Gwrangon

Gwrangon was not a personal name but a title. It was a British corruption of the Latin word for governor, and even that was a generous title for the man who bore it. Sidonius Cassiodorus was a plump man. His heavy jowls and nose were networked with varicose veins from an overly luxuriant lifestyle that bore no resemblance to the hard, military existence of those who had held his position in days gone by.

In an earlier time he would have been known throughout Britannia as *Comes litoris Saxonici*; Count of the Saxon Shore. One of three military titles created during Roman Britain's final days, the Count's command once covered the forts on the east coast of Britannia and northern Gaul, ensuring safe waters against Saxon and Frankish pirates.

Little more than camps in their earliest days, the forts saw significant improvement under Carausius, a general appointed by Rome to clear the sea of raiders. In 287, Carausius seized Britannia for himself and strengthened its shore defences against Roman repercussions.

Britannia had been drawn back into the Roman fold after Carausius's assassination by his financial advisor but ever since, the island's history had been a troubled one. The near fatal disaster of the Barbarian Conspiracy of 367 was only a symptom of the rot that had set in. Barbarians continued to plague the island on all sides and the legions stationed in Britannia grew ever more rebellious, plucking candidate after candidate from their own ranks and putting them forward for the position of 'Emperor of the West'.

One of these was Magnus Maximus; a general who had fought with Theodosius I against the Barbarian Conspiracy ten years previously. His vision had been promising but was ultimately shattered by his defeat and subsequent execution by that very emperor.

Rome's last real attempt to save Britannia came in the form of General Stilicho. With the young halfwit Emperor Honorius more interested in the welfare of his pet chickens than that of the Western Empire, it left his highest military officer more or less regent in his stead. General Stilicho's measures in Britannia included pushing the Picts back beyond Hadrian's Wall and creating a number of military positions to safeguard the island, one of which was the *Comes litoris Saxonici*.

The British legions had tried again in 407, proclaiming another of their generals - Constantine - as Emperor of the West. Constantine III had departed Britannia taking all his legions with him. His rebellion was as ill-fated as that of Magnus Maximus and considerably shorter. The Britons, feeling abandoned by his departure, booted out his officials claiming that they wanted nothing further to do with him. But with Saxons settling in droves on the east coast and Picts swarming down over the defences in the north, the situation grew ever more desperate.

Pleas were sent to Emperor Honorius begging for assistance but the empire had its own problems. In 410 the unthinkable had happened. Rome was sacked. Alaric and his Goths had won the ultimate symbolic victory. For the first time in nearly eight hundred years, a barbarian army had swept into the former capital and ransacked it. Honorius, cowering in his new capital at Ravenna, scribbled a reply to the Britons' request. It was simple and damning; 'Look to your own defences'.

Rome had officially washed its hands of the province.

The chaos and terror that had followed had necessitated action on the part of the Romano-British nobility who found themselves cut off from their former overlords and at the mercy of the barbarians at their gates. It was then that the Council of Britannia had come into being. The island had been split into four sub-provinces many years before with a separate governor for each. These governors, along with the three military titles created by Stilicho formed the body of the council and, with the addition of the Bishop of Londinium and Master of Coin, the Council represented the last remaining form of government on the island.

It was little more than an aping of the old Roman administration and the titles of the late empire became mere formalities. Sidonius Cassiodorus, son of Roman aristocracy on his father's side and British on his mother's, weaselled his way into the position of Count, although he lacked a major portion of its command. Gaul was not his concern, neither were many of the forts on the north east coast of Britannia. Cantium - a former civita of the empire - was the only land granted him by the Council. But the value of Cantium lay in trade. Most of the important ports on the island lay in Cantium and the profits they brought meant wealth, power and privilege.

Sidonius Cassiodorus was enjoying some of those privileges now. He set his wine cup down and ran his fingers through a bolt of green silk that had travelled all the way from Parthia to the shores of Britannia, left to him by a merchant as a gift. Vastly expensive, the bolt would make fine tunics for he and his son as well as stoles for his wife and daughter.

A corporal entered the room wearing chain mail and a ridge helmet. He crossed the mosaic floor and threw out a salute.

"Sir," said the soldier. "Scouts have reported a large body of men on the Londinium Road. They are headed this way."

"How large?"

"They are disorganised and undisciplined but are large enough to be called an army. Roughly three hundred. They look to be Saxons. They are on foot."

"From Rutupiae?"

"Very likely, sir."

Cassiodorus rubbed his shaven chin, his brow creased with concern. "Probably those two pig-spawned brothers who killed Eldred and then refused my tax collectors. I had no idea that they could muster so many men. Have the villagers brought within the walls of the villa and post as many archers as you can. Get word to the auxiliary cavalry and have them conceal themselves beyond the tree line. Act quickly, corporal. We do not have much time."

"Yes, sir!"

"Must you allow your soldiers to tramp their muddy sandals across our floors?" asked his wife, entering the room in the soldier's wake. "They were only washed yesterday."

"Not by you, my flower. We have servants aplenty to wash them again. Besides, I am a military man. My soldiers do not have time to unlace their sandals to bring me news of Saxons on the warpath."

"Saxons? Coming here?" she asked with alarm in her voice.

"Oh, we are quite safe, dear. I still have some military might at my command and these Saxons are lost on land. They are sea rats. Without their boats they are little more than landed fish. Nevertheless, fetch Antonia and Flavian and join me in the chapel. We shall pray for salvation from these pagan hounds."

# Hengest

When the sun had fully risen, the army set out once more, following the lead of the scouts. Barely a few miles had been traversed before the red roofs of the villa could be made out, tucked away in a little valley with trees at its back. The surrounding farmland looked deserted but the fields were well tended.

"They know we're here," said Horsa. "Probably got everybody holed up in the house. What's the plan?"

"I want you and Beorn to take half of the men around to the side and march upon the house from the left," said Hengest. "Kill anybody you encounter and burn the buildings. I shall take the rest of the men to the right and do the same. Anybody trying to escape will be caught between our two forces."

"A simple plan."

"Simple is often best," replied Hengest, thinking back to the wars of their homelands when such a plan was enough to take a single hall or cluster of buildings belonging to an enemy chieftain.

"I think we've brought far too many men for such a task."

"Perhaps, but better to be safe than sorry. Besides, the sight of such a massive force approaching from both sides might be enough to make Gwrangon cower in terror and surrender without a single blow."

The army set about dividing itself into two equal forces and Horsa led the way with Beorn bellowing on his horn. Their men marched behind, chanting a popular war-song of their homelands.

"Guthlaf! Ordlaf!" said Hengest, calling for his two trusted Danes. "I want you both to flank me with the rest of our force behind."

"You're going to lead the attack yourself?" asked Ordlaf in surprise. "Is that wise?"

"Do you see my brother loitering in the rear ranks of his army?" Hengest snapped. "I march at the front, and you with me."

Mud was churned up underfoot as they set forth, the dual horse banner fluttering high above their heads, their voices bellowing chants of death with all the gusto they could muster. Deserted farmhouses drifted past them, with smoke still flowing from their chimneys; abandoned in the face of the attackers and Hengest dispatched squads of men to ransack them and torch their thatched roofs. This they did but not a single person did they see.

The villa rose up before them, its waist-high wooden fence pitiful in the face of the marching horde. An abandoned cart lay across the path and Hengest ordered Guthlaf to plant his banner atop it to form a rallying point for his men. Across the field he could see his brother ordering the fence to be torn down. The men chattered excitedly but from the house came nothing but eerie silence.

"Walk up and knock, I suppose," remarked Ordlaf with a grin.

"Form a line!" Hengest bellowed to his troops. "Shields in front, archers at the rear!"

There was a great shuffling as his order was put into action. When they were ready, he took his place in the shield wall. He gave the signal to march and the row of interlocking shields shifted forward at a sluggish, disorganised pace.

As soon as they were within bow shot of the house, several arrows were loosed from some courtyard within and sang through the air finding marks in Hengest's ranks. There were cries of alarm as the men, not ready for this sudden attack, stumbled and jostled each other.

"Shields up!" shouted Hengest. "Archers! Fire when ready!"

The rear ranks halted and fixed arrows to their strings, letting them fly. But the walls of the villa were too far and too high to penetrate and they fell short for the most part with a few bouncing harmlessly off the plastered walls and falling back down to earth.

Then the villa responded with a resounding peal of vengeance. Near on a hundred black shafts sprang from behind its walls and rained down on the attackers, thudding into shields and puncturing leather, mail and flesh with deadly force. Men fell dead in their tracks and others screamed at their wounds.

Hengest's archers responded with another unsynchronised volley which did as little harm as their first. Then came another hail of death from the villa.

"Damn, they're disciplined!" protested Guthlaf under the cover of his upraised shield. "He must have at least a hundred archers in there, all firing in unison with scouts on the walls telling them where to aim!"

"Enough of this," said Hengest. "If we stay put they'll cut holes in us, but if we get close enough to the walls, they'll have to come out and fight. March forward! Shields high!"

The order was given out and passed along to Horsa's force on the other side of the villa and as one shambling mess, the attackers moved forward, stepping over the bodies of their dead comrades. Another volley issued forth and wrought havoc amongst the ranks, felling men as they marched.

"We're nearly there," shouted Hengest over the noise. "They've got one more shot at us, and then we'll be upon them."

But the expected volley never came. Instead there issued forth a great bellowing of horns from the trees on the left side of the villa and two hundred horsemen came charging down to slope towards them.

"Gods protect us!" exclaimed Hengest. "He's got cavalry!"

There was no time to issue an order to break apart and even if there had been, Hengest's army was too disorganised to have put it into action. Instead the mounted warriors slammed into the left flank of his troops, driving spears into flesh and swinging out with great swords and axes, harvesting a bloody path through his men.

Terrified, they stumbled and fell against each other, trying to get out of reach of the scything blades of the horsemen. War-cries from the charging cavalry thundered to the beat of their horses' hooves and Hengest's ears pricked up at them. Something horribly familiar about those guttural shouts and bellows.

"They're Saxons!" he cried to no one in particular. "Damn them all, they're Saxons!" His force driven in two, he watched in dismay as the cavalry continued onwards towards his brother's forces. There was nothing he could do as a similar fate was exacted upon them. Men fled in terror as limbs and heads were lopped off and bodies picked up on the ends of spears and hurled end over end as the cavalry burst through the other side and galloped up the slope, wheeling about to begin another pass.

"Retreat!" roared Hengest. "Retreat! Before they come at us again!" It was a word he had never wished to utter in his life; a coward's cry that could cost him a seat in Waelheall should he die that day. But there was no choice if he wished to save most of his army. Warriors on foot could never stand up to a cavalry unit.

His men needed no repeat of the order. Terrified, they began to flee for their lives, away from the villa. Hengest grabbed Ordlaf by the shoulder and pulled him away. "Come on!" he shouted as men thundered past him. "The fight is lost! Come on! Where's Guthlaf?"

"Dead," replied Ordlaf, his face streaming with tears.

Hengest followed the young Dane's finger to where the body of their comrade lay in the mud, his helmet and skull split by a Saxon axe, the blood pumping from the crack in the iron. Tears of sorrow and frustration broke forth from Hengest's eyes. What a fool he had been! He had led his men on a foolish quest into foreign lands without having the first clue of what lay ahead. How many others were dead because of him? *Decimated by Saxon cavalry! Damn the gods and their jests!*

His bitter thoughts were cut short as the cries of terror rose up around him once more. The horsemen had caught up with them. His ears filled with the terrible noise of slaughter as they tore through the fleeing ranks. A heavy blow landed on his shoulder followed by a sharp pain and then all was mud and spinning sky as he felt himself hurled forward. The drumming of hooves echoed through his mind and faded away as he sank into blackness.

# PART II

*(Ac) Ac byþ on eorþan elda bearnum
flæsces fodor, fereþ gelome
ofer ganotes bæþ; garsecg fandaþ
hwæþer ac hæbbe æþele treowe.*

(Oak) The oak fattens the flesh of pigs for the children
of men.
Often it traverses the gannet's bath,
and the ocean proves whether the oak keeps faith
in honourable fashion.

# Vitalinus

Vitalinus was not a young man. His once black hair was now streaked with grey. He had always been thin - never active enough to be muscular, nor lazy enough to be fat - but now in his winter years, his body had something of the skeletal about it. As head of the Council of Britannia, he was no stranger to luxury and he ate moderately and drank perhaps excessively, but something seemed to be eating away at him, something *corrupt.*

Even after his many years as the most powerful man on the island, Vitalinus was not of the old Roman aristocracy. His father - Vitalis - had been a British chieftain with lands in the west and had married Sevira, the daughter of the usurper Magnus Maximus, in an attempt to fuse his family with the blood of a new dynasty of emperors. Their son, Brutus, had been his father's hope for an heir to the whole island. As grandson of a Roman emperor and descendant of the British chieftains, Brutus would be a symbol of a new age of order emerging from the chaos that had reigned unchecked for generations. Perhaps he would even become the first King of Britannia.

This plan had been dashed with the failure of Maximus's rebellion and execution in 388. It mattered little to Vitalinus. He had been six years old when his father had married the rebel general's daughter and, with no Roman blood in his veins, he had never been a part of his father's plans. Vitalinus had to hide his pleasure at his father's dashed hopes for Brutus. The younger half-brother he hated had been destined to

56

usurp his place as heir to the family estate but with Maximus's failure, Brutus became obsolete more or less overnight.

Vitalinus's common British lineage and the disgrace of his stepmother's family did not dissuade him from his own political ambitions however. Before he was twenty-five he had consolidated his father's lands and at twenty-seven, General Stilicho bestowed upon him the governorship of Britannia Prima; one of the four major provinces that comprised the island. One of the others, Maxima Caesariensis – which included the town of Londinium – Vitalinus arranged to be ruled by his eldest son, Vortimer.

Vortimer was a weak ruler and was effectively his underling. Although the other two provinces were not ruled by his family, Vitalinus had achieved what his father had failed to do; he had lifted his family to the top of the aristocratic heap in Britannia and brought the lion's share of the island under its command.

But descendant of swine-herds and cattle-thieves he may be, even Vitalinus had certain standards.

He stared at the man in front of him. The stench pervaded his nostrils even though the expanse of the broad oak desk, littered with scrolls and writing implements, lay between them. It seemed to radiate from the stinking rags the man probably considered clothes and the stiff leather armour soaked in many years worth of sweat and the blood of several battles, to drift free and contaminate the cool air of the stone chamber right up to its vaulted ceiling. Personal hygiene was an alien concept to these northern savages. There were no bath houses where they came from.

The savage was a tall man. Long black hair fell down in a matted cascade of grease and filth to rest on his broad shoulders. A cloak stitched together from many colours reached nearly to the floor and his massive mailed arms hung slack at his sides with his thumbs jammed into a wide belt. Most alarming of all to Vitalinus were the ritual markings on the man's face. Three parallel scars had been etched into the man's cheek denoting some barbaric rite of passage. There would be more, Vitalinus knew, about the man's body, carven into the skin representing kills or other such achievements worthy of trophy.

It had been the way with all the Britons once upon a time. The writings of Caesar and Tacitus told of the primitive tribes who painted themselves with the blue dye of the woad plant before battle in addition to the ritual scarring and tattooing that indicated rank and social standing. God be praised for shedding the light of civilisation upon this island!

*Even if it only extended to the southern part.*

The north was still as wild and savage as it had always been. Only now, with the iron legions of Rome gone from the island, the northerners were free to venture south. The great wall put up by the emperor Hadrian was but an unguarded fence for them to scramble over. For years now they had been plague upon the northern Britons. They must be brought to heel, whatever the cost, but it was amusing to Vitalinus that these Picts were presently asking for his help.

"We are willing to pay generously for your aid," spoke Prince Talorc mab Aneil of the Pictish clans. He spoke in the common British tongue, layered with his own northern dialect for Latin was unknown to the Picts.

"With what?" Vitalinus enquired, discretely shielding his nose and mouth with a scented handkerchief.

The Pict motioned to two of his men who lurked at the rear of the chamber. They were equally filthy and primitively dressed and they staggered forward carrying a small but sturdy chest between them which they laid at their master's feet. Talorc flipped it open with the toe of his muddy boot.

Vitalinus peered over the desk. Within the chest, he saw the faces of Honorius and Theodosius I among others. There had been no minted coins in Britannia for decades, making most of the loot useless as currency, but the gold and silver quotient of them may be valuable and the gems and bracelets twinkled temptingly.

"We have much more where this came from," replied the prince.

"Looted from northern British towns, no doubt," said Vitalinus with a knowing smile.

The smile was returned, equally knowing. "Our own lands in the north are overrun with invaders. They push us ever southward. We have no choice but to take food and cattle where we can."

Vitalinus knew whom the man referred to. Gaelic raiders from Hibernia known as the Scotti had besieged the western coast of the Pictish territories much in the same way that the Saxons plagued the south east. The Picts fought the Gaels fiercely but had nevertheless been pushed from their territories and, in turn, raided the northern Britons with increasing frequency.

"What else can I offer the great King of the Britons to encourage him to aid me in my war?" Prince Talorc continued.

Vitalinus smiled again. *King of the Britons?* He was no such thing. This barbarian was flattering him. There had been no kings in Britannia since before the days of the Caesars. Vitalinus, like the other members of the Council, was merely filling the shoes left vacant by the governing body of the Roman Empire. True he was head of the Council, and that might make him a king in the eyes of this savage, but his colleagues would have some very strong words to say should such an idea ever reach their ears. *Still, it was a pleasant notion...*

"And your sister?" Vitalinus inquired, "How strong is her force?" *Blessed Lord, what a poor state of affairs!* That the Britons should share their island with a people who allow their women to attain such lofty heights of power! It was easy to see why such a system could not work. This Pictish prince was in line to his throne upon the death of his father, but his half-sister, Galana, through some damnable pagan tradition, also had a claim through her mother.

"My sister is but a puppet of her advisors," Prince Talorc replied. "She is weak and indecisive."

Vitalinus smiled. The man had not answered the question, merely skirted it with some positive piece of information designed to allay his concerns. Perhaps these savages were not so stupid after all.

"And why did you come to me specifically, rather than put your case before the Council?" Vitalinus knew the answer but asked anyway. This Pictish prince hoped to buy his support before risking refusal by the other council members.

"You are their leader," replied the Pict. "You have to power to sway the Council's vote."

"There is one thing that concerns me," said Vitalinus.

"Name it."

"You and your warriors, what God do you follow?"

This seemed to confuse the prince. He thought on it for a moment before answering. "We follow the Mother Goddess who has been worshipped by my people since the beginning of ages."

Vitalinus thought as much. He would have a hard time convincing the Council to aid a bunch of howling pagans.

"Would you and your men agree to be baptised and receive the blessing of the Christian God?"

Talorc frowned.

"With the blessing of God comes the blessing of the Council," Vitalinus urged.

"We may... consider it," said Talorc at last.

"Do," encouraged Vitalinus. "With the light of the true Lord on your side, the odds would be greatly in your favour." He rose and poured another goblet of wine for his guest, watching as the savage knocked it back in one thirsty gulp. "Return now to your fellow delegates and discuss the matter with them. I have had rooms set aside for you. When you are decided, send word to me and I shall prepare your case for the Council."

The prince nodded respectfully before making to leave.

"Oh, you can leave the chest," said Vitalinus.

Talorc nodded, turned on his heel and, patterned cloak sweeping the mosaic floor, left the chamber followed by his two attendants.

Vitalinus removed the scented handkerchief from his nose and dared to sniff the air. It smelled a little better now. He stood up and walked over to the window that looked out on the great, sluggish waters of the River Tamesis. Gulls cawed as they wheeled in the air above the fishing boats and terracotta roofs of the warehouses that made up the river front. He sucked the salty air in deeply through his nostrils. The stone hallways of the governor's palace - his son's palace - were as straight cut and angular as Roman law itself. And like that esteemed institution that had once ruled the known world, the palace was a relic of a bygone age.

"Scribe," he said to the small, bent man who sat in the corner of the room, still scribbling away at some task he had been set earlier. "Send for Aurelianus. Tell him to come at once."

"Yes, my lord," said the small man before scurrying away, dropping scrolls as he went and scrabbling about to pick them up.

"Oh, and scribe?"

"Yes, my lord?"

"Have that girl sent to my chamber; the daughter of that merchant who was unable to repay his debt to me. You know the one. I have decided to take payment in kind. Tell him he may return to his villa but his daughter stays with me until I tire of her."

"Yes, my lord."

An hour later, Vitalinus arranged his robes and exited his chamber. Ambrosius Aurelianus was waiting in the antechamber, not sitting on one of the couches but standing to attention as if he was a common guard. Vitalinus wondered how long he had been there.

He was a tall, strong man, young in years. His red cloak and tunic were spotless and his armour was polished to a high sheen. He was a soldier of the old style; discipline and order above all else. He hailed from a very old family of Roman descent and this showed in his bearing and swagger; a fact that always irritated Vitalinus.

He ushered the girl out of his chamber and sent her on her way. She scuttled off, clutching her stola to her body and allowing her tangled hair to shield her tear-stained cheeks. Vitalinus caught a tiny curl of disgust cross Aurelianus's face. *Damn his prudish impudence!* Admittedly the girl was a little young; no more than twelve summers perhaps. But he was a man with large and varied appetites. And besides, who had the right to deny the lord of the island whatever pleasures took his fancy?

"Are we to war with the Picts, then, my lord?" Ambrosius Aurelianus asked.

"That remains to be decided," Vitalinus replied. "Although prolonging the civil war between the tribes may have its benefits. Wine? Vortimer keeps a good cellar stocked here in the palace. That's about the only thing my son is capable of doing properly."

A servant was called for, bringing a tray with two cups and a decanter. Vitalinus gulped half his cup and refilled it, thirsty after his exertions. "Shall we take a walk in the gardens?"

Gravel crunched under their feet and was the only noise that broke the stillness of the gardens other than the trickle of the fountains. A servant clipped away at a bush on the other side of the open area, shearing the plant into regular, sharp order.

"Tell me, Aurelianus, how many men have you under your command at present?"

"Seven-hundred cavalry plus two-thousand infantry," came the immediate reply. "By recruiting local militias and cohorts of the northern cities, we might rally five-thousand men."

Vitalinus winced. It was a pathetically small number compared to the old days. Since Rome had abandoned them they had had to make do, forging order out of chaos to the best of their abilities. Together the British leaders held a fragile alliance that could be the beginnings of a new nation, a new era of order and unity, an era of *Britons*. There had been some of course, who never possessed the backbone to fully embrace such a concept and constantly wanted to run back to the Romans, begging for protection like weak children. Aurelianus's father had been such a man.

The resulting war of 437 between the house of Vitalinus and the house of Aurelianus had been a nasty but brief affair. Both factions commanded large forces of men, comprised of ex-legionaries and newly recruited auxiliaries. A few battles were fought and eventually, inevitably, Vitalinus won. The senior Aurelianus was cut down at the battle of Wallop. His head had decorated the bridge of Londinium for three months until, ravaged by birds and the elements, it had tumbled into the River Tamesis where it lay still; a ghost of a lost age.

Aurelianus's son, Ambrosius however, showed more promise. A military genius, even at a young age, he was too much the patriot to show any of his father's pro-Roman failings despite his rigid sense of Roman discipline and order. Vitalinus had encouraged him to side with the Council and had given him the highest military position in Britannia. If Vitalinus and the other council members filled the shoes of the old Roman governors, then Ambrosius Aurelianus filled the role of *Comes Britanniarum*; the chief of the three military commands created by Stilicho.

"We may need to levy more men from the countryside," said Vitalinus. "Prince Talorc's sister commands a large force."

"The nobility will not be happy come harvest," said Aurelianus. "There is already a shortage of manpower to work and till the fields. Perhaps if the family of Cunedda had remained in the north, then there would be no need to send an army to deal with the Picts."

Vitalinus frowned at the implied criticism. Cunedda had been a fierce chieftain of the Votadini; a tribe whose territories began just on the other side of the Wall and had been little more than Picts themselves. They were somewhat friendly to the northern Britons; contact with Roman civilisation having curbed their savage natures. Some years earlier, Vitalinus had sent Cunedda and his many sons to combat the Gaels who were ravaging the western part of Britannia Prima. The move had been successful in that respect, but it had left the north open to the Pictish tribes. One could not fight one front without leaving another undefended it seemed.

"I received word this morning from Sidonius Cassiodorus," Vitalinus said.

"Ah, our brave *Comes litoris Saxonici*," said Aurelianus, with all the irony he could inject it with. "What news from the east?"

"He's having trouble with the Saxons again."

"Well, that's hardly worth reporting. The Saxons have been a menace for decades. What is it this time? A new *Barbarica Conspiriatio*?"

"Not exactly, but they do seem to be becoming more organised. A small force attacked Cassiodorus's villa last week. They were repelled by his auxiliary cohort, but it was a near thing. Cassiodorus fears that if he is not reinforced, then a second attack could be disastrous."

"Is it not his responsibility to keep these savages pacified?" asked Aurelianus. "With all the wealth he leeches from piracy and trade payoffs, I would have thought that he could buy up every sword arm in Britannia."

"There have been newcomers," replied Vitalinus. "Two brothers, I hear, have overthrown the local tax collector of Rutupiae and taken command of the town. More and more Saxons join their ranks every day. If these barbarians decide to start using cavalry, then the entirety of Cantium could fall."

"Cassiodorus is a corrupt imbecile," said Aurelianus. "If he invested as many resources into defending the shore from barbarians as he does into his own whores and elaborate feasts, then Britannia would have no Saxon problem."

"You don't need to tell me that," sighed Vitalinus. "Just when I may have to send our forces north to fight one lot of barbarians, he goes and lets another group have the run of the place on our right flank! We cannot afford any weakness in our defences. Cassiodorus's usefulness, I fear, is at an end."

"What do you propose to do?"

"I wish you to go to Cantium, Aurelianus. There you will deliver a customary letter of our support to Cassiodorus, but also you will fulfil a clandestine mission on my authority."

"My lord?"

"Seek out these Saxon brothers. If they are as charismatic as I am led to believe, then they may well be worth bargaining with. Tell them that if they are willing to lay down their arms against us, they may enter my employ as protectors of the Saxon Shore."

"Client barbarians?" protested Aurelianus.

"It is time we began to use our heads, Aurelianus. We have barbarians at every gate and few Christian Britons left to protect them. What better way to ensure the safety of the Saxon Shore than to use the Saxons themselves to guard it? I think it is time to employ the age-old trick of *foederati*. If these two brothers are as ferocious as they are rumoured to be then they will not let Cantium fall to a second such group of barbarians. They will be defending their own turf, so to speak."

"But with respect, my lord, would such a plan not have the same result as if the Saxons took the east by force?"

"Let them take it by force and they will revel in their victory and look to other lands to conquer. But give them the land, and they will be grateful and not think of attacking us further. Let them fight over the land between themselves if necessary, and then, when all sides are weakened, we can march in and reclaim it."

"And what of Cassiodorus?"

"Yes, what of Cassiodorus?" mused Vitalinus. "Should the Saxons accept our offer, you are to bribe his cavalry force. They're Saxons themselves, and would probably join their countrymen for a single amphora of wine."

"Then Cassiodorus is to die?"

"He has failed us time and time again. We cannot allow such weakness. Yes, he is to die. And his replacements may have a force under their control large enough to be of further use to us."

"So, after giving the Saxons the run of the eastern shore, you intend to use them against our other enemy?"

"You see, Aurelianus? We must fight fire with fire in such times so that our own brave soldiers are not all used up."

Aurelianus was silent. Vitalinus knew that he strongly disapproved of dealing with barbarians.

"Scribe!" Vitalinus called, his voice echoing across the garden. Never far out of earshot, the same, small frightened man came scurrying along, fumbling in his robes for wax tablet and a stylus. He squatted down at the feet of Vitalinus with a wooden board in his lap and, after marking down the customary salutations, began to write as his lord dictated;

*"In order to safeguard the eastern lands of Britannia, your continued vigilance is required. At present, we are unable to send reinforcements due to our concerns in the north. Ambrosius Aurelianus however, who is bringing this letter to you, shall provide you with advice on how best to fortify your position against further attack. Make use of him. He is the greatest military mind left in Britannia."*

Vitalinus reached out a hand to take the tablet from the scribe. He took a seal from a fine chain around his neck and pressed it into the soft wax. The seal had been his father's and depicted a man astride a horse ringed by a single word. It was not the family name, rather a title his father had used at the height of his royal pretentions and which Vitalinus now used as head of the Council. It was a Latinisation of an old British title which meant 'overlord'. The bold Latin script that had been impressed into the wax read;

VERTIGERNVS

# Hronwena

Hronwena peeled back the bandages that covered her father's wound. It had been deep; a nasty blow to the shoulder that had torn the flesh almost down to the bone. But he had survived the attack and for that she thanked Woden, despite the infection that had set in during the journey back to Rutupiae.

"I swear by Frige," her mother had said when they had inspected the wound together after Horsa and Ordlaf had lain him down on the bed in his room above the bakery, "men couldn't keep a wound clean if it could prevent the end of the world."

The hastily applied field dressing had consisted of a dirty rag wrapped tightly around the shoulder. It had soon become stiff and dark with clotted blood.

He had been delirious with fever for the best part of a week and Hronwena rarely left his side. Her knowledge of herbs and rune lore surpassed that of anyone in the town and she had taken it upon herself to be her father's personal nurse. She dressed his wound with poultices of Wegbrade, water and ash to draw out the poison and gave him ale laced with Mucwyrt to raise his strength.

It was good to have something to do. She found life in the old bakery so tedious and she dared not venture out into the streets. It was a way to be close to her father at least; this man she vaguely remembered bouncing her on his knee and tickling her a lifetime ago. It was odd to see him so weak and entirely at her mercy.

The pain of having his bandage changed stirred him and he began to return from between worlds and speak sense. He demanded to know what had happened.

"Ordlaf pulled you to safety," Hronwena told him. "You were knocked unconscious by the blow and fell."

"And I didn't even redden my sword," he said, gritting his teeth in frustration. "I am ashamed, daughter. I led my men into a trap and was nearly killed by my own folly. You must think me a pretty poor man to have as a father."

"Do not speak so, father. You couldn't have known how well fortified the enemy was. Your men look on you with respect for leading the attack."

These words cheered him a little, but he still clearly burned with shame. Later that day, her uncle Horsa came to visit him.

"I'm a damn fool, brother," her father said as he entered.

"If that's supposed to be some sort of apology then forget it," Horsa replied. "I've never seen an enemy so well organised and equipped. No man could have done a better job with what we have."

"That's just it, isn't it? We are Jutes, by all the gods! How could I neglect the one advantage that our people have over all the rest? We are horsemen by birth! Born in the saddle as some say. I've been at sea for too long. I've forgotten how our ancestors fought and won battles. They didn't win by numbers, they won by their horsemanship!"

"Well, be that as it may, the battle is over now and we are both still alive. That has to count for something."

"How many men did we lose?"

"Who knows? Most of them were mere hangers on looking for booty. We never took a proper headcount anyway. It doesn't matter."

"And Guthlaf? What of him?"

"You missed his funeral, I'm afraid. We gave him a good send off and buried his body upon the headland beneath a mound. I thought that would be what you would have wanted for him."

"Help me up. I need to visit his grave."

"You'll do no such thing!" cried Hronwena. "I've not stitched you up and spent night and day helping you fight this fever for you to burst apart like an overstuffed sack!"

"Oh, damn your fussing, daughter. I'm your father not a sick whelp!"

Horsa grinned at the exchange between the two of them. "Perhaps you had best heed her words. You are in no fit state to go walking about."

Her father grabbed him by the arm. "Listen to me, Horsa. Guthlaf was more than a good thegn. He was a friend and a mentor. When we were facing death at Finnesburg, he convinced me to lead the Danes when he could have done it himself. And then, when Finn offered him his freedom, he chose to remain by my side out of loyalty. It was I who led him to his death. I am the cause of his fate. Will you just help me pay him the smallest respect by visiting his barrow?"

Horsa nodded silently and began to help him out of bed, ignoring Hronwena's protests. He managed to dress himself and the two of them walked downstairs and out into the street.

# Hengest

Petals lay strewn across the hulk of the barrow; tokens of many visitors. An arch made by slabs of rock barred the entrance. At a later date this too would be covered with earth, forever sealing Guthlaf's body within. The cold sea wind blew in and over the mound, scattering the petals.

Hengest knelt at the entrance and placed his hand upon the cold stone. He began to weep. "Forgive me, Guthlaf. Would that I had not let my pride stand in the way of my reason you might still be alive. I am sorry, my loyal friend, I am sorry."

Horsa placed a hand upon his shoulder. "Do not blame yourself, brother," he said. "I have seen many men meet their fate. Some cower like frightened sheep from the butcher's knife while others greet it with open arms for they know that they have fulfilled their wyrd and that their time on Middangeard is over. Guthlaf was one of these men. Even as we mourn for him now, he is sitting in Woden's hall, drinking and laughing at us for our melancholy. Come now, let us honour him properly by drinking to his name and getting on with our lives, never forgetting his noble end."

Hengest rose. "You are right, Horsa. Thank you. Guthlaf was a warrior all his life and his end was a good one. We shall never forget him and when hostilities are renewed with Gwrangon, we shall kill ten extra Britons in his honour."

"You plan to attack again?" Horsa asked.

"As soon as I am healed and as soon as I can get hold of some horses. We'll crush that damned Saxon

74

cavalry of his and burn him alive inside his own home." A thought suddenly struck him. "What of our banner? What became of it?"

"It tumbled to the ground during the retreat. One of our men grabbed it as we ran and passed it on to me later. I rewarded him adequately."

"What kind of shape is it in?"

"You'd better take a look at it for yourself."

When they were back in the room above the bakery, Horsa produced the banner for Hengest's inspection.

His face turned grim as he held it up to the light. Apart from being nearly black with dried mud, a great hole had been ripped in it, disfiguring the intricate knot-work that Hronwena and Halfritha's hands had so delicately stitched. He gazed upon the ruined emblem of the dual horses with intense sadness.

Hronwena took the banner from him and said; "I shall repair it, father. With mother's help of course. It will look as good as new in no time. I promise."

"Do you see what a fine family I have, Horsa?" Hengest said, turning to his brother. "A man couldn't ask for better."

But his affectionate words did not sway his daughter's sternness in confining him to his bed for the next few days. She brought him broth and fresh bread and tended the wound with herbs and poultices. After three days of staring at the thatched ceiling and listening to the activity drifting up from the wharfs outside, Hengest felt he was going insane with boredom. There was so much to do! And every day wasted was another day Gwrangon surely spent replenishing his troops and strengthening his position.

One afternoon, when the bakery was unusually quiet, Hengest got out of bed and dressed himself before heading downstairs to the kitchen.

When he had first set foot in the building two years ago, the kitchen area had been little more than a dusty storeroom. But Halfritha and her theows had set about transforming it into a sweet-smelling grotto of the culinary arts. Herbs grew in pots along the windowsill, the storeroom was kept filled with salted meats and vegetables and one of the ovens, long since disused, was cleaned and kindled into use and had rarely been cold since, producing fresh bread every morning and roasting and baking meats and fish every evening.

Halfritha liked to see no man under her husband's employ go hungry and ensured that the kitchen was an ever popular addition to the old bakery. The men were eternally grateful for the hot meals it produced and many looked to Halfritha as they might look to their own mothers, despite her being a good deal younger than most of them.

Hengest found his family deep in discussion in the kitchen. Aesc was sitting at a table working his way through a bowl of stew and Horsa sat on the stone sill of the oven, basking in its heat. Halfritha and Hronwena sat at a bench loaded with carrots and cabbages, their faces worried.

"What is it my family finds so important to discuss that I may be left in the dark?" Hengest said as he entered the kitchen.

They started and turned to face him as he took a seat at the table.

"We didn't think it worth telling you until you were healed," said Horsa.

"Oh, damn that, I'm as well as any man, apart from the severe malady of boredom. Come on, out with it. What's the cause of all this secrecy?"

"An ambassador has come from some town to the west," said Horsa. "Name of Aurelianus or something to the like. He represents a British nobleman who runs things."

"What does he want with us?"

"Well, I couldn't really make head or tail of it myself. I spoke with one of his servants. This ambassador wants to meet with us to discuss a truce."

"Truce? Why would we want a truce with a man we haven't even heard of?"

"That's just what I said, but apparently this western nobleman is the master of our good friend Gwrangon."

"Sounds like a trap to me," Hengest muttered. "Why does this man want to parley with ones who have just attacked one of his own and been defeated?"

"He didn't say. He just wants to meet with us on neutral ground on the outskirts of Rutupiae. No weapons, no warriors. Just talking."

"What do you think, Horsa?"

"I think we should tell him where to stick his truce. We don't need any dealings with British noblemen from places we've never heard of."

"What was the name of this western town?"

"Londini... Londoni..." said Horsa, struggling to get his mouth around the Latin name.

"Londinium?" Hengest asked.

"That's it."

Hengest heaved a sigh of exasperation. "Horsa, we are going to sit down and have a proper look at my map one of these days. Londinium is only the most important town on the whole island! Some western town he says! This nobleman is probably the most powerful Briton on the island. And you want to ignore his offer of alliance?"

"You want to accept it?" Horsa returned.

"Why not? It can't hurt just to talk with his representative. If he truly is running things in Britta, then it may be prudent to have some sort of talk with him before we attack Gwrangon again. We don't know what he might be offering. Where is this servant of his?"

"Holed up in some tavern nearby, so he's not going anywhere. No rush."

"Send for him."

"Surely you're not intending to march off to battle again so soon?" Halfritha asked.

"I only intend to see what this man is offering us."

"But are you up to travelling?"

"He may think he is, but I can tell you he is not," said Hronwena with a scowl. "He needs rest and that wound needs daily attention."

"What sort of daughter have you raised in my absence?" asked Hengest in jest as he grabbed his wife around the middle and pulled her down onto his lap. "One after your own heart, I'm sure."

"Well, we've nearly lost you more times than I care to remember during the last few years," Halfritha said, squirming about, embarrassed by such treatment in front of her children. "Maybe she just wants you here so she can keep an eye on you for once. And I can't say that I blame her."

"Gods save me from women's shackles!" Hengest exclaimed. "I'm only going to the outskirts of the town to talk with somebody. Anybody would think that I am off to war in foreign lands by the way you two carry on!"

"Are you so sure that you aren't?" Halfritha asked him with her eyebrow raised. "You don't know anything about this Aurelianus fellow or what he wants."

"I know that if he tries anything unfriendly, Horsa and Ordlaf will be by my side to ram his parley up his damned arse and send him limping back to Londinium."

"Language, dear," chided Halfritha. "Not in front of the children."

"Don't worry about me, mother," said Hronwena. "I'm sure I've heard all the foul words known to man since moving into this place. I don't know about Aesc though," she added, hugging her little brother tightly around the neck. "He's only a little boy." She kissed him on the top of his fair head, making him writhe with embarrassment.

"Get off!" he exclaimed, still trying to eat his stew. "I'm no such thing. At least I wouldn't be if father let me go on one of his campaigns for once."

"Campaigns!" said Hengest. "Listen to the lad! Only eleven summers and he speaks like a seasoned warrior! Aesc, my boy, you shall go to war with me one day and learn that it is not as the scops would tell it. For the most part it is hard, dirty work."

"Well, how about taking me with you to see this Briton?" Aesc asked hopefully.

Hengest considered this for a moment whilst Halfritha looked at him with concern. "Certainly, boy," he said. "You shall come with your old man and see how he deals with these British fools."

"Are you sure that's wise?" Halfritha asked. "You're barely in a fit state to go yourself, and as you said, Aesc is only eleven."

"A father's duty is to rescue his son from his mother's apron strings, isn't that right, Aesc?" Hengest said with a wink to his son. "It's time you came with me and learned what real men do."

"And then can I fight?" Aesc asked, his eyes alive with excitement.

"We'll see," his father replied. "If there is a fight to be had, then I may need every able sword arm in my service."

# Aurelianus

*Damned good oysters*, thought Aurelianus to himself as he finished off the last of the shellfish he had sent for from Rutupiae. He would have to bring some back for his daughter to taste. She was fond of fine foods. *But how to transport them without them going bad?* He would have to think on it.

With his business concerning Cassiodorus finished, he and his small retinue of guards had set up camp on the outskirts of the town beneath the branches of a large oak tree that was so old it had probably seen Julius Caesar land his army here five centuries ago.

Aurelianus had no desire to go into Rutupiae. He didn't approve of the coastal towns, thinking them decadent, vulgar and overrun with Saxons. Besides, the sight of his highly disciplined British troops in their shining armour might give these Saxons the wrong impression. Better to play it safe and let them come to him in their own time.

It was a bad business, this game with the barbarians and he didn't approve of Vitalinus's decision. But who was he to question his lord? He had sworn loyalty to the Council and its leader in the holy house of God; loyalty to the death. Besides, he owed Vitalinus his life. After the battle of Wallop and his father's death, Vitalinus could have demanded the execution of the whole House of Aurelianus. Things rarely ended well for the families of traitors.

Aurelianus had been a very young soldier and, his wife having died the year previously, was the only family his infant daughter had left. He would have done anything to protect her. When Vitalinus offered him a pardon in exchange for his eternal allegiance, he had jumped at the chance and so he and little Aureliana were allowed to live.

He had raised Aureliana practically by himself with the aid of a few servants. Now she had reached eighteen summers and the two of them were the only remaining members of the once great House of Aurelianus; centuries of breeding from the old Roman stock whittled away to a soldier and his daughter. She was everything to him. That was why he had refused the many offers of marriage proposed by various noblemen. Some said that he was overprotective, but he didn't care. He'd be damned if he let his Aureliana marry into any of the decadent families that now ruled Britannia, acting like petty monarchs, living off the power given to them by General Stilicho.

Deep at heart Aurelianus was a Roman, through and through, just like his father had been. His family had served the governors and emperors since time immemorial. Such loyalty had quickly gone out of fashion after Rome had abandoned the province. But Britannia was too fragmented, too engrained on its old tribal lines to rule itself. Despite his sworn loyalty to Vitalinus and the Council, Aurelianus harboured secret beliefs. If Britannia was truly to survive then Roman military leaders such as Aetius of Gaul would have to step in once more and bring order to the island.

But that was a futile dream. Despite the fact that Aetius was currently fighting the Huns, the majority of the Britons would never willingly send to him for aid. They were too proud. An artificial spirit of patriotism and rebellion had been raised in the aristocracy despite the chaos surrounding them resulting from their own ineptitude as rulers. That was the root of their current predicament. That was why madmen like Vitalinus would rather enlist barbarian savages as allies rather than send to Gaul for help.

"General," said one of his soldiers, poking his head into the tent. "They approach."

"Good," Aurelianus replied, moving the platter of empty shells off the table. "How many of them?"

"About ten to fifteen. On foot."

"Very well. They must have an escort I suppose. But let only the designated ambassadors approach the camp. Have my men form a line just to show them that we are not fools to come here unready for combat. I will come out and meet their delegation."

He waited a couple of minutes for his man to put his orders into action before leaving the tent and making his way down towards the hastily formed line of troops. He was proud of his men; each highly trained and disciplined. At least something that still looked Roman existed in Britannia. Each of them bore large oval shields emblazoned with the Chi Rho symbol; the first two letters of the word 'Christ' in Greek.

In the distance he could see the Saxons; a rag-tag group of savages in mismatched garments of coarse cloth, boiled leather and matted furs. Four of them broke off and approached the British line. The tallest of them bore himself proudly and walked a little ahead of his comrades; the leader no doubt, and eldest of the two brothers. He had long, fair hair that reached almost to his waist and a beard that was of equally barbaric length. Both had plaits woven into them and objects of bronze and bone swayed about amidst the wavering sea of hair. His face was strong and pale with blazing blue eyes beneath a heavy brow.

Two of the other men were shorter and had darker hair although the same blue eyes of their race, but the fourth was significantly younger; little more than a boy. He had the fair hair and fine features of the tallest man and Aurelianus guessed that this was the son of the leader.

"I greet you in the name of Vertigernus, leader of the Council of Britannia," Aurelianus said to them.

They looked at him in confusion. *Of course,* he thought with an inward sigh. Too much to hope for that they spoke Latin. He repeated his greeting in British, hoping that they at least understood a smattering of the common tongue.

The leader replied in broken but understandable British; "Greetings, Briton. We have come to hear what you have to say, but I must warn you that I have my best warriors nearby. Any sign of trickery and they attack."

"Please," said Aurelianus. "There is no need for hostile words. I come as a friend. I would invite all of your men into my camp were it but a simple question of hospitality, but I fear, my soldiers get fidgety when armed Saxons are in such close proximity to them. My name is Ambrosius Aurelianus. I represent the Lord Vertigernus, ruler of Britannia Prima and leader of the Council of Britannia. Whom do I have the honour of addressing?"

"You speak to Hengest, son of Wictgils, son of Witta, son of Wecta, son of Woden," said the tall man. "This is my brother, Horsa, also son of Wictgils and Aesc, my son. Also here is Octa, my lieutenant."

"Let us speak in the comfort and privacy of my tent," Aurelianus said, extending his arm in welcome. The Saxons seemed reluctant at first, but he led the way, smiling in a way he hoped looked friendly.

Once they were seated inside, he poured goblets of wine for all and handed the first to Hengest who looked at it suspiciously. "Good wine," Aurelianus said. "From Armorica. Know where that is?"

Evidently the Saxons would not drink unless he did so first and so, with exaggerated movements, Aurelianus took a long draught from his own cup. At this they smiled and drank in turn.

"And now, let us turn to business," said Aurelianus, seating himself behind his table. "I understand that you have been having some trouble with Sidonius Cassiodorus."

"Do you speak of Gwrangon?" Hengest asked.

"I do believe that he is known by that name amongst the commoners, yes."

"I have trouble with any man who steals from me and threatens my family."

"Indeed. Now, my lord Vertigernus has a proposition for you. He has heard of the great things you have done in Rutupiae; of how you whipped the local gangs of criminals into line and ousted the previous corrupt ruler. You have been doing Gwrangon's job for him, for it is he who the lord Vertigernus set up as a protector of the eastern coast.

My lord's proposition is this; oust Gwrangon as you ousted that crime lord in Rutupiae, and you may rule the coastal towns from Regulbium to Anderitum here as free men. This territory would, in effect become yours in the legal sense of the word."

Hengest considered these words and then replied; "Why should I risk the lives of my men to destroy Gwrangon for your benefit when I can rule here with or without your permission?"

Aurelianus smiled. "Perhaps you do not understand the ways in which Britannia is governed. Lord Vertigernus is effectually in command all four provinces of the island. He has armies the size of which you have never dreamed of. At the snap of his fingers, he could crush the eastern coast and all who dwell here."

"Then why does he require our help?"

"He does not wish to rule Britannia with an iron fist. He is after all, a lord elected by the Council, not a tyrant. He wants to keep his people happy and safe. In order to do so, he must regulate subjects of his such as Gwrangon and bring them to heel if they do not measure up. This is where you come in. Rather than send his armies here to raze the towns to the ground, he would rather employ such men as you to govern the local populace. It is a much less bloody stratagem and also less costly."

Hengest said something then to his brother and the Saxons appeared to enjoy a private joke. When they were done chuckling, he spoke again; "Am I to understand it that Rutupiae and the other costal towns would be the permanent territory of me and my descendants, free from the interference of your master?"

"In a way, but there is the matter of trade to be considered. Gwrangon's role as ruler of the Saxon Shore was to keep the pirates in line and ensure that the merchant ships from Gaul had an easy passage up the River Tamesis to Londinium. It is imperative that this trade continues. As rulers of the coastal towns, Lord Vertigernus will require you to maintain the peace and keep commerce flowing. I understand that you command a strong fleet of ships and many brave warriors. It should not be too much of a problem for you to stop the merchants from being attacked."

"There are many pirates in these waters," said Hengest with a smile. "It is impossible to safeguard every single trader from being raided."

"Of course, but Lord Vertigernus would expect such attacks to be kept to a tolerable minimum should you agree to his terms."

"Your master's proposal is not unappealing," said Hengest after a few minutes deliberating with his brother. "And we would be happy to accept his offer to run the coastal towns for him and ensure that trade continues. There is but one problem with such a plan however. My army recently engaged Gwrangon and I am embarrassed to say that we were defeated. He is well fortified and his strength lies in his cavalry. Unless my army is equipped with fine horses also, we will be unable to oust him."

"Ah yes," said Aurelianus. "The famed Saxon cohort under Gwrangon's control. With regard to them, you may put you minds at ease. I have spoken with these men and they have already accepted terms set down by Lord Vertigernus. They will aid Gwrangon no more. Should you desire horses, I can arrange for this cavalry unit to go to war under your own standard."

Hengest blinked at these words. "These mounted warriors would be mine?" he enquired.

Aurelianus nodded. "Lord Vertigernus suggested that as they are your own countrymen, perhaps it would be prudent to side them with you against Gwrangon's men."

Hengest and his men grumbled at these words and it became apparent to Aurelianus that he had insulted them somehow. He decided to refill their empty wine cups.

"I accept your offer," Hengest said finally. He rose and raised his cup. "We salute the agreement."

Aurelianus rose also and lifted his own cup. "To our eternal friendship," he said and watched in surprise as Hengest knocked back the wine in one gulp. Aware of some savage custom and fearful of appearing rude, Aurelianus did the same and winced as the stinging wine rushed down his throat and into his belly. "It is agreed then," he said, coughing. "Ready your men and send word to me when the attack is to be made. I shall then arrange a meeting between you and the Saxon cohort. God be with you."

Hengest smiled and said; "May Woden protect you and your family."

As the Saxons turned and filed out of the tent, Aurelianus sat back down in his chair and exhaled slowly. *Woden?* The name was unfamiliar to him. Some barbaric heathen deity they sacrificed chickens to no doubt. Never mind. It was done. The alliance had been struck with these godless men from across the sea and control of the most important trade route on the whole island had been handed over to them on a silver platter.

May God help the Britons now.

# Hengest

"I still don't like it" said Horsa. "This isn't freedom. We are now the lapdogs of the Britons. Theirs to command."

They were back in Rutupiae and were sitting in an upstairs room of the old bakery with Beorn, Ordlaf and a few other warriors, discussing the meeting that had taken place with the Britons.

"Only so far as trade is concerned, Horsa," said Hengest in irritation. "Did you expect them to hand land over to us without a price attached?"

"We seem to be doing them a favour already by killing off their underling that they have tired of. Now we have to comply with their demands of running the coastal towns in their name while they take all the profit?"

"There are more than enough traders for us to plunder without arousing the suspicions of the Britons. You know as well as I that Eldred made a fortune by skimming the trade that passed through Rutupiae. And we shall have five such towns under our control."

"And all the while we are puppets on the string of this Vertigernus. I don't like it."

"Well, it is something we must bear for the time being," said Hengest in exasperation. "Once we have this Saxon cavalry under our command, we will be stronger than ever before, both on land and at sea."

"And that's another thing," insisted Horsa. "How can you be so trusting of this Aurelianus, or the Saxons for that matter? Was it not they who killed Guthlaf and nearly severed your arm from your shoulder? Or have you forgotten that already in your eagerness to play ball with the Britons?"

Hengest caught the look in Ordlaf's eye at the mention of his recently departed friend. The young warrior had not been himself since Guthlaf had been killed. The two of them had been inseparable and the older man's death had hit him hard. "I have not forgotten," he replied. "But war is war. People switch sides. There isn't a man here among us who has not done work at one time for a cause that did not sit well with him. Guthlaf met his end fighting for us. Although it may seem dishonourable to his memory to recruit his killers, I do not believe that he would have protested were he alive today. What say you, Ordlaf?"

The Dane looked up at Hengest, his eyes bloodshot. "Guthlaf always trusted you, my lord. He never questioned your motives or your ability as a leader. I will not dishonour his memory by doing any different. If joining with the Saxons is the best way forward in your mind, then you will hear no objections from me."

"Good man," said Hengest. "Then we shall send word to Aurelianus and ask him to set up the meeting. In the meantime I want our army replenished with fresh recruits and outfitted for battle. If anybody knows any carpenters in the town, I want them to send them to see me."

"Carpenters?" asked Horsa. "Have we not furniture enough?"

"I am devising a way that will make our second attack on Gwrangon's house less costly."

"And me, father?" asked Aesc, his face expectant.

Hengest smiled. "Yes, Aesc, you shall march with us this time. But I want you and Octa working extra hard on your spear and sword skills. Hear me, Octa?"

"I'll have him ready" replied the Saxon, patting Aesc on the shoulder. "Have no fear as to that."

Hengest's preparations for war were put into action immediately. A messenger was sent to Aurelianus and two days later, word came that the Saxon cohort had marshalled on the outskirts of Rutupiae beneath the very same oak that the Britons had camped under. Despite Horsa's pessimism, Hengest went out to meet them although he took the precaution of bringing as many able bodied warriors with him as possible.

The Saxons displayed a mixture of fashions, their time fighting for the Britons showing in their dress. As well as the usual Germanic garments of furs and leather breeches, there was also evidence of Roman-style helmets and colourful tunics and cloaks fastened with Celtic brooches. This mixture of styles gave them a mongrel look.

Hengest was acutely uneasy walking into their camp, his aching shoulder and furiously itching stitches strong reminders of the sharpness of the axes held by the men he was about to welcome as friends. Guthlaf was also on his mind and he wondered if he were doing the right thing. But then again, he had forgiven the crew of the *Fafnir* who had kidnapped his wife and children and they had served him as loyally as he could have hoped for right up to their deaths.

The Saxon leader was a tall man in a Roman helmet and scale armour. He was older than Aurelianus and his hair showed signs of grey. He came forward and took Hengest's arm in greeting, speaking in his Saxon language; "*Hwaet*, fellow warrior! I am Ebusa, leader of this cohort."

"I am Hengest, ruler of Rutupiae," he replied, staring hard into the man's eyes. "This is my brother Horsa and my son Aesc. The other three men are my thegns; Ordlaf the Dane, Beorn the Angle and Octa the Saxon."

"Well met, fellow men of Germania" the Saxon replied.

"I understand you wish to join us," said Hengest.

Ebusa shrugged. "Loyalty goes to the highest bidder in these times. The Briton leader paid us well to switch sides. So, for the time being, we are at your service."

"How are we to be sure that you will not switch sides on us for some higher price?" Horsa demanded.

Ebusa laughed. "You can't. But few men in Britta can match Vertigernus's purse if that makes you feel any better. Will you have mead with us?"

"Gladly," said Hengest and they were led further into the camp to where Ebusa's tent was set up by the old oak tree.

Hengest looked around at the Saxon camp. There was a vast amount of horses, hobbled or tied to posts while their owners fed them and brushed down their glossy coats. There was even a small forge where a blacksmith hammered away at a glowing horseshoe while his apprentice shod a mare nearby. The warriors who were not attending to their horses were sitting around fires eating and talking in a mixture of British and Saxon.

"What type of horses do you use?" Hengest asked Ebusa.

"British mares mostly," Ebusa replied. "Not as powerful as the horses of the continent, of course. Frisia in particular. Now those are some fine horses."

"Indeed, I have ridden them," replied Hengest.

"I envy you. Would that I could get hold of some. But it is poor treatment for such a fine animal to transport it across rough seas in the small confines of a trading vessel. I understand the Jutes hold the horse in particularly high esteem."

"We do. It is our most sacred animal, sacrificed to Woden alone. We are born to ride, so they say."

They sat down at a hearth fire and clay jugs of mead were passed around. There was meat also and the evening grew merry. Despite the brutal attack that had almost claimed his life, Hengest grew to like Ebusa. The man possessed a certain kind of polite civility that was undoubtedly a result of growing up in a land so recently vacated by the Romans, but he was also a Saxon at heart and as he called for his scop to sing old songs from the Germanic homelands, Hengest found tears of homesickness welling up in his eyes. Even Horsa seemed to be enjoying himself and drank enough to impress the Saxons before challenging one of them to a wrestling match that had more than a few of them cheering him on.

"When did you two come to Britta?" Ebusa asked Hengest.

"About two years ago."

"Came seeking land and plunder, I bet. Just like the rest of them."

"Something like that. Are you so different?"

"I was born here. My father was leader of this cohort under Constantine. I was too young when he took the last of the Roman legions off to Gaul. They never came back. With the Goths breaking down Rome's doors, the empire was too wrapped up in its own troubles to remember this little island."

"The Goths? I have heard of them."

"Some say that they are descended from the Geats. Though how they got so far from their homelands is beyond me. Alaric was their king in those days. He was employed by the Romans as a barbarian confederate. A paid ally who turned on his masters. A bit like me!" He laughed and handed the mead horn to Hengest. "Leave Britta to the barbarians, that seems to be the Roman policy these days."

"And yet you still serve the Britons? Surely you could set yourself up as a king with such a fine force behind you."

Ebusa laughed. "*Eala!* I am not such a barbarian as you, Hengest with no offence intended. I grew up under Roman order, such as it was in those chaotic days. But the idea of kingship is something best left to others."

"But Rome's days are over," pointed out Hengest.

"When the Romans left things sort of carried on in Britta; run by the offices of the same men General Stilicho had set up. There were a few changes of course, but mostly the Britons like to stick to what they're used to."

"Are the Britons so used to their warriors betraying them?"

Ebusa took a long swig of mead and wiped his mouth. "Gwrangon is a fat fool. No tears will be shed on account of his passing. Besides, this land could do with some new leadership and I'm not averse to seeing some Germanic influence in the running of things. But let us now discuss tactics. Having my troops on your side would be a mighty advantage in open battle, but Gwrangon likes to stay holed up in his villa. Cavalry are no good against stone walls and hidden archers."

"The mere fact that you will not be fighting against us is enough to ensure victory," Hengest said. "Besides, I have devised a plan that will bring his gates down without losing a single man."

"I am intrigued," Ebusa said. "What is your plan?"

"That will be a surprise to you as much as it will be to Gwrangon," laughed Hengest. "Suffice to say that I have learned much from my two years here in a land once ruled by the mighty Roman armies."

# Aesc

The second attack on Gwrangon's villa came swiftly and without mercy. Unlike the first time, there was no warning and the farmers and villagers were still at work in the fields by the time the invading force marched into sight.

Aesc rode with his father and his uncle Horsa. Ebusa and his Saxons rode on the left flank as they descended the slope towards the farm. The villagers fled in terror, dropping their tools and making for the villa. Those who were not fast enough were cut down by the front ranks of the horsemen. The great wooden doors of the villa creaked closed, cutting off the flow of stragglers, leaving them to their fate.

Hengest gave the signal to halt before his front ranks were within bow shot of the walls. The cavalry slithered to a standstill and the mass of footmen led by Beorn and Ordlaf behind slowed up, jostling each other for room, their spear tips wavering above them. The dual horse banner, newly repaired as promised, fluttered in the silent wind, held by Ordlaf who had replaced his late friend as Hengest's standard bearer.

Hengest turned in his saddle to speak to Aesc. "How are you finding it, son? Are you enjoying your first battle?"

Aesc beamed at him and nodded. "I haven't killed anyone yet though."

"You'll have more than enough chances for that once we get inside. Just stay close to me. Your mother would have my pelt as a hearth rug if anything happened to you."

"Cutting down fleeing villagers is poor sport," said Horsa leaning in his saddle so his nephew might hear him. "But the real battle awaits us beyond those gates."

"As to that, Hengest," said Ebusa, "is it not time you showed us your plan for bringing the gates down?"

Hengest turned and gave a signal to his rear ranks. The army parted and a large construction of wood and leather was pushed forward. It looked like a miniature wooden hall on wheels. It had a sloping roof protected by interlocking shields that housed twenty men who walked in two lines, pushing the construction along. Between the lines hung a massive timber with a sharpened tip that had been hardened by fire. Chains supported it so that it swung freely and could be drawn back and forth.

"Ingenious," said Ebusa as they watched the small hut on wheels being pushed up towards the front gate, its men totally protected from the arrows that hailed down on them. "Where did you get the idea?"

"I understand the Romans used similar techniques," Hengest said.

"That is so," Ebusa replied. "Their armies were full of craftsmen who could build things never dreamed of by barbarian minds."

"In this strange land of mixed cultures, a man must use his head to crush his enemy," explained Hengest. "The simple but courageous tactics of our homelands will not suffice here, where minds are mightier than swords."

There was a great booming sound as the ram was pulled back and released, slamming against the doors like a thunder clap. It was drawn back again and again, each strike accompanied by a cheer from the army.

"Get ready," his father said to the mounted men at his side. "I may be adopting these cowardly Roman tactics, but I still want to be the first to have blood on my sword!"

"Are we to lead the charge on horseback?" Ebusa asked.

"Yes, but only us four and ten of your best riders," Hengest explained. "Tell the rest of your men to hold back so my warriors can work their way into the courtyard where there will be plenty of room for sword and axe work. Have them circle the villa to ensure none of the Britons escape through other doors, but tell them to keep out of bowshot from the walls."

There came a great cracking sound from the gates as the wood splintered and the two massive doors began to fall inwards. The archers on the walls had resorted to using flaming arrows and the roof of the battering ram was burning in several places. The men at the rear of the army were going wild with enthusiasm.

"Come on!" shouted Hengest, drawing *Hildeleoma*. "Move that ram out of the way! In! In and kill them all!"

The fourteen horsemen charged quickly followed by the host of footmen, howling war-cries to their gods as they ran. By the time they reached the gates, the blazing ram had been dragged out of the way and the twenty men inside left it to burn by the side of the track while they joined their comrades in storming the courtyard.

The resistance offered by the Britons was a shadow of what they had previously put forward. Disorganized and unready, the soldiers within the walls were cut down by the invaders in moments. Blood spattered the flagstones and the walls rang with the sounds of steel meeting steel as the awful stink of guts and opened bowels rose up in the confined air. Men were trampled under hooves as Hengest pressed forward, making room for his infantry.

From his saddle, his reddened sword waving around in the air, Hengest ordered men up onto the walls to take down the remaining archers which they did so gleefully, sending the unfortunate men plummeting down to shatter on the courtyard below. The riders dismounted and charged up the steps to the front door.

It was bolted and barred from within and the surge of attackers broke upon it like the crashing waves of the sea. Sword hilts, boots and shoulders hammered on the doors that stood as the last barrier between the villa's inhabitants and the onslaught of the foreign horde. Soon it was smashed down and Hengest was the first in, leading his men down dimly lit corridors of stone decorated with rich hangings.

The invaders split up, taking the many corridors and rooms at random, hacking down any Briton that stood in their way. Each room afforded new glimpses of obscene Roman luxury the like of which was totally alien to the Germanic warriors whose muddy boots defiled mosaics depicting unknown gods. Their bloodthirsty shouts rang in the halls and rooms that were accustomed to polite civilisation. Sculptures and busts were smashed. Hangings and curtains torn down and trampled. Gold, which was more than plentiful, was swept up by greedy hands and the cries of unfortunate serving girls could be heard from many rooms as they were violently taken on beds of silk and satin.

Aesc, for his part, was content to marvel at the wonders of Romano-British civilisation. In one room he found a sunken pit in the ground lined with blue and green tiles. It was filled to the brim with water and he concluded that it must be one of those baths the Romans had introduced to the island. Another room revealed itself to be a shrine to their one god who hung on his cross in an alcove. The walls were painted with bright frescoes depicting men and women with strange circles of light surrounding their heads. He surmised that they must be the Christian saints the priests spoke of in the marketplaces; martyrs who had died horribly for their beliefs.

But the youthful bloodlust that raged within him had still not been sated and he was ever more eager to wet his blade. He tore through various chambers, ignoring the obscene acts that were being carried out around him by his father's men, intent on finding his own opponent. He found himself in the villa's kitchen – a large room with tables strewn with vegetables and herbs. He ripped down the wooden door to a storage room and stepped back at the sight of a tubby, balding man cowering within with a woman and two children. They all looked on him with expressions of abject terror.

This, he surmised, was Gwrangon and his family. Not much to look at now that his great stronghold was being torn apart around him. The man gibbered something in Latin and held out a short dagger in defence. He was wearing armour; the polished, sculpted stuff the Romans wore. It looked ridiculous on this fat, frightened man and for some reason that made Aesc angry at him.

He grabbed Gwrangon by the rim of his breastplate and hauled him out of the storage room, sending him sprawling on the tiled floor of the kitchen. The man scrambled to his feet, still brandishing his pathetic weapon.

"If you are so intent on using that breadknife," began Aesc in his best British, "let's see you do it."

He lunged at the nobleman, cutting wide enough for his blow to be deflected with ease. But Gwrangon screamed and lashed out with his knife, scratching the leather armour Aesc wore. He had obviously never wielded a weapon before and the utter uselessness of the man as anything other than a corrupt landowner irritated Aesc intensely.

He lunged again, this time cutting closer and drawing blood from Gwrangon's arm. His family screamed in terror and Gwrangon stumbled against a kitchen table, clutching at his wound as the blood seeped through the cloth of his tunic.

"Come on!" Aesc shouted. "Fight!"

The man stuck his knife straight out as if he were trying to pluck a sausage from the fire and Aesc brought his sword down hard and fast, severing the hand that held it. Gwrangon reeled backwards, his own screams mingling with those of his horrified family as his hand landed on the floor, still holding the knife.

"Enough!" Aesc shouted and he swung his sword again, this time at Gwrangon's throat. The Briton stumbled backwards, his head lolling from its nearly severed neck, an expression of dumb horror on its chubby features as blood pumped down the sculpted muscles of his breastplate. He fell heavily, crashing to the tiles where he lay lifeless. Aesc ignored the screams of the man's family and gazed down on the corpse that, but a few moments ago, had been walking about, talking, moving, *alive*.

He had finally killed a man.

And suddenly, he wasn't at all sure how he felt about it. Part of him wanted to congratulate himself but another part – a part that was growing steadily stronger – felt a little ashamed of killing a man who didn't even know how to fight. The shame grew and turned into mild disgust. He had killed a man who had only been trying to protect his family.

For the first time the weeping of the woman and her children penetrated his fevered mind. They were guilty of nothing. This nearly headless corpse at his feet had been their world and he had taken him from them. He had butchered a woman's husband in front of her. He had killed the father of two young children before their very eyes.

He hated himself for it. There was no glory in this. Of all the men in the house that could have fought him, killed him even, he had decapitated a defenceless man in front of his family.

The door to the kitchen burst open and his father and uncle strode in, blood plastered to their swords and spattered all over their clothes and faces. His father looked down at the corpse of Gwrangon.

"Well, my boy," he said proudly. "You have had your first taste of blood. And the very leader of our enemies too! How does it feel?"

"Awful," said Aesc truthfully. "I didn't think it would be anything like this. I feel sick."

His father laughed and Aesc looked at him in bewilderment. "I was the very same when I killed my first man, Aesc," he said. "Every man finds his first one hard. It gets easier, so have no worries as to that."

At that moment Aesc never wanted to kill another man for as long as he lived, but he kept silent.

"A sad and sorry end to a sad and sorry man," Horsa commented, nudging the corpse with his boot. A little blood spurted from its neck. He looked up at the dead man's family who cowered in the storage room. "What about them?"

Hengest shrugged. "Make theows of them." He motioned to a couple of his men who loitered in the hallway behind him and they came in to drag the wretched creatures away.

Aesc watched them go, still consumed by his own self-loathing.

Ebusa entered the kitchen. "Well, that's the last of the resistance cleared up," he said. "The men are enjoying their victory as you can no doubt hear. The villa is yours now."

"I don't like these Roman dwellings," Horsa said as he looked around him while he wiped his sword on a piece of cloth torn from Gwrangon's tunic. "Too cold and hard. Everything is stone!"

"We shall not live here," Hengest told him. "I have a spot picked out on Thanet to build a mighty hall in the style of our homelands that will stand for a hundred generations. An island makes for a formidable fortress."

"I am surprised," Ebusa said. "I had thought that you would consider a fine villa like this to be part of your spoils."

"You can live in it if you like," Hengest said. "If you are so familiar with these British homes, then it's yours. For me nothing can beat the comfort of wood and the welcoming hearth of a hall."

"I'll not have it," Ebusa replied. "I barely have enough servants to till my own land without taking this mansion on as well."

"Then we put a torch to it," Hengest said. "As a testament to our eradication of the British hold on these lands. They are ours now! Burn it! Make its flames a beacon; a statement to all of Britta; we are here! And here we shall stay!"

A fire was stoked in the belly of the villa and soon the building was up in flames. There was drinking and singing that night as the victors revelled in their success. Piles of treasure looted from the home served as thrones for the warriors who feasted on meat taken from the kitchens and wine from the cellars. The few servants who had been spared death lay bound and under guard nearby, awaiting the cold light of dawn that would herald the start of their new lives as slaves.

As the fire increased, terracotta tiles cracked and slid off the roof and the flames leaped out through the holes, tickling the belly of the night. A short while later, the timbers gave way and the entire roof caved in on itself in a mighty shower of sparks and embers that drifted up into the blackness amidst the cheers of the conquerors.

# PART III

*(Epel) "Epel byþ oferleof æghwylcum men,*
*gif he mot ðær rihtes and gerysena on*
*brucan on bolde bleadum oftast."*

(Estate) An estate is very dear to every man,
if he can enjoy there in his house
whatever is right and proper in constant prosperity.

# Vortimer

Light flooded in through the high windows of the basilica and caught the rim of the golden cup held high by Bishop Lentilus as he recited the words of the Eucharist;

"We give thanks to Thee, our Father, for the holy vine of David Thy servant, which thou hast made known to us through Jesus, Thy servant: to Thee be the glory for ever."

Candles flickered and danced in the aisles of the cavernous chamber. The apse was all that was left of Londinium's original basilica and forum; the rest torn down by the Romans as punishment for Britannia's support of the rebel Carausius. Now its ceiling been painted and a new nave and roof had been constructed around it and the building served as the holy house of God amidst the ruins of what had once been the largest public complex north of the Alps.

Bishop Lentilus was an elderly man with a stooped posture and a snow-white mop of curled hair crowning his lined face. He continued the Eucharist as he crumbled bread onto a golden plate. "As this broken bread was scattered upon the mountains and gathered together became one, so let Thy church be gathered together from the ends of the earth into Thy kingdom, for Thine is the glory and the power through Jesus Christ for ever."

Vortimer, lord of Maxima Caesariensis and ruler of Londinium, stood with his father at the front while the Bishop rambled on. Vortimer was clearly his father's son; just as tall, but darker and smoother. Anybody looking at him would see a glimpse of the handsome young man Vitalinus had been once been. He kept his hair short and a neat little beard completed the appearance of a man keen on cleanliness and organisation. But where his father's eyes blazed with a fiery ambition, Vortimer's were duller and many often said that he lacked his father's cunning.

Once the ceremony was complete, the congregation began to dissipate and voices and laughter rose up to the ceiling as friends met and gossip was shared.

"Greetings, Aurelianus," Vitalinus said as the soldier moved towards them. "And Aureliana, how good to see you!" This was directed at a pretty, young woman by Aurelianus's side. She possessed the dark hair and eyes of her noble line but nature had refined it into a feminine beauty as soft and smooth as milk. "You have been well, I hope, during your father's absence?"

"Very, I thank you," Aureliana replied. "It gave me some peace and quiet to continue with my studies without father's usual blustering."

Vitalinus laughed at this and Vortimer enquired; "Have you been away visiting relatives, Aurelianus?"

"I sent him on a small errand to Cantium to settle a dispute amongst the Saxons," his father answered.

Vortimer glanced at him. "With respect, father," he said, "Aurelianus is commander of the armies at the Council's disposal, not your personal lackey to send on errands."

"I am the Council, boy," his father replied through a forced smile.

"Your father is right, Lord Vortimer," Aurelianus said. "As the leading council member, I am answerable directly to him."

"And what was this errand?" Vortimer asked. "I thought that fellow Cassiodorus took care of the Council's interests in Cantium."

"Cassiodorus has been replaced," said his father.

"By whom? And under whose authority?"

"He has been replaced by a Saxon chieftain. And the authority was my own."

"Surely you jest, father," Vortimer asked incredulously. "A Saxon in charge of Cantium?"

"Not all of Cantium, merely the coastal towns. I thought it prudent to place a stronger line of defence in the south east than was there previously. These Saxons are a ferocious people. With them guarding their territories in the east, no foreign army would dare land on those beaches and our trade routes will remain protected."

"Are you sure that they can be trusted? What's to stop them from marching further inland?"

"I have further plans for them that should keep them busy. Our coming war with the Picts will be a good ground to put the Saxons' loyalty to the test."

"That war has not yet been sanctioned by the Council," warned Vortimer.

"If the Council refuses it then they are fools willing to die with their dreams," said his father. "The only way to keep peace in the north is through an alliance with Prince Talorc against his sister. The Saxons will help us win this war. You see, my son, I have plans within plans that will ensure the safety of Britannia."

"What are these Saxons like, Aurelianus?" asked Vortimer. "You met with their leaders one assumes."

"They're not too bad as far as barbarians go," Aurelianus said. "Pagans of course. Hair down to their middles and faces as bristly as pine trees."

"How fascinating," Aureliana commented. "You never said you met some. What do they wear?"

"Whatever they can get their hands on by the look of them. Skins, furs and crude bits of chain mail and leather armour. They never wash and they stink to high heaven."

"Good lord!"

Vitalinus laughed. "They shall be in for a shock when they arrive in Londinium. Perhaps they will even be coaxed into taking a bath. Prince Talorc, I hear, is most fond of our bathhouses and takes at least one a day now."

There was a stunned silence from the other three.

"When they arrive in Londinium?" Vortimer repeated. "These savages are coming here?"

"Yes, I had thought to invite them to our feast at Pascha."

Vortimer looked at him with a horrified expression. "You wish to invite these barbarians to one of our most holy festivals? To sit at table with us as we celebrate the Resurrection of our Lord? Bishop Lentilus may have something to say about that!"

"He will come to understand the importance of having such allies," his father said. "Besides, the old fool is happy as long as we keep drumming up enough Pelagian heretics for the executioner's block." He noticed the look of shocked excitement on Aureliana's face. "I apologise, Aureliana. I did not mean to criticise His Eminence in your presence."

"Not at all, my lord," Aureliana replied. "I am quite thrilled by such scandal!"

"I think it is time we left, my dear," her father said hurriedly. "We must make a move if we are to be back at the villa before dark."

"Always a pleasure to see you, dear Aureliana," Vitalinus said.

"And you, my lord. I hope your plans with the Saxons work out. I very much look forward to meeting them at Pascha."

Vitalinus smiled as she was pulled away by her father and the two of them disappeared into the throngs of people exiting the church. "In future, Vortimer," he said, "do not question me in public. Even in front of Aurelianus. It looks most ill."

"I apologise, father. But do you not think you are taking your powers as head of the Council a little too far by having Aurelianus recruit barbarians?"

"It is no different than when I had Cunedda and his sons relocated to the west to fight the Gaels."

"That was different. That was sanctioned by the Council. Eventually. And the men of the Votadini are almost Britons, for all their living on the wrong side of the Wall. But these Saxons..."

"Are you aware that the territories once belonging to the Votadini are now overrun by Queen Galana's tribesmen?" his father interjected. "The Picts have swallowed up the lands of the Novantae and the Selgovae too and even occupy Din Eidyn; Cunedda's old royal seat. It is just as it was in the days of the

*Barbarica Conspiriatio*. They reach right up to the Wall now and there is a very real danger of some sort of unification of the tribes under Galana. I for one would very much like to see her brother stand up to her with some degree of success and rule the tribes as an ally of the Britons."

Vortimer was saved from further lecturing by the arrival of Bishop Lentilus.

"Ah, Your Eminence!" said Vitalinus. "Another fine delivery. I do believe I saw tears in the eyes of some as they left."

"You do me too much credit," Bishop Lentilus replied. "I am but a servant of Our Lord. I had hoped to speak with you both before you departed, on the matter of the poisonous heresy that is being conducted in this very town."

"I can assure you that my agents are working their hardest to root out these Pelagians," Vortimer replied. "And my father's lands have been clean of their heresy for many years."

"I am sure, I am sure, and for that I and my superiors are most grateful and we pray for you both. But news has reached my ears of a group of heretics who meet on a weekly basis in some undisclosed location across the bridge. As you are aware, I am in correspondence with Bishop Germanus of Auxerre and he is most interested in the progress of the British clergy in stamping out this evil."

Vortimer did not miss the implied threat in the old man's words. Bishop Germanus was a man whose ire was not to be roused for any reason. Eighteen years ago, he had been sent to Britannia by an assembly in

Gaul to undo the heretical teachings of Pelagius who had insisted that man was responsible for his own good and evil without divine aid and that the concept of Original Sin was false. Germanus had been moderately successful, winning many around to the Augustinian teachings, but the heresy had continued in small cells around the country. If left untended, the clergy claimed, Britannia could fall to sin and evil beyond anyone's aid.

Vortimer knew that the last thing his father wanted was another visit from Bishop Germanus who was an iron-willed old warhorse by all accounts. In addition to having the full and unconditional support of the clergy in Gaul and Rome, Germanus was also a military man with connections to Aetius of Gaul. An impromptu visit from Germanus or worse still, Aetius, would be a serious hitch in his father's plans. He knew that Vitalinus would do everything in his power to keep Britannia an independent nation, free from the shackles of Roman interference. He had heard that lecture more than enough times.

"Rest assured, Your Eminence," said his father, "My son's men shall search every house, in every cellar and under every bridge until this nest of vipers is uncovered and brought to task. You may trust us on that."

The old bishop smiled. "I hope so, Lord Vertigernus. I hope so."

# Hengest

"Octa!" bellowed Hengest at the sound of shouts and breaking furniture coming from the bakery floor below. "Tell those sons of whores that if they must fight, to take it outside!"

He was trying to hold a meeting of sorts between his highest thegns and the noise downstairs was very distracting. He poured over a map of Britta spread across the desk in his office. The very concept of a drawing that marked out the rivers, towns and forests of Middangeard had been an alien concept to him before he had arrived in Britta. Once he had got his head around the idea, he had decided that it was a wonderful thing. Everything was there to see; Thanet, the coastal towns, and the great winding River Tamesis that lead all the way up to Londinium to which they had been invited.

"Are you seriously considering going?" Horsa asked him.

"Why should I not?"

"For one thing, it may be a trap. Another would be the question of what benefit it could possibly be to us."

"This Vertigernus helped us out before and no harm came of it. Have our businesses suffered since we destroyed Gwrangon? Have armies from the west come hammering on our doorstep? No, we have been left alone and our businesses thrive."

"So you think that further dealings with these Britons will bring more fortune and prosperity to us, eh?"

"I think father is right," said Aesc. "The Britons have given us no cause to distrust them."

"Besides," put in Ordlaf with a grin, "they may have more of their own chieftains they wish us to dispose of."

"But this Londinium place," said Horsa. "It sounds a little too much like wandering into the bear's cave to me. I just don't like the thought of marching in there when we know so little about its rulers."

"We will not be going alone. I plan on taking a good-sized band of warriors with us. Besides, Vertigernus has asked us to bring our families. His intentions are clearly peaceful."

"What?" exclaimed Horsa. "You mean to tell me that you are bringing Halfritha and Hronwena?"

Hengest nodded. "Vertigernus says that it is to be a family affair. Some sort of Christian feast day or something." He ran a finger along the rough surface of the map. "We shall sail up the Tamesis on the *Bloodkeel* and put in at one of the docks in the town. Ordlaf and Octa shall remain here to protect the bakery and our other vessels and ensure that everything keeps running smoothly."

"There is also the festival of Eostre coming up," said Horsa. "Have you forgotten that?"

"I have not. We shall only be a few days in Londinium and back before the spring festival. Don't look so glum, Horsa. I should think that this feast Vertigernus has invited us to is merely a chance for him to get to know his neighbours and allies better. If such an invitation had been offered in our homelands by a neighbouring chieftain, you would not have batted an

116

eyelid. But because it comes from the hand of a Briton, you instantly think of treachery."

"Well, what of it?" asked Horsa irritably. "I don't trust these Britons as a matter of fact. Or their devotion to their one god."

The meeting concluded and Hengest soon found out that his brother was not the only one who had misgivings about Vertigernus's invitation. As he slid beneath the skins next to the warm body of Halfritha, he stroked her golden hair. She was still as beautiful to him as the day he had seen her in that blue dress in his father's hall all those years ago in Jute-land. He kissed her bare shoulder and curled his legs up beneath hers. Normally she giggled at this and snuggled closer to him but this time she seemed cold.

"What's wrong?" he asked.

She sighed. "Must we go to Londinium?"

"Gods, not you too!"

"It's so far," she complained.

"It's barely a few miles! You who have travelled from Jute-land to Angle-land and then here to Britta across the great Western Sea, are you now afraid to take a short trip up river?"

"All right, it's not the distance then. I just don't see what business we have with these Britons, that's all. When you decided to come to Britta, you said you wanted to build a safe and secure home for your family."

"That's what I am doing," he reassured her. "Already my men are cutting down timbers and building my hall on Thanet. I plan for it to be complete in time for Eostre."

"I just don't like it here, that's all. This town is so seedy, so crowded. And so unlike our homes across the sea. All the crime and piracy that goes on. It's not honourable. And now you want further dealings with the Britons..."

"I promise you, wife, that soon we shall have a home far away from this place on good, clean open ground beneath blue sky. It shall be so big and so grand that it will put Waelheall itself to shame. And it shall have a great hearth around which we shall sit in winter and listen to songs from our homelands. The kitchen will be so large and well stocked that you shall need an army of theows to keep it running."

At these promises Halfritha smiled and Hengest kissed her.

"And I shall be a king," he continued, "and you shall be my queen, and all the men in Britta shall be envious of my beautiful queen. But only I shall make love to her like this..."

He ducked under the sheepskin covers and Halfritha squealed with delight at his touch.

# Horsa

The *Bloodkeel* drifted inland on the tide, its sail down and oars shipped. Hengest watched the muddy banks slide gracefully past with wonder at the strength of this island that could drag the water back to it day after day. Some said that it had something to do with the moon, but Hengest put it down to the work of some powerful gods.

Halfritha and Hronwena sat in the stern, enjoying the sights of the countryside of which they had seen nothing of since coming to Britta. Horsa sat with Beorn and the rest of the crew at the oar benches, talking and sunning themselves in the glorious spring weather, glad that the journey did not require much rowing despite the still wind.

Fishing boats and traders drifted past, watching the gargantuan Germanic ship creep along in confused terror. Large birds strutted about looking for fish in muddy patches of reeds and beyond stretched farmlands for as far as the eye could see where herders tended to their livestock and men and women worked in the fields, sweating under the hot sun.

It was late afternoon by the time the outskirts of Londinium could be seen from the bow. The light was golden and it swept across the fields to catch on the angular corners and rooftops of the Roman town. Voices quietened on the *Bloodkeel* as the sight unfolded before them. Never had any of them seen, nor dreamt of such a place. The ramshackle buildings and hovels of Rutupiae and the other coastal towns paled in comparison to the massive fortifications that rose up before them.

Encircling the whole town was a stone wall that ran along the water front. Several gates stood at regular intervals flanked by bulging circular towers topped with battlements. The wall was in poor repair with several sections of it crumbled away exposing broad views of the town behind where a kaleidoscope of colours treated the eye. Pale yellows, oranges and pinks glittered as the rooftops of villas, palaces and temples caught at the fading light. Smoke rose from hundreds of homes and drifted on the river air where gulls cawed and wheeled.

The docks took up almost the whole of the waterfront: a massive area of quays, jetties and moorings where a hundred vessels of all functions and sizes were tied up. Warehouses and granaries towered behind them, reaching up to the foot of the wall and men beetled around on the muddy banks, carrying goods back and forth. Further downriver a stone bridge stretched across the water to an expansive suburb on an island in the middle of the river.

"I had no idea that men could build such things," Horsa said in awe as they crept closer.

"Do you still regret coming?" Hengest asked.

Horsa remained silent.

"Where shall we put in, do you think?" Beorn asked.

"There's a free jetty over there," said Hengest, pointing to a stone quay where a group of people had gathered. "I suppose that's our welcoming committee."

They dropped oars and manoeuvred the *Bloodkeel* alongside the stone quay which lay in the shadow of the great wall. Ropes were tossed to men on the ground and the ship was securely moored.

"Greetings, friends!" called out a man dressed in rich robes as Hengest and Horsa stepped onto the quay. He was mature in years and wore a good deal of gold about him. He spoke British clearly and slowly so that they could understand him. "I am Lord Vertigernus, ruler of Britannia Prima and leading member of the Council of Britannia."

"I am Hengest, son of Wictgils and this is my brother Horsa," said Hengest. "We thank you for your hospitality. Allow me to present to you my wife, Halfritha, my son Aesc and my daughter Hronwena."

"Ah! Delighted, delighted!" Vertigernus said, casting his eyes upon the women and letting them linger especially on Hronwena. Hronwena's colour rose and she looked away.

"Allow me to introduce you to your host; my son Vortimer, ruler of this province and the town of Londinium." He indicated a younger man next to him with short black curls and a pointy beard. "Ambrosius Aurelianus you know already, of course; our ferocious war-leader."

Hengest nodded politely at the stern-faced soldier but the gesture was not returned. Behind him stood a row of British soldiers bearing their huge oval shields and gripping their spears tightly. An elderly man who stood next to Vertigernus raised a golden staff with a curled end and spoke in Latin with his arms outstretched.

"What's he saying?" Hengest asked.

"His name is Bishop Lentilus and he welcomes you in the name of our Lord and Saviour Jesus Christ, and may God grant you peace and happiness during your stay with us," Vertigernus translated. "I have made arrangements for your men to be housed in the old Roman barracks in the north west of the town. My son has also set aside rooms in the palace at the disposal of you and your family."

"I thank you," said Hengest. "But I would prefer to leave my men here on board my ship rather than put you to any inconvenience."

"Oh, it's no trouble," Vertigernus said. "Aurelianus here will see to the bed and board of your men as he has a large body of his soldiers stationed there already and there are plenty of huts to spare."

"Very well," said Hengest. "I shall house my warriors with your men but I still insist on leaving a small detachment with my vessel."

As Beorn had stated that he would be damned if he would eat and bed down alongside Christians, the guarding of the *Bloodkeel* was left to him and a few select men whilst the rest of the crew, led by Ebusa, followed Aurelianus through the town to where their accommodation awaited.

Hengest and his family were shown to their rooms in the governor's palace which lay but a short walk from the docks and their eyes widened as they drank in the scenes each room afforded. Never had they seen such luxury, not even in the villa of Gwrangaron. Mosaics spilled across every floor depicting old Roman gods and characters from mythology. Busts of governors and Caesars from the old days stood on pedestals, glowering at all who passed them. Gold and gemstones decorated every room.

"The men who could loot this place would become richer than all the ealdormen in Jute-land put together," Horsa whispered to his brother.

"Don't even think about it," Hengest warned. "We are here as friends, not raiders." But Horsa could see the same glint in his brother's eyes.

They were left to explore their chambers while the servants departed. Aesc and Hronwena ran from room to room, each new discovery lighting up their faces with excitement. The beds were magnificent high things with silk and satin sheets, a far cry from the straw-filled pallets they were used to, and in another room there were baths filled to the brim with hot, steaming water.

"More of these famous Roman baths," Horsa said, peering into the watery depths. "I think I'll pass. It's not natural bathing indoors. It doesn't hold a candle to the cool, refreshing water of rivers and streams."

"At least this way, one can bathe during winter," replied Hengest. "And besides, when have you ever been so keen on bathing?" he added with a grin.

After settling into their rooms, Hengest and Horsa decided to step out and see the sights of Londinium. Naturally, Aesc wanted to come too and, despite his mother's stern disapproval, Hengest allowed it, seeing that the youngster was thrilled to find out what this capital of the Britons had to offer. Hronwena was only too happy to keep her mother company in the palace as she didn't appear at all comfortable being in this strange town.

In some ways Londinium was similar to Rutupiae. Only much, much bigger. The buildings were of the same pale plaster and terracotta tiles only these were in better condition and without the wooden extensions and other Germanic modifications. Large villas belonging to the wealthy rose up on hills above the straight streets and their owners could be seen being carried through the town on litters by their servants, hidden behind silk curtains. The rest of the populace consisted of Britons from all walks of life; soldiers, craftsmen, traders and even long-haired, trouser-wearing Britons from the further reaches of the island who seemed to be considered little more civilised than Hengest and Horsa by the rest of the populace.

Most did not pay much more than a passing glance to the three Jutes as they prowled the town, telling them that their countrymen were not wholly unknown in Londinium. Indeed several Germanic dialects could be heard in passing and Horsa's head turned with interest to stare at fellow Jutes as well as Saxons and Angles.

The market stalls and squares were filled with the bustling activity of commerce where outdated coins were broken and weighed in exchange for exotic goods like olive oil, spices, pottery, coloured glass, silk and fish sauce. Horsa smiled as he noted that these were the very goods that flowed in through the coastal towns under their watchful eyes and provided them with such a lucrative income.

It was evening by the time they discovered the forum. A sprawling courtyard of crumbling pillars and ruined wings surrounded the remains of the great basilica that stood tall in the midst of the chaos. People still flocked about it engaging in business and chattering away as if they did not know that the centre of their once great town was little more than ruins and the Caesars who had ruled it were long dead.

As it grew dark, Aesc began to complain that he was hungry. Horsa shared his complaints and, reluctant to return to the palace when there was still so much left to see and discover, they decided to try one of the local eating houses.

To their surprise, many were closed and a few questions put to some locals revealed that Christians were in a state of fasting in honour of their messiah whose resurrection would be celebrated the following day by feasting.

"What kind of god demands that his followers starve themselves?" demanded Horsa with a sour expression. "Besides, I'm hungry now. I can't wait until tomorrow evening."

They eventually found a wine shop whose clientele did not take their faith quite so seriously and food and drink could be purchased for a few broken coins.

It was a thriving place tucked away beneath a ruined wall that had once been part of the old amphitheatre in the northern part of the town. Dim and poky, the place radiated warmth from oil lamps and the hot press of bodies. They shouldered their way towards the back and grabbed a table just as a pair of soldiers vacated it. Horsa winked at a serving girl and ordered food and wine to be brought for three.

She promptly returned bearing a wooden board with bread and cheese along with three clay cups which she filled with wine from a small amphora. They ate ravenously and slurped at the strong wine, tired after their walk through this strange town.

"I need a piss," said Aesc, looking around for an appropriate place to relieve himself.

"Not much straw here," said Hengest, looking at the bare flagstones beneath their feet. "But there's a door over there. Probably leads out back. Best to follow local customs, whatever they may be."

Aesc nodded and rose from the table to make his way through the crowd. He passed a table of Britons who were engaged in a high stakes dice game. Hengest caught Horsa's eye.

"Take your hand away from your purse, brother," he said. "The last thing we want while we are guests at the palace is to get involved in a tavern brawl."

"Relax," Horsa replied. "Although I feel lucky I'm not sure that those fellows would appreciate me taking all their money."

One of the Britons turned at the sound of Germanic tongues and Hengest's face froze. "Horsa!" he hissed. "That man! Do you recognise him?"

"Of course I do," Horsa replied, his fingers itching for his saex. "It's that cocky bastard who came to demand tribute from us at Rutupiae. I wondered what happened to him. We didn't encounter his ugly face when we burned Gwrangon's home."

The Briton had recognised them and had risen from his seat, swaying slightly from the drink. His friends had risen also, intrigued by their companion's interest in the two barbarians.

"Just what this town needs," said the Briton in a loud voice. "More damned *Saeson*. Why don't you scum stick to the coastal towns where sea rats belong?"

Horsa drew his saex and stuck it point down into the wooden table top. "We're Jutes, not Saxons, you ignorant bastard. Get it right! And as for the coastal towns, if you ever show your filthy head in them again, I'll stick it to the prow of my ship!"

The Briton's face burned with rage. "You're not in Rutupiae now, *Sais*. And this time, I think, there are more of us then there are of you."

He was right, but neither Horsa nor Hengest were the type to let an insult slide in the face of greater odds. Hengest drew his saex also and stood up.

"Brave man," said the Briton. "Unusual quality in a people who take land that does not belong to them and butcher British families. That's, right," he added, speaking to the room at large. "These are the two barbarians who murdered Gwrangon and burned his villa! These are the two who now control the coastal towns instead of honest Britons! And now they wander into our capital as if they own that too."

Horsa felt like pointing out that the death of Gwrangon had been ordered by so-called 'honest Britons' but decided that it would not be believed and may even damage their position with Vertigernus. Such damage may have already been done however, as the majority of the customers in the tavern were flexing muscles and testing blades in preparation for violence.

"I didn't see you hanging around to protect your master when we marched on Gwrangon's stronghold," said Horsa. "If that's indicative of the British spirit then perhaps we shall own Londinium too one day!"

That had done it. The outraged Britons hurled themselves towards them, one of them picking up a chair and swinging it at Horsa. Hengest lashed out with his saex at the man, but could not halt the act and Horsa was knocked sideways amidst a shower of splintered wood. A bottle smashed against the wall by Hengest's ear and he ducked, flipping the table over to form a barricade between them and the enraged Britons.

Their main enemy had drawn a short dagger and was egging his comrades on. When some of them showed hesitation in the face of Hengest's swinging knife arm, he advanced, intent on finishing the two Jutes singlehanded.

He didn't hear the door swing open and was only aware of a presence behind him just as it was too late. He spun on his heels to be confronted by a young boy with a face showing an adult's rage. He gasped as Aesc's blade sank between his ribs and toppled forwards, pushing Aesc to the ground beneath him.

The crowd hung back, shocked by the brutal killing of a man by a youth half his age. Aesc scrambled out from beneath the corpse, his tunic smeared with blood. He looked up at Hengest and Horsa with a pale face but bravely made light of the matter, despite his trembling voice; "You're right, uncle. It is more satisfying when they have a weapon in their hands."

Hengest roared with proud laughter.

The dead man's friends quickly overcame their shock and advanced on the boy. Hengest grabbed

Horsa by the arm and hurled the table aside, desperately trying to get to his son before the Britons did.

A voice rang out from the rear of the tavern. "Stop! For the love of good God, stop!" Few paid it much heed but the voice was persistent if not particularly intimidating. "Stop by order of Lord Vertigernus!"

That got their attention. The crowd parted to let a small man in a green cloak through. He had a thin, weak face and was dwarfed by nearly everybody in the room. "These men are guests at the palace!" the small man explained in a hurry. "They are under the protection of Lord Vertigernus himself. Any man who harms them will be hanged from the town bridge come morning!"

He stopped at the feet of Hengest and Horsa who were shielding Aesc from their enemies.

"Who are you?" Hengest demanded.

"My name is Caradoc," the man replied. "Or Ceretic, depending on who speaks it; Briton or *Sais*. I think it is best if we leave, and the sooner the better."

Hengest eyed him suspiciously before nodding and they followed the man out. The crowd let them pass, unwilling to interfere in palace business. The corpses dangling from the town bridge were more than enough incentive to mind one's own business in such affairs.

Once they were outside, Ceretic turned to the three Jutes and said in perfect Saxon; "I was sent by my lord Vertigernus to assist you should you get into any trouble."

They looked at him in astonishment.

"You speak our language!" exclaimed Hengest.

"Indeed," replied Ceretic. "My father was a Saxon who married a British farmer's daughter. I serve the palace as an interpreter. That is why I was chosen to follow you today."

"You mean to tell us that you've been spying on us all evening?" asked Horsa.

"Not so much spying..." said Ceretic. "More of a helping hand should you need it."

"I'm not sure that we like that," said Hengest. "But you did get us out of a sticky spot in there so for that you have my gratitude."

"Not at all," replied the man. "Your people can often be unpopular in Londinium. The Britons are not too happy about the situation on the east coast and many of them resent the fact that all trade seems to be controlled by Saxons. But that is of no importance now. Come, I think it is time we returned to the palace."

All agreed upon that being the best course of action.

# Hengest

Upon entering the large reception room of the palace, Hengest realised that whatever hardships the Christians had put themselves through during the forty days leading up to their holy festival - whether it be fasting or holding an all night vigil in the basilica to welcome the light of dawn - they more than made up for it with the climactic celebration.

Tables had been set up and laden with a feast to make the benches of Waelheall pale in comparison. An extraordinary variety of dishes met the eye and tantalised the nose. Salmon baked in vine leaves, birds stuffed with olives, oysters by the platterful, venison, pork and fowl, great pastries filled with game that billowed steam when cut open and vegetables of every kind were heaped up alongside cheeses and fruits. Wine and ale were in abundance but there was no mead being considered fit only for the commoners by the British nobility.

Hengest and Horsa were seated at the highest table with Vertigernus and his son Vortimer. To Hengest's left sat Ceretic the interpreter and beyond him, Halfritha, Aesc and Hronwena. Bishop Lentilus, Ambrosius Aurelianus and his pretty daughter sat opposite Horsa. The meal was blessed by Bishop Lentilus who raised his arms and praised Christ who, the Britons believed, on this day hundreds of years ago, had returned from the dead three days after his crucifixion. A prayer was said and Hengest and his family politely bowed their heads and closed their eyes as the others did, letting the unintelligible Latin words flow over them. Then the feasting began.

Feeling totally out of his depth, Hengest picked at the strange food and sipped at the stinging wine amidst the finery and polite conversation of the Britons. He saw his family doing the same and was proud of them for their efforts.

Opposite him, Lord Vertigernus was engaged in conversation with a man to his right that Hengest did not recognise. They spoke in Latin and Hengest struggled to comprehend the words. It was so unlike the British tongue he had picked up since coming to these shores. He marvelled that the Britons should find their own ancestral language too common for polite usage, preferring instead the language of the people who had conquered them.

"Lord Elafius here is ruler of Britannia Secunda," explained Ceretic who had clearly perceived his floundering. "They are discussing his son who was injured in a hunting accident last summer."

"My apologies, Hengest," said Vertigernus. "I forget that you do not speak Latin. Lord Elafius's son is gravely injured, you see. His leg was shattered when his mount fell upon it. The physicians and the priests assure us that he will be well but he may never walk again."

"I am sorry to hear that," Hengest said to Lord Elafius. "Was it a very temperamental horse?"

Elafius seemed a little taken aback by the politeness of this barbarian. "Not unreasonably so," he replied, clearing his throat. "It was given to him as a present for his eleventh birthday by his aunt. The horse is dead now of course. Broke its leg in the fall and I had to end its misery. My son's however, continues."

"Do you know much of horses, *Sais*?" asked Vortimer, his use of the term a little barbed as if he had meant to say 'barbarian' instead but had thought better of it.

"All Jutes do," Hengest replied. "To our people the horse is a brotherly creature and symbolises strength, honour and freedom. The Jutes make magnificent warriors astride their fellow creatures."

"I should very much like to see your ferocious people in action," Vertigernus said.

"Few can stand against a hundred mounted Jutes when the battle-lust is upon them," added Hengest.

"I wonder how they would fare against mounted Picts." Vertigernus seemed to direct this towards a man sitting further down the table who had been silent until now.

He was an extraordinary looking man with long, black hair and beard – most uncommon in British high society – and blue markings on his face as if he had been purposely scarred and the raw flesh stained with the dye of some plant. He wore clothes so garish and multi-hued that they made him look extremely out of place amidst the tunic-wearing Britons as did his accent which was deep and slow. "Horse-riding is not a common feature of Pictish warfare," he answered. "With so much of our lands covered by forest and the rest steep hills, and mountainside it is not a custom my people have much adopted. But our noble folk do on occasion ride into battle atop horses."

"This is Prince Talorc of the Picts," Vertigernus explained to Hengest.

"Picts?"

"A wild people in the north," said Aurelianus, chewing on a chicken leg. "Pagans. Not too different from your own people, I imagine."

"Well, I don't know about that," said Hengest, eyeing the Pict, for truly, he had never seen any man so strange looking.

"Aurelianus is joking, of course," said Vertigernus, although the sternness in the soldier's face suggested that he was anything but. "The Picts are all that is left of the old Britons. Believe it or not, the whole of Albion used to be filled with people like Prince Talorc here. Of course the Romans subdued them in the days of the mightiest Caesars, but they were never able to fully conquer the north of the island. Too hilly, some have said."

"Or the inhabitants are too ferocious," added Prince Talorc with a touch of pride in his voice.

"One Caesar even built a wall from one side of the island to the other to keep them out," Vertigernus said.

"A wall across the whole island?" Hengest asked incredulously.

Aurelianus nodded. "The greatest achievement of the empire in my belief. Eighty miles long and twenty feet tall in places."

"I refuse to believe it until I see it," said Hengest.

Vertigernus smiled. "What a portentous thing to say, my *Sais* friend. I very much hope that you do indeed see it. Aurelianus here is organising an expedition north to fight the Picts. Not Prince Talorc's people, of course, but his bitter enemies. His sister, Galana has laid a claim to his throne. She is a wicked witch of a woman. If she takes the Pictish throne, then she will soon set her eyes on the rest of Albion and that would be bad news for all of us. Naturally, the Council wishes to support Prince Talorc in his quest to oust his sister. I had hoped that our newly forged friendship would entice you to join us, Hengest."

There was a silence at the table. Hengest was aware that several of the British noblemen were eyeing Vertigernus uneasily.

"My lord," began Elafius, "I really think that such a matter should be put to the Council before you decide to hire barbarian mercenaries."

"Mercenaries?" exclaimed Vertigernus. "Who said anything about mercenaries? I am merely suggesting that these fine *Saeson* warriors enter into an alliance with us to fight a common enemy. They have already proven themselves more than loyal by safeguarding the coastal towns and ensuring that trade continues uninterrupted. We Britons need friends such as these. Of course, I am not suggesting that they help us purely out of unconditional loyalty, for I am, if anything, a realist. No, should they join with us, then there would certainly be further benefits for them."

"What kind of benefits?" Hengest asked, eyeing the British lord suspiciously.

"Complete control of Cantium. From the Tamesis to the ocean."

There was an outcry at these words. Aurelianus glared at his lord and master as if he were a madman and the rest of the nobles gaped and murmured to each other. The conversation grew heated and Latin took over from British, leaving Hengest and his family to watch in embarrassed silence. Hengest leaned over to Ceretic and asked him to translate the conversation which he did.

"You cannot be serious, father!" Vortimer exclaimed. "Give them Cantium! Why not give them the run of all Britannia?"

"Silence, Vortimer!" bellowed Vertigernus. "Do you dare defy me and insult our guests to their faces? And as for the rest of you, what are you all chattering at? Am I not the leading member of the Council, chosen by the men seated at this very table?"

"The whole point of the Council is to discuss these things," said Elafius.

"There is nothing to discuss," Vertigernus snapped. "Did any one of you question my logic when I sent Cunedda and his sons westwards to fight the Gaels? Did that plan prove faulty? The west is now as secure as the walls of Londinium itself. But yet you question my judgement in making the east just as secure. We are an island, gentlemen. We cannot look to Rome for protection any more. We must build this island into a fortress if we are to survive the hordes that hammer on our gates."

"Bishop Lentilus," pleaded Vortimer, "What say you?"

"I am a simple man of God, my boy," the bishop replied. "Politics is not my game. But I know this; Lord Vertigernus is a fine ruler who has not failed us in the past. He was chosen, not only by the people of

Britannia, but by God himself to lead us through these dark days. I for one, trust his judgement."

This, while clearly not appeasing the angered nobles, at least pacified them a little and many simply lapsed into silence, gazing into their goblets as if the key to the safety of their land was hidden somewhere in those crimson depths.

"I thank you, Bishop," said Vertigernus. He returned to using British and addressed Hengest. "I apologise, my friends. As you can see, we Britons are often as keen to fight each other as our enemies. But I put the question to you now; will you continue your loyal defence of this land by marching to war with us against those who would destroy it?"

Hengest needed no time to meditate on the notion. A chunk of land greater than any he had ever dreamed of ruling had been offered to him and the only price attached was the death of a few northern tribesmen. He rose from his seat and held out his wine goblet. "I accept," he said, feeling the eyes of the whole room on him.

Vertigernus, evidently pleased, rose also and lifted his own goblet. "Then with this room and God Almighty as witness, let it be an agreement!"

Every cup in the room was raised to lips, however reluctantly by some.

# Horsa

Horsa glared at his brother over the rim of his goblet. What nonsense was this? He wanted no war with northern savages. But as usual, Hengest had taken the lead, spoken for both of them and played his role as the eldest just as he had done when they were children. Weren't the five towns already under their control enough for him? What did he want with the whole of Cantium? Did he not know how much his ambitions rankled with his family? Did he not feel their eyes on him?

Halfritha looked to be on the verge of tears at the prospect of losing her husband in some new pointless war. Hronwena's face matched her mother's. She had nursed her father back from death's door after their fight with Gwrangon. What new wounds would he return with this time? And Horsa had a feeling that something else was bothering her. On several occasions he had looked up from his plate to see Lord Vertigernus staring at her from the corner of his eye. He recognised the dirty leer of a man who wanted to tear the clothes away from a young woman's body and he disliked their host for it.

The only one of them who looked pleased was Aesc, no doubt eager for a further chance to prove himself in his father's eyes. The little lad was a fool but Horsa was fond of him. He was not too different from him when he had been a boy. But he had more of a conscience than Horsa had ever had at that age. Aesc had admitted to him in private that his killing of Gwrangon haunted him. It had not been a particularly honourable kill, even Horsa had to admit that, but it wasn't bad for the first blood on a boy's sword.

Conversation turned to other topics. All the Britons were eager to put the distressing moment of dissention far from them. Horsa turned his attention to the food and drink. He was acquiring a taste for the wine that kept appearing in his goblet as if by magic. He smacked his lips at the taste of venison cooked in some unknown way with some foreign spices.

Opposite him sat a girl who had been introduced to him as Aureliana, daughter of Aurelianus. She was no Germanic woman, but still, she was very beautiful with dark hair held up in the Roman fashion spilling a few loose tendrils down on either sides of her perfect face.

"The venison can hardly be so bad," she said to him in British.

"What?" he replied, not understanding her meaning.

"That you must sit with it on your tongue without swallowing."

He realised that he had been staring at her and swallowed hastily, washing down the half-chewed meat with a gulp of wine. "Excuse me," he said. "The food is excellent. As is the company."

She smiled at him and said; "Tell me, *Sais*, do they celebrate Pascha in your own lands?"

"Not as such," he replied. "Although we do celebrate the onset of spring with feasting and dancing in honour of the goddess Eostre."

"Goddess? How curious. You mean to tell me that the word of Christ has not yet reached those lands?"

"Indeed it has not. We have many gods. Woden is their chief but Eostre is the feminine embodiment of spring and the light of dawn in the east. She must be paid the proper respect if the fields are to be fertile and the women and livestock are to bear offspring."

The overhearing of these remarks set Bishop Lentilus into a bout of coughing and spluttering as he choked on his wine in outrage at such pagan barbarity displayed at the table of Pascha.

Vertigernus reached over and patted the old cleric on the back gently, saying; "You have upset our dear bishop, my heathen friend. We are not used to the customs of pagans in Londinium. You must forgive us."

"I think it all sounds fascinating," Aureliana said. "To think that there are some people in the world who have no inkling of God and instead worship idols fashioned by their own imaginations."

"That's enough, daughter," warned Aurelianus. "Do not encourage these men to further heathen outbursts."

Horsa glowered at the man and met his steely eye, searching for some retort that would surely have put the poor bishop into a seizure, but quickly remembered where he was and held his tongue.

"They are not to blame," Vertigernus said. "Albion herself was a hotbed of pagan evil once, before the word of our Lord came to this island. Indeed, some parts of it still are, isn't that so, Prince Talorc?"

The Pict nodded politely, but Horsa detected something of an affront in the strange man's eyes.

"Our Pictish friend here agreed to be baptised by Bishop Lentilus," Vertigernus went on. "By accepting Christ into his body, he has purified himself and ensured a victory over his wicked sister. With British aid of course."

"That is an important prerequisite," stated the bishop, now recovered from his coughing fit. "You yourselves must accept the authority of the one true god before marching to war with Aurelianus."

"I beg your pardon?" Hengest said.

"You must of course, give up your pagan ways and agree to be baptised," Lentilus went on. "It is the only way God can ensure victory against the Picts."

"Victory will be ensured by our strength of arms and our iron spirit," interjected Hengest testily. "We require no god to aid us. If ever we do, then we shall sacrifice to Woden." He was angry at the flippant remarks of the Britons regarding the gods of their homeland.

"Then there will be no alliance," snapped the bishop.

"Now, friends," said Vertigernus. "Let us not allow wine to lead us towards heated words. I'm sure that this is something we can discuss before coming to some arrangement."

"There is nothing to discuss," said Lentilus. "These men must be baptised if they are to fight under the British banner. I will not have it any other way. We cannot allow pagans to fight in the name of our Lord."

Vertigernus looked to Hengest and Horsa, an expression of pleading on his face. "Will you not reconsider, my friends?"

"We will not," answered Horsa. "Asking us to give up our gods is like asking you people to cast down those crucifixes you wear around your necks."

"Does your brother speak for you?" Vertigernus asked, turning to Hengest.

Hengest thought for a moment. "He does. We will not turn our backs on the gods of our homelands. Do not ask it of us."

Vertigernus sighed. "You disappoint me. Well, as long as you are sure of it, then there is no point discussing it further. But we should not let this disagreement ruin the feast before us. Let us eat and drink more as friends."

And that is what they did, but the evening was not far from its end. With bellies full and heads swimming with wine, the guests drifted off to their rooms one by one. It had been a tiring and eventful evening for all.

# Bishop Lentilus

The following day was no less taxing for Bishop Lentilus  and he yawned as darkness fell on the town. His many clerical duties often kept him up late into the night. He rubbed his sleepy eyes and picked up his candle to light his way down from his office in the upper rooms of the ruined basilica.

Vertigernus had been to visit him earlier in an attempt to sway his opinion on the baptising of the barbarians. They had been drawn to anger and harsh words had been spoken for he, Bishop of Londinium, would not allow himself to be swayed on such a crucial matter. It weighed on him heavily; yet another burden upon an old man's shoulders. But enough of such thoughts. Now he needed sleep.

The long, dark colonnade stretched out in front of him, lit only at occasional intervals by the moonlight that shone in through the high windows. He held onto the stone banister with the flickering candle in his other hand and the great black void on his right leading down to the floor of the nave below. His bedchamber was in the annex on the other side of the forum and this night, as he did every night, he promised himself that one of these days he would have his things moved from his office to a room closer to his sleeping quarters. This nightly journey in the blackness was too much for a man as old as he.

He halted abruptly, startled by some noise. He may have seen more than seventy summers, but there had never been anything wrong with his hearing and he was sure that he had just heard something. He listened.

Nothing.

He shook his head and moved on but then, he detected a slight shadow in the corner of his eye. Somebody was there! Watching him!

"Who's that?" he called, peering into the black shadows that seemed like liquid. He was certain that a figure stood a few feet from him but he could not fix his eyes on any outline. He stepped forward, holding out his candle to banish the shadows and reveal the one who lurked within them.

He had no time to turn or even cry out before the unknown assailant was on him; hard hands gripping his arms and pushing him, forcing him against the banister.

He screwed up his face in agony as his brittle bones broke against the stone columns of the banister but that was the least of his worries as he felt the whole thing move under his touch. The banister was loose! Rock grated against rock as several pillars gave way and plummeted to the floor below. Lentilus screamed – a small, frightened and pitiful scream – as he felt himself tumble over the edge and fall into the blackness.

He fell for what seemed to him like and age and he tried to pray. But his words to God were never completed as his body hit the stone floor of the nave with a crunch.

He died before the pain had any chance to sink in.

# Vortimer

"Have you heard?" exclaimed Vortimer as he strode into the hall. "Bishop Lentilus is dead!"

Vitalinus sat at the table eating a breakfast of porridge and fruit. He looked up at his son without a trace of surprise on his face. "I am aware of it."

"Fell," said Vortimer, as if not hearing him. "Fell to his death in the basilica. Apparently the banister was loose and he tumbled to the nave below."

"Old building, the basilica," replied Vitalinus, returning his attention to his porridge. "Falling apart really. A terrible accident waiting to happen."

"Odd that he should fall to his death within hours of having an argument with you."

"Are you suggesting anything, boy?" Vitalinus's eyes flashed dangerously at his son.

Vortimer sighed. He hadn't intended to make accusations. He didn't really believe that his father was capable of such a thing but it was hard to ignore the coincidence. "The townsfolk are murmuring things against you. They are saying that it is far too convenient..."

"I care little for what the townsfolk think," snapped Vitalinus. "And so should you. Let them suspect what they want for it is of little consequence. I have the real perpetrators already in custody."

"What? Who?"

"Pelagians. That cell Lentilus was so worried about was discovered by Aurelianus's men last night on the other side of the river. Three of the wretches confessed in the early hours of this morning to killing the bishop."

"Confessed under torture?"

"What of it?"

"It's hard to believe! Pelagians are a misguided lot, but they are still men of God. Killing a bishop? I would never have dreamed that they could go so far."

"They are dangerous radicals. With our troops and magistrates coming down on them like God's army of avenging angels they have grown ever more desperate. Lentilus was a good man who sought to eradicate their kind once and for all. With him out of the way, perhaps they thought that they would have an easy time of it. Well, they thought wrong. These three animals are due to be executed tomorrow and following that, I'll not rest until every vile cell of this blasphemy is wiped off the face of Britannia in Bishop Lentilus's name."

"A noble mission, father. It would certainly win more of the populace around. And it would also ensure that your plans with the Saxons suffer no interference from Bishop Germanus. Your power would continue uninterrupted."

"You are becoming just as your mother was, Vortimer. If you have an accusation against me then speak it. Don't dance around the subject like a woman!"

Vortimer's gut churned at the mention of his mother. He had been twelve years old when she had died giving birth to his younger brother. His father had quickly remarried and more children had followed, relegating his mother to a mere memory, seldom spoken of. With his older sister now dead too and a younger brother he had never particularly wanted or liked grown to manhood in the west, Vortimer rarely returned to the family estate. Londinium was a comfortable world away from the dreary, rain-swept hills of his childhood.

"I am merely pointing out that the death of Lentilus has worked in your favour, father. Perhaps the Saxons no longer need to be baptised now that Lentilus is no longer here to demand it."

"It would seem so," said Vitalinus.

"Lord Marcellinus has arrived," Vortimer said. "I saw his horses being stabled on my way over here."

"Good. That is everyone then. The Council can meet a day from now."

"Everything seems most timely," said Vortimer, seating himself at the table and taking the ladle from the pot.

"Yes, it does rather," said Vitalinus and Vortimer caught a ghost of a smile on the old man's lips.

The execution of the three Pelagians was received with great acclaim by the people of Londinium. The town had been in a state of shock and mourning at the news of the Bishop's death. It was not that he had been a particularly well-loved figure but the brutal murder of such a holy man was a crime unheard of in its blasphemy. 'Is nothing sacred these days?' was the question that bounded about the town. Crowds flocked to the forum to see the execution of his murderers and the air crackled with the anticipation of justice about to be dispensed.

Vortimer watched from the balcony of a building that faced the forum as the prisoners were brought out in chains to the cheers and jeers of the crowd. He would have much rather had not been there. Such entertainments were not enjoyable to him. But he was the ruler of Londinium. The people expected him to oversee the executions of traitors and many would be watching his face from below. He tried to keep his expression rigid; devoid of both pleasure and distaste at the proceedings.

Guards parted the throngs to form an aisle through which the Pelagians were led and the crowd pelted them with mouldering food and stones. The prisoners looked about them in terror with the wide-eyed expressions of trapped animals as they were led to the centre of the forum where the executioner's block stood.

It was a massive slab of stone that had once been part of a supporting pillar. Streaked with the brown stains of dried blood, it stood as a reminder and a deterrent. Soldiers had formed a ring around it to keep the crowds back and the executioner stood to one side, the large sword held in his hand, keenly sharpened that very morning for the task at hand. The barricade of soldiers closed behind the prisoners as they entered the ring of execution; sealing them in with their fate.

An elderly, white-haired magistrate came forward and addressed the crowd; "People of Londinium! We have gathered here today to see justice done under the eyes of God!"

There was a great cheer from the crowd.

"The Pelagian Heresy has plagued this town and this island for a generation," he went on. "Despicable blasphemers such as these three men here are a canker upon this land, thankfully kept in check by our good Lord Vertigernus. But can there be punishment enough for three wretches such as these who have taken the holy life of a bishop chosen by God?"

The crowd cried out that there was not. One of the prisoners began to weep.

"There is not," agreed the magistrate. "Only God can dispense true justice in this matter and so we must hasten these men on to their judgement at the gates of heaven."

The magistrate had no more to say and nodded to the guards who held the weeping Pelagian. He was dragged forward and forced to kneel at the block and place his shaking head upon the cold stone. The executioner stepped up and placed the keen edge of his blade against the trembling pale neck. The crowd fell silent in barely controlled anticipation. The blade was raised and the executioner brought it down in one single, clean chop. The crowd went wild as the head was sent spinning across the flagstones, sending out a cart wheeling jet of blood.

Vortimer cringed. He was unused to the sight of blood, having never seen a battle, but he forced himself to watch. This was the reality of his father's rule; blood in the forum, heads on spikes. The other two prisoners were executed in the same way, mumbling prayers as they knelt at the block. The second's head was removed just as easily as the first but the third took three blows before the executioner resorted to stamping on the nearly severed head until it finally tore free.

Vortimer turned away, that morning's porridge threatening to rise up in his gullet. As he turned he saw his father standing on an adjacent balcony, surrounded by various fawners. He seemed to be enjoying the spectacle almost as much as Vortimer was hating it. And for that, he hated him.

The following day the Council convened in an upstairs chamber of the palace. Vortimer, always punctual, had been the first to arrive. Aurelianus, also a man of strict timekeeping came soon after. Lords Elafius of Britannia Secunda and Marinus Marcellinus of Flavia Caesariensis swept into the room together followed by Brochfael; the Master of Coin. Although Britannia no longer minted coins, there was still a treasury and a treasurer to command it. Lord Vertigernus was, of course, late, having developed a reputation for being the last to arrive and making the others stand on ceremony for him.

The chair of the late Bishop Lentilus was lamentably vacant and would remain so until his replacement was chosen. The election of a new Bishop of Londinium was one topic on today's agenda. The only other chair that remained empty was that of Sidonius Cassiodorus; Count of the Saxon Shore. Vortimer noticed that the others occasionally glanced at it nervously. Perhaps they, like him, were wondering if his father would dare to go so far as to fill it with his self-appointed replacement. Surely even he would not be so stupid as to put a pagan Saxon on the Council?

Lord Vertigernus swept into the chamber with a man closely following. All eyes turned to this man and there was an almost audible sigh of relief when it became immediately apparent that it was not Hengest the Saxon. It was a young, meek-looking man wearing the robes of a deacon. Such was the relief of the gathered council members that the man was immediately disregarded as Vertigernus took his seat.

"Greetings, my friends," Vertigernus said. "I apologise for my lateness. Shall we get down to business?" There were nods and murmurs of agreement. "After the tragic death of Bishop Lentilus we must turn our hearts to the unpleasant duty of naming his successor. The Bishopric of Londinium cannot be allowed to stand vacant for too long. Unless anybody has any other candidates in mind, allow me to put forward Fabius Calvinus for the Council's consideration. He has been a loyal supporter of both the Council and of the late Bishop Lentilus."

"Calvinus?" asked Lord Elafius. "I am unfamiliar with the name."

"This is him beside me," Vertigernus replied, indicating the frightened looking deacon who fiddled with the sleeves of his robe nervously. "A fine young man who has a mind for the fast moving game of politics. Bishop Lentilus, for all his achievements, was sadly, a romantic. He believed that the British clergy was an isolated body independent of the Council. As a result, there were some disagreements. Calvinus here is a man born in Londinium and a man who can juggle religion and politics with all the grace of a circus performer."

There was a stunned silence from the Council.

"Make a deacon the Bishop of Londinium?" exclaimed an astounded Lord Marcellinus. "Is this a joke?"

"I would not joke on such a matter during this time of mourning for our lost bishop," said Vertigernus sternly.

"But this is most irregular," said Elafius. "Surely one of our priests would be more qualified for the job."

"What is it about this deacon that makes him so appropriate, father?" asked Vortimer.

"I have already mentioned his qualities," said Vertigernus in a tired voice. "The time has come to choose a bishop that is more sensitive to British needs and not so hasty to hold the authority of Rome up as a threat to us."

"As a threat to you, you mean," said Elafius. "We all know how much you begrudged Lentilus his friendship with Bishop Germanus of Auxerre. With this lowly deacon here as bishop, your position of power will be secure from interference from Gaul."

There were murmurs of agreement from the Council and Vertigernus glared at Elafius with hate in his eyes. "You misjudge my character and my intentions, Lord Elafius," he said coldly. "Perhaps you would rather Rome sent her armies back to Britannia to crush us under her boot once more?"

"Rome is too busy with the Huns to worry about us," Elafius said.

"Yet Germanus has much influence with the military," said Vertigernus. "He stuck his nose in Britannia's business once before, and he will not hesitate to do so again, perhaps with the aid of his friend Aetius this time."

"But Germanus's expeditions against the Picts and the Saxons were wholly successful," said Marcellinus.

"One must wonder why you dislike the man so much. Was it that he achieved peace where you yourself failed?"

Vertigernus's eyes spat fire at the Lord of Flavia Caesariensis. "As the Picts are still ravaging the north and the Saxons are settling in droves in the east, I would say that Germanus's expedition was anything but successful," he snapped. "Besides, our own armies are more than adequate under the leadership of Ambrosius Aurelianus."

"And yet we need to employ Saxon mercenaries?" asked Elafius.

"The method of *foederati* has been used for centuries," said Vertigernus. "Bolstering our forces against the Picts can only to be to our advantage."

"And when the Picts are defeated, father," spoke Vortimer, "what then? Who will we employ to fight the Saxons when they, inevitably, turn on us?"

The Council voiced their agreement at this, impressed by the young lord's will to stand up to his father. But Vortimer knew that it was hopeless. The army followed Aurelianus and all knew who Aurelianus followed. Vortimer looked at the soldier sitting there in his polished armour. He had been silent so far. Was the man really so craven? His father had been killed by Vertigernus and yet he clung to the robes of 'the overlord' like a frightened child might cling to his mother's apron. Did he have no honour? No self respect? He suddenly cringed inwardly. *Am I really any different?*

"You misjudge our barbarian friends," insisted Vertigernus. "They wish land to build their homes on.

In exchange for this they will fight our enemies for us. In time, they too may come to be called Britons."

Finally, Aurelianus did speak. "What has all this to do with the choosing of a new bishop? The agreement with the Saxons has already been struck. If we take Cantium away from them now, we will not only lose their support in the war in the north, but we will make enemies of them forever. It is a done deal."

Vortimer heard the futility in the soldier's voice. The man clearly disagreed with his master's ideas but was a prisoner to his own cowardice.

"Quite right, Aurelianus," said Vertigernus. "Now, if there are no other candidates for the position of Bishop of Londinium, then I suggest we take a vote on Calvinus."

The chamber was silent. There were no other candidates. His father had not allowed them enough time to find any. Eyes flitted from Aurelianus to Vertigernus. Together the two of them were Britannia. One; a simple-minded soldier who sat there, stolid as a rock, his polished armour a symbol of his military might that might be used against any physical rejection of his master's proposal, and the other; an insidious snake who commanded a legion of spies and assassins to enforce his will. Resistance was pointless. The expressions of the faces of the council members could have been summed up with a single sentence; 'Look at what had happened to Lentilus.'

"Bishop Calvinus," Vertigernus said after allowing the silence to become a deadweight in the chamber, "you may take your seat. Your appointment ceremony will take place as soon as possible."

The young man shuffled over to the seat that had so recently been vacated by Lentilus and nervously sat down in it. The eyes of every single council member watched him as if he were the sole symptom of Britannia's sickness.

After the Council had adjourned, Elafius caught up with Vortimer in one of the corridors.

"A noble attempt, my boy, but a futile one under the present conditions," he said.

Vortimer turned to him. "What do you mean?"

"Your father holds too much of Britannia in his pocket. With Aurelianus under his command, he can bully the Council into accepting whatever decision he wishes them to make, as we saw today."

"You are speaking out of turn, Lord Elafius," Vortimer warned.

"And for that I apologise. But you must see it as plainly as I and the rest of the Council do. Your father is trying to take control of Britannia in the fullest sense of the word."

Vortimer turned angry. "Take care, Elafius. Your words could be your downfall. One only has to look at the stains on the executioner's block in the forum to see what becomes of those who speak out of turn."

"Oh see sense, Lord Vortimer," said Elafius in exasperation. "You have witnessed your father's actions over the last few months. The sanctioned death of Cassiodorus by those Saxon dogs, the invitation extended to their leaders to join us at the feast of Pascha. And now the sudden and mysterious death of Bishop Lentilus - the one man who had the power to overturn your father's rule – and his replacement by a deacon, a young pup of a boy, who is little more than your father's lackey."

"Bishop Lentilus was killed by Pelagians," Vortimer insisted, but he knew that Elafius saw the half-heartedness in his voice.

"So your father is so keen to remind us. His persecution of the Pelagians was his only card to play to keep Lentilus from sending to Gaul for the intervention of Bishop Germanus. With Lentilus dead, your father's rule is all but cemented. I am not the only councilmember who feels that perhaps the time for some action has come."

"Action?" Vortimer hissed the word, not wishing it to be overheard in the echoing corridors of the palace. "You mean treachery against my father? A man chosen to lead this Council by its own members?"

"I was no such member in those days, nor were any of us. Your father's powerbase began a long time ago and he has been gradually strengthening it, year by year. There are many who think that the time has come for a new leading member to be chosen. Some have even suggested you. You hold all of Londinium in your hand..."

"I warn you, Elafius, do not put such things to me," said Vortimer. "My father was ordained by God to lead this council and such a thing cannot be undone by the blathering of old men. Good day." He turned and walked quickly away. He felt Elafius's eyes on his back, and he cringed from them as he cringed from himself.

# Hengest

Hengest sat down in the cushioned chair before Lord Vertigernus's desk. There were two other men in the room; one was Ceretic the interpreter, here no doubt for his benefit. The second he did not recognise, being a youngish man dressed in some sort of ceremonial robes. They all sat around the desk informally like women at their sewing and Hengest wondered what this was all about.

Vertigernus smiled at Hengest as he poured some wine for them all and Hengest winced at the sight of the dark red liquid sloshing around in the goblet. Horsa had insisted on drinking with the men up at the fortress the previous night. Hengest's head hammered like a war drum. They had stayed late, singing, drinking and betting on the wrestling matches that were struck up between the Britons and their own men. Hengest had not yet got used to the fruity drink of the Romans, preferring the mead and ale of his people. Wine was not disagreeable in taste or effect, but it did give one the most terrible hangovers.

"You are wondering why, I am sure," said Vertigernus, sipping his wine, "I have called upon only you and not your brother."

"It did cross my mind," Hengest replied, reluctantly reaching for the goblet.

"I called you only because it is a personal matter I wish to discuss. You will have heard, I am sure, of the tragic death of our good Bishop Lentilus."

"Yes, my condolences," Hengest replied.

"A nasty business, but not as it turns out, without benefits for our friendship. You will remember that the good Lentilus was very much of the opinion that you and your family were to be baptised before any alliance between our two peoples could be reached. A proposal that you did not relish, I understand."

Hengest smiled, seeing the Briton's point. "And with Lentilus dead, there is nobody to make such demands, do I understand you correctly?"

"Yes and no," Vertigernus replied with a smile. "Whilst Lentilus was very much set in his ways, I am afraid that his opinions are shared by a good many more. Our union will still have to be cemented in a formal ceremony under the eyes of God. Thus the people and the Council will be appeased and will give our alliance their full blessing."

He had lost Hengest. Even with Ceretic translating the more tricky British words for him, he did not understand Vertigernus's point. Did the demand to abandon the Ese still stand? "What do you have in mind?" he asked.

Vertigernus turned to the man in the ceremonial robes beside him and said; "This is Bishop Calvinus, the new Bishop of Londinium. Lentilus' successor if you will. He and I have been discussing this point and have thought of a possibility which we now put to you." He nodded at the young man encouragingly as if suggesting that he should speak.

Calvinus looked a little flustered but did his best to compose himself before addressing him. "Ah..., yes...." he began. "In order for the agreement to be recognised by the Council and the people of Albion, we have decided that a union between your two families would be the most desirable route to take."

Hengest blinked. "A marriage?" he asked.

"That is more or less it," stammered Calvinus.

"I am already married."

Calvinus looked dumfounded at this and turned to his lord for aid.

"No , no," Vertigernus said with a smile. "We were thinking more of your lovely daughter in fact."

"My daughter?"

"A marriage between your daughter and the ruler of the Council would cement the alliance between Briton and *Sais*," urged Calvinus. "It would be an act witnessed by God Almighty and would receive his blessing."

"You?" said Hengest in astonishment, turning his eyes to Vertigernus. "You wish to marry my Hronwena?"

Vertigernus nodded. "A very attractive girl, incidentally. I would have no qualms with marrying her for the good of this land."

*Qualms indeed!* thought Hengest in irritation. His Hronwena marry this old Briton? "Are you not already married?" he asked.

"Alas, no. My third wife, Brina, passed away last year. I was reluctant to remarry for she was a very fine woman, but then, so is your daughter."

Mixed emotions fought each other inside Hengest's gut. By marrying his daughter to this man he could secure the alliance that he so greatly desired without offending the Ese. But forcing Hronwena into marriage to a man many times her age? He thought back to his courtship of Halfritha in Jute-land a lifetime ago. He had been terrified that his father would refuse the marriage and force him into wedlock with some nobleman's daughter for his own political gain. Now, he was the one deciding such things. Could he now treat his own daughter in such a way?

But think of what could be gained through such a union! This war with the Picts would see him return victorious as the ruler of all Cantium; a land that stretched beyond any borders he had ever dreamed of! He would be a king! The hall he would build and the warriors he would command flashed before him like prize horses at a fast gallop. And what was to be lost? Hronwena would marry an old man who would surely be at death's door soon enough. In the interim, she would live with him in some British palace where she would be treated like a queen and showered with riches and luxury. Even she would be only too happy at that prospect, surely?

"Very well," he said. "Such a union would indeed be beneficial for all concerned."

"Then you accept?" Vertigernus asked eagerly.

"I accept."

Vertigernus rose, his face beaming and lifted his wine goblet. Ceretic and Calvinus followed suit. "Wonderful!" he exclaimed. "Then let us drink to the alliance between *Sais* and Briton and the union between the house of Vitalinus and Hengest!"

Hengest forced a smile as he raised his goblet. His insides churned mercilessly at the thought of it, but he ignored his hangover and swallowed the wine, grimacing at the stinging taste that rushed down his gullet.

## Aesc

Tears stung Hronwena's eyes as she raged at her father. "He's even older than you!" she exclaimed.

"Then all the shorter your marriage to him will be," Hengest said. "He'll be dead within a few years, and then you can return to us and marry whoever you like."

"And in the meantime I must share my bed and my body with that disgusting old Briton? I won't!"

Hengest glared at her, disapproving of her defiance. They were in their chambers in the palace, packing their things in preparation for their departure on the morning tide. Aesc was sorry to be leaving the town, but still looked forward to seeing Octa again and continuing with his training. "You will do as you are told, girl," his father said. "It is not the place of a daughter to question the choices of her father."

"Nevertheless," put in Halfritha, "I would have thought you might have discussed this with us before agreeing to the arrangement."

"There was point in dallying," Hengest snapped. "I made the decision for the good of the family."

At this, Horsa let out a derisive snort from where he lounged on a cushioned bench. Hengest looked at him expectantly, but the younger brother remained silent.

"Do you remember when we were her age?" Halfritha continued. "Our love for each other was so strong that nothing your father could have said would have swayed your intentions."

"I don't see any man Hronwena loves here," Hengest replied. "Nor has she ever mentioned one. The situation is completely different. By marrying this Briton, the advantages to this family will be innumerable. Without it, we cannot ally with the Britons formally and must remain the guardians of Rutupiae, that flea-infested shithole that you both have told me you hate. Hronwena shall marry Vertigernus, and that's an end to the matter."

Hronwena let out a stifled cry of frustration and hurled the bundle of clothes she had been carrying to her chest onto the floor and stormed from the room. Halfritha glared at her husband with more anger than Aesc had ever seen in her eyes before and followed after Hronwena.

"Well?" Hengest asked, turning to his brother. "Are you going to berate me for my decisions also? Siding with my wife seems to be what you are best at these days."

"You think you're so fucking high and mighty, don't you?" Horsa spat. "Harping on about your decisions being for the good of the family! I think that in your quest for a crown, you have forgotten what family means."

"Am I the only one who can see beyond my own nose?" said Hengest in exasperation. "What of it if I want something better for all of us? Would you be content to spend the rest of your life extorting silver out of traders and merchants?"

"But that's just it, brother! You'll always want something better. Your family has never been good enough for you. Even as children you always wanted to rise above the life of an ealdorman's son, as if such a life was beneath you!"

"You're a fine one to talk, Horsa. You who left the family at the first sign of trouble to fight and whore your way around the northern world with a bunch of raiders! You didn't show such trepidation when you skewered Eldred's gullet for him or when we stormed Gwrangon's house and burnt it to the ground."

Horsa leaped up at this and Aesc thought he was going to strike him.

"At least I know my place in the world!" Horsa raged. "What of it if I'm happy with a whore in my lap and a drink in my hand? It's a damn sight more noble than entertaining dreams of kingship and sacrificing my own family's happiness to achieve it. You are a raider and a gang leader, Hengest, nothing more! Not a king, not a ruler of a people. You are a man just like me!"

"You have no idea of what I can achieve!" Hengest roared. "I may have been born the son of a drunken ealdorman, but before I die I shall wear a crown upon my head, this I swear before Woden!"

"So it's come to vows now, has it? Perhaps you remember the vow I once swore that I would save your life. You were not so high and mighty when I rescued you from Finn of Frisia. You were a king's prisoner, not royalty. Perhaps I should have left you there where you could learn some humility!"

Hengest was taken aback by his brother's venomous words that he could not reply before Horsa stormed from the room, slamming the door behind him.

"He's wrong, father," Aesc said. "They're all wrong." He hated to see his father deserted by his family, humiliated.

"Thank you, my son," Hengest said, sitting down at the table and cradling his head in his hands. "But I wish they would come round to my way of thinking."

"They will in time. When they see the wealth and land Hronwena's marriage to Vertigernus will bring us and the crown you shall wear, they will quickly change their tune."

"I hope you are right, Aesc, I really do."

## Aureliana

"We really must be getting back, my lady," Seren called out to her ward.

"Not just yet," Aureliana replied, galloping ahead. "The season is so beautiful and it is a shame to waste God's great wonders by sitting indoors with dour-faced men and dusty old tomes."

The season was indeed beautiful. Spring was in full sway and the forests were humming with new life. Bluebells grew thick in large patches and birdsong chattered above the chuckling waters of the streams. Above stretched a seemingly endless jade canopy of leaves that cast wavering shadows.

The two women – the lady and her maid – rode their horses onwards, the former drinking in the sights and smells whilst the latter trailed behind, occasionally looking about her as if nervous.

"It will be getting dark soon," Seren warned. "And your father will skin me alive if we should return after the sun has gone down."

"Oh do not nag, Seren," Aureliana said irritably. "You always spoil things with your incessant worrying and coddling. I'm eighteen summers. Much too old to have a nurse still."

"There's not many who would disagree with that excepting your father," the older woman replied. "Most would say that he should have found you a husband a long time ago, instead of keeping you in his home to live the life of a spinster."

"Spinster indeed! Besides, father would never let me marry. He thinks that there isn't a decent man left in all of Albion these days. And I'm inclined to agree with him."

"Then you shall die old and alone with only your father's overprotective nature and your own stubbornness to blame."

"I don't care! I'd rather die alone than marry some stiff old nobleman who would want me to bear him twelve sons and spend my days weaving and embroidering and praying and confessing my sins to priests and bishops I don't even know."

"Well, what's wrong with that? We all have sins to confess, God knows."

"I don't," replied Aureliana with an angelic smile.

"There," said Seren with a disapproving frown. "That's a sin. And if you were a little younger I would tan your hide for it. Such a thing to say!"

"Well, honestly," Aureliana replied with her nose in the air, "how can anybody know that a person has a sin to confess without them actually confessing it?"

"All people have sin in them," said Seren. "And to suggest otherwise borders on Pelagianism; a wicked, wicked path of thought."

"Pelagianism, pah! A lot of fuss about nothing if you ask me. Who cares what other people believe? A person should be able to choose their own ideas when it comes to religion."

"Lord have mercy!" squawked Seren. "If only Bishop Lentilus could hear you now!"

"Bishop Lentilus is dead."

"And may the Lord rest his soul. But his successor is sure to continue his good work in stamping out that wicked heresy. And you would do well to mind your tongue, my girl."

"I shouldn't think so. Father says that Bishop Calvinus is a dribbling fool on Vitalinus's payroll without an inch of backbone in him."

"Goodness..." said Seren, looking as if she were worried that some of Lord Vertigernus's spies were lurking in the forest watching them.

"I heard father say that Calvinus is simply a puppet with Vitalinus's hand up his arse."

Seren shrieked with indignation and reached out with her riding crop to chastise her but Aureliana laughed heartily and galloped on ahead. The old maid urged her horse onwards but was not the rider Aureliana was and could not keep up.

"You'll have to ride faster than that if you want to catch me, Seren!" she called, showing great merriment at her maid's poor horsemanship.

They galloped around a copse and suddenly halted, both letting out a small cry of alarm for a little way ahead, a rider blocked their path. He was clearly a barbarian of some sort with long, light brown hair that reached to his shoulders. He wore a pair of leather breeches and a sheepskin jerkin that showed off his thickly-muscled arms which were marked with many scars. At his belt he wore a long dagger.

"Let us fly, my lady," Seren whispered, "Perhaps we can outrun him but we shall surely be killed if we stay."

"No," Aureliana replied, gazing upon the barbarian's blue eyes and the several days of growth on

168

his strong chin. She called out to him. "It's Horsa, isn't it?"

The barbarian cantered forward and smiled at her. "Indeed it is, lady. Aureliana, I believe?"

"Why, yes."

"My lady, please, I beg you!" hissed Seren, watching in horror as her ward trotted ahead to speak with the barbarian.

"What are you doing here?" she asked him.

"Just out for a ride. Seeing what the countryside north of Londinium has to offer."

"And how do you find it?"

"Very pleasant. Forests are unusual for me. My homeland is open like the sky. But the sea is my real home."

"Are you here alone?"

"Yes. My brother has many things to occupy his attention in the town. Some of them we do not meet eye to eye upon. I needed to clear my head. Will you walk with me?"

"Certainly not!" put in Seren before Aureliana could answer.

"Be silent, Seren!" Aureliana snapped. "I shall walk with whoever I please."

"But he is a Sais, my lady. And a pagan! Your father would have us both whipped!"

"My father is not here. And you shall not tell him, is that clear Seren? Besides, Horsa here is not a Sais, are you? You are a... what is it?"

"A Jute."

"There you go, Seren, he's a Jute."

169

The maid looked at Horsa with the kind of expression that said she didn't much care what he was. He was a barbarian and that was cause enough for them to ride away in the opposite direction immediately.

"And what's more," said Aureliana as she dismounted, "I have never walked with a Jute."

Horsa dismounted also and they walked side by side, leading their horses by their bridles. Seren stumbled along behind, leading her own mount and never taking her frowning eyes off the couple in front of her.

"What is a Jute exactly?" Aureliana asked. "Is it like a Sais?"

"In the eyes of the Britons perhaps we are similar," Horsa replied. "But between ourselves there are a great many differences. Our languages for one."

"Are they so different?"

"Not as different as the British tongue which I find so hard to get my mouth around."

"I think you speak British wonderfully," said Aureliana, but his expression told her that he didn't believe her. "You should learn Latin," she continued. "Then again, maybe not. It is so dreadfully dull, especially the grammar. I much prefer British, even if it is the language of the commoners. It is much more musical and emotional. Do they have songs in your homeland?"

"Oh yes, our *scops* are the most gifted in all the northern world."

"*Shops?* I am unfamiliar with the term."

"*Scops*. They sing songs. Poetry. That sort of thing."

"Ah, you mean bards. Is that what they call them in your language? *Shops?* How strange! What do they sing of?"

"Heroes, kings, warriors and battles mostly," Horsa replied. "Some are sung to praise the king or ealdorman they are written for and to celebrate his deeds. Others are about victories over monsters such as trolls, fire-wyrms and ettins."

"Fascinating. Much like the old tales the Britons used to sing. I love those. Romance and magic and heroic deeds. But nobody sings them anymore. Now singing is only used to praise God. It's so very dull and doesn't have any of the passion of the old songs. Will you sing one of your own songs to me?"

Horsa gaped at her. "Sing? No, I don't sing. I am no *scop*, no bard."

"Oh, please do. I'm sure you have a very nice voice. And I would love to hear a song from your own lands sung in your own language. What is your favourite?"

Horsa thought for a moment. "*The Lay of Earendel*, I would think."

"Who is Earendel?" asked Aureliana, her eyes lighting up at the unfamiliar name that sounded so exotic to her ears.

"He is a wanderer and a friend to all seafarers. His is the first light to arise each and every dawn."

"Do you mean Venus, the morning star?" asked Aureliana.

"Perhaps. All I know is that he has been a comfort to me in many hard times. Seeing him arise each day brings me hope that I will live to see that day end."

"Sing me his tale," persisted Aureliana.

Horsa sighed and took a moment to collect himself. He took a deep breath and then began to sing.

When he had finished Aureliana gaped at him and turned to share a look with Seren. "It is true," she said. "You are no bard. I have never heard such a guttural singing voice!"

"Well I did say so!" Horsa snapped angrily. "But you demanded that I sing."

Aureliana burst out laughing. "I did not mean to offend you, Horsa. It was a very lovely song. Even though I did not understand the words. It sounded sad to me. Is it a sad tale?"

"Very," Horsa replied. "Earendel was a born wanderer. He voyaged all over the world and saw many fine things, but one day, he came upon a woman bathing in a stream. Esel was her name and her hair was as gold as barley in autumn and her skin as pale as milk. He desired her greatly. But she spurned him for such a romance could not be as she was one of the *Waelcyrie*; a shield maiden of *Waelheall*."

"Of where?"

"*Waelheall*. It is the place all warriors go to when they die in battle."

"Like heaven?"

"I suppose so. But only men are allowed and only if they are not oath breakers. The *Waelcyrie* collect the dead souls from the battlefield and carry them to Woden's golden halls where they feast until the end of the world when they will be called upon to fight for the gods."

"No women at all? Doesn't sound very fair to me, but do go on."

"Esel returned to *Waelheall* and left Earendel behind, broken hearted. But his love for her was so strong that he followed her there, all the way to Woden's hall. This made the gods very angry and they cursed him to wander the stars between worlds for all eternity. Esel took pity on him and gave him a parting gift; an Aelfstone that would glow to light his way and it is this light, from the prow of Earendel's ship that is seen in the early morning as he rises up over the rim of *Middangeard*."

"*Middangeard?*"

"It is our name for the land upon which we stand. 'Middle earth', I think it would be called in your tongue. There are many worlds containing many different peoples and all are connected by the branches of a massive tree."

"Tell me of these worlds," Aureliana asked, utterly spellbound by such a concept.

"Well, apart from the world of men, there is the realm of the Light Aelf-folk who are all poetry and beauty, but can be wicked and spiteful if one crosses them. The Dark Aelf-folk dwell deep in the earth and are blacksmiths. It was they who made the weapons and tools of the gods including my brother's sword *Hildeleoma*. There are Frost Ettins and Fire Ettins too who are massive creatures that make the ground tremble when they walk. They dwell in harsh lands uninhabitable by men folk."

"Sounds like a lot of evil, pagan nonsense to me," piped up Seren who had been doing her best to make sense of the Jute's broken British, but she was ignored.

"And then there is the land of mist and shadow where all souls that are denied entrance to *Waelheall* go; murderers and oath breakers," Horsa continued.

"And women too?" asked Aureliana. "Surely if they are denied entrance to *Waelheall*, then they too must go to this other place."

"Yes, women too," admitted Horsa.

"Well that sounds utterly monstrous," Aureliana said. "As bad as the priests and bishops of this land who are so quick to condemn everybody without even knowing if they have done anything wrong."

"But of course some women – the very best of women – are chosen by Woden to be his shield maidens. Those are allowed into *Waelheall*. I have no doubt that you would be chosen as one of the *Waelcyrie*."

"Really?" asked Aureliana, her eyes lighting up. "And what qualities must a woman have to catch the eye of your god?"

"They must be strong willed," Horsa said. "And have kind souls. But what our god truly admires is beauty. All his shield maidens are the most beautiful of women whose perfect hair and shapely bodies can bewitch even the hardest of men so that they would do almost anything to lie with them, even for only one night."

"Well, I must say!" Seren exclaimed, clearly scandalised.

"And you say that I am such a woman?" Aureliana asked, looking deep into the frozen blue of Horsa's eyes, the colour rising in her cheeks. "What could your god want from a woman like me?"

"The same thing he wants from all his shield maidens," Horsa replied. "Who else is going to serve his warriors mead and keep them warm in their beds at night?"

Aureliana blinked at this and then realised that he was jesting with her. "Oh! Oh, of all the beastly...! Horsa the Jute, you are the most frightful barbarian! The most barbaric man I have ever met in fact!" She pouted and frowned at him as he roared with laughter, but she could not keep it up. His cheeky humour was infectious and appealed to her greatly though she tried her best to hide it. "You are also the most fascinating man I have ever met." He stopped laughing suddenly and they stared at each other in silence, their lips parted as if tasting the air between each other. Aureliana wondered what it would be like to let those lips touch hers.

"My lady, we really must be getting back!" said Seren in a state of great alarm.

Aureliana looked up at the sky between the treetops. It had paled somewhat and the day was not as warm as it had been. "I suppose you're right," she said. "Well, Horsa, it has been lovely meeting you again, but now I must return home or my father with rouse every soldier in Albion to find me. And if he caught me with you, then both our lives would take a drastic turn for the worse."

"Not so fast," Horsa said. "You still owe me something."

"Owe you? What on earth...?"

"For that insult about my singing voice earlier. And as I sang for you, I think that it would only be fair to expect a song from you in return."

"You wish me to sing? But it's getting late!"

"Then you had better be quick about choosing a song. Something British I think, one of those old ones you are so fond of."

"Well, um..."

"My lady, we must be away!"

"Alright, Seren! Let me think! Right, I know. It's called *The Love of Culhuch and Olwen*. I'll only sing a few verses as Culhuch had many adventures in seeking her hand. Ready?"

Horsa nodded and she began to sing.

*When Valens sat on throne in Rome,*
*And Pict and Goth stayed at home,*
*A northern lord ruled full fair,*
*In Celyddon he sired his heir.*
*Culhuch this good prince was named,*
*And to his house he brought no shame.*
*His mother died to give him life,*
*In a pig's pen she raved and bore her strife.*

*When Culhuch reached the age of seven,*
*With his mother naught but loved in heaven,*
*His father took a bride to bed,*
*And to her stepson she said,*
*'I have a daughter, full fair of life,*

*And to you she would make a comely wife.'*
*To his stepmother Culhuch said,*
*'I wish no bride for my bed,*
*For I am young and have not shown,*
*That I have valour of my own.'*

*At this the lady grew full of wroth,*
*'You dare reject my daughter's troth?*
*You I curse to love no other,*
*But Olwen who can have no lover,*
*For Ysbathaden is her father*
*The giant-lord who would rather,*
*His daughter meet a maiden's fate,*
*For he is full of jealous hate.*
*No maiden matches Olwen's grace,*
*No beauty rivals her fair face,*
*Born is she of Annun's powers,*
*For in her footsteps grow white flowers.'*

*A broken arch above a mere,*
*Where crystal water glittered clear,*
*In Roman ruin ivy-gripped,*
*Knelt Olwen fair and full-lipped.*
*Her hair sparkled like foaming mead,*
*And as she bathed she did not heed,*
*Culhuch who lay in grass nearby,*
*Upon her body he did spy.*

*A grim, grey keep of rock and stone,*
*Ysbathaden called his home,*
*A mighty tyrant, tall and wide,*
*Who could clear a forest in a stride.*

Culhuch came to his board,
Red of hand and wet of sword,
For he had slain every guard,
And every hound within the yard.
'Mighty giant,' Culhuch cried,
'I desire Olwen for my bride.
Do not deny me your daughter fair,
For we are slaves to the love we bear.'
'Wretched cur!' the giant roared,
'You dare defy your mighty lord?
No man may take her to his bed,
But one who agrees to shave my head,
Turch Trwyd's tusk you must seek,
Only then will I forget your cheek,
Because my bristles are so tough,
His tusk alone is sharp enough.'

Culhuch sought Turch Trwyd's lair,
Which only the brave and mad do dare,
In it he met the monstrous beast,
And chased him north, west and east.
Finally the brute he slew'd,
And through his tusk Culhuch hew'd,
And brought it before the giant's board,
Sharper than the sharpest sword.
True to his word he began to shave,
And cut the giant's face most grave,
Through flesh and bone he drew the tool,
 And proved to all he was no fool,
For Ysbathaden had he slain,
And Olwen was his to claim.

When she had finished, Horsa only gazed on her with wide blue eyes. She mounted her horse.

"Will that do?" she asked from her saddle.

He nodded. "But what is Turch Trwyd?"

She smiled and said; "That is for you to find out."

"When can I see you again?"

She looked at the ground. "I don't know," she said. "Perhaps never. Will you be in Londinium for long?"

"No. We are leaving on the morning tide. But I expect we shall return for my niece's wedding to the Lord Vertigernus. Will you be attending?"

"I should think so."

"And afterwards," he continued, "I am off to war under your father's banner. I may get to know him well in the coming months."

"Don't expect much from him. I love him dearly but he despises your people with a passion. If he knew that we had met, he would probably never let me out of his sight again."

"Then he must not find out. And I will see you again. I will make it my business."

"Until next time then," she said and before she turned away from him, she blew him a kiss.

# Horsa

As he entered Londinium Horsa saw the Roman town in a new light. No longer was it a seedy, foreign lair filled with hostile faces. He saw families, children playing in the streets, old people sunning themselves. The goods in the market places smelled sweeter and the painted plaster and tiled roofs more vibrant. There were even flowers. In a run-down town infested with corruption and poverty with war-clouds looming ever nearer, somebody had thought to put out flowers. Why hadn't he seen those before?

*Aureliana.* Even her name sounded like a flower and he wondered what it meant. Her song had found a home in his head and dug in there with sweet stubbornness. He couldn't remember many of the words, only the voice and he kept replaying it over and over in his head, fearful that he might forget it.

He led his horse down the mud-slicked wooden walkway to the jetty where the *Bloodkeel* lolled at its moorings. His men were loading supplies into its keel. He could see Beorn's bald head bobbing about as he argued with Hengest about something.

"You can't put all the casks in the bow," he was saying. "She'll ride too low in the fore. Her keel'll be scraping every sandbank from here to Thanet!"

"But there's no room in the aft because of all the wool and cloth we've purchased," Hengest replied.

"Well, who told them to load it all in the aft? Not I! It'll all have to be unloaded..."

"That'll take hours! We are growing short of time and we all long for our beds, do we not?"

Horsa couldn't help but smirk. "Best get started now then," he called to them. Both men turned to gape at him.

"I was wondering when you would turn up," Hengest said. "I was half afraid that you had turned native and were planning to remain here with the Britons you love so dearly."

Horsa grinned sheepishly. "I spoke out of turn earlier, Hengest. I'm a hot-headed bastard."

"Yes, you are. But I've never held that against you and I don't intend to start now." Hengest clambered onto the jetty and embraced his brother. "Are you ready to return home now? Eostre will soon be dawning on us and we need to pay her the proper devotions if we are to have success in the days to come."

"And Hronwena's marriage to Vertigernus?"

"We will return to Londinium in a month's time. The wedding will take place here and then we are off to war. Are you with me?"

Horsa nodded.

# Hengest

Hengest's hall on Thanet had been completed during their absence. It was a fine thing; more than he could have hoped for and he could not help beaming with appreciation as they approached it. A small settlement had emerged over the recent weeks formed of huts and storage houses surrounding hard packed earth where the people involved with the building of the hall lived with their theows. Workshops and ironsmiths showed signs of recent industry; sawdust and cut-offs were piled up in small mountains and the forges had barely cooled from their constant production of rivets. Beyond this, upon a small rise, was the hall itself.

New wood and clean thatch seemed to glow in the afternoon light and gave it an otherworldly sheen that almost suggested that it was made of gold. Its huge doors were flanked by pillars carven, at the insistence of Hengest, with beasts and creatures and faces, much like those on the hall of King Finn of Frisia. When they entered the hall they found men still at work on the supporting pillars, carving them from top to bottom with glorious intricacy. Light from the smoke holes in the thatch shone down, illuminating particles of chipped wood that floated in the air.

Hengest walked down the centre of the room, stepping down into the hearths and up again as he traversed the length of the hall. The space was cavernous and the lack of benches, tables and hangings made it seem hauntingly empty. He gazed this way and that, imagining the roaring fires and close company that would soon warm it and the richly woven tapestries that would decorate every wall. At the far end of the room was a dais with enough space for several chairs and a long table.

"Is that to be your throne?" Horsa asked him.

Hengest did not answer. He stepped up onto the dais and paced it, wondering if there was enough space for all his family to be seated there. Of course, Hronwena would be absent from his table for quite some time, but she would return. He would always put aside space for his daughter. It was her sacrifice that allowed him to build this hall for his family and keep it safe from attack. He hoped that she would one day understand this.

There was one other building he wished to see. Beyond the hall he had given orders for a complex of stables and paddocks to be built. There was enough land to spare and Hengest had not skimped on size. He heard the intake of breath from his family as they exited the hall through its east door and gazed down on the complex.

"It's enormous!" gasped Halfritha. "Just how many horses are you planning on keeping?"

"Never again will it be said that Hengest the Jute was outnumbered by horsemen," he replied.

A man exited the stables and approached them. It was Octa.

"My friend!" Hengest called out to him in barely contained excitement. "Have they arrived? Do we have them all?"

Octa beamed. "Every last one of them. The crossing was peaceful and all the boats arrived safely just the other day."

"What is this, husband?" Halfritha asked.

"Come inside and see," Hengest said.

They entered the stables and, other than the fact that the building with its rows of stalls was even larger than the hall, there was another thing that amazed Hengest's family. Nearly every stall was occupied by a horse.

"But, there must be near on a hundred beasts here!" exclaimed Aesc.

"Exactly one hundred Jutish and Frisian mares," said Hengest proudly. "Beorn told me he knew a dealer back in his homeland and so I set Octa the task of trading with him while we were gone." He allowed a nearby dun mare to sniff his hand while he ruffled its mane.

"You did it, brother," said Horsa, his face clearly impressed. "You brought them all here. Now you have a cavalry force unmatched in all of Britta."

"Most of these beasts will go on to the coastal towns," Hengest explained. "I want every town of ours garrisoned by a small cavalry. That way our interests on the mainland will be protected from assault on land and can easily band together to repel larger attacks. I have given orders to repair and enlarge the stables already in existence in all the five towns under our control."

"You really are building a kingdom, aren't you?" Horsa asked him.

"We are. *Together*," he answered. "A kingdom to last the ages. When we are all dead and naught but dusty bones in our barrows, the world will still remember our names and they will say that we founded one of the greatest kingdoms in the world."

# Hronwena

"Hold still, Hronwena," said her mother irritably as she knelt at her feet. "I know you don't want to get married, but don't make me prick my finger."

Hronwena stood with her arms outstretched as her mother inserted pins into the long, sea-green dress that was to be her wedding gown. She fumed at her mother's acceptance of her father's plan to marry her to Vertigernus. Was this the strong, brave woman who had protected them with her own body when they had been captured by raiders two years previously? It seemed hard to believe.

Aesc watched them from the corner of the room with an expression of amusement as he bit into an apple.

"There, I think that should do it," her mother said, standing back to admire her handiwork. "Such wonderful material. They tell me it came from Parthia, wherever that is, but it's perfect for a wedding gown. Now, don't move, Hronwena, I need to see what can be done with this stola. Funny way of dressing, these British women have, but Lord Vertigernus wants you to look like a British bride so a stola it is. What do you two think?"

Her husband to be had sent two British handmaidens back to Cantium with them to instruct his betrothed in British customs and her mother in the ways of Romano-British dressmaking. So far they had been utterly useless and had only wept and cowered in her father's hall, shrinking from every man and staring wide-eyed at the barbarism that surrounded them.

They scampered off to pray to their one god every morning and again before meals and never strayed from the chambers unless commanded to do so. Whenever Hronwena or her mother had tried to practice their British with them, they had merely nodded and replied with one syllable answers, never daring to correct any faults. The pair of them were exapsterating. Even now they seemed reluctant to give any opinion, positive or negative, on her mother's attempt at making a British dress.

"Well?" her mother asked them in British. "Have I got it right?"

"Very good, my lady," said one.

"Beautiful," said the other.

Hronwena rolled her eyes, despairing at all this concern with dressmaking when she was about to be married off and sent away to some remote part of Britta.

"Oh, don't make that face, Hronwena," pleaded her mother. "You can't turn up to your own wedding with that expression."

"I've got several days yet," Hronwena said bitterly. "I'll save my smiles of joy for then."

"Look, I know it's a nasty business and I'm sorry if I seem preoccupied with trivial things. But that is just my own way of dealing with it. Your father is head of this family. If he decides that you are to marry this British friend of his, then that is what you must do."

"But it's not fair! And what makes it all the worse is the reason I am marrying him. It's just so that father can have his dreadful treaty with the Britons and he and Aesc can march off to war and possibly never return."

She caught the expression on her mother's face and stepped off the pedestal. "I'm sorry mother, I didn't mean..."

"You're right, my girl," her mother said miserably. "The gods know you are right. If I could do anything to stop this awful marriage then I would do it in a heartbeat. But your father won't listen to me anymore. He has changed since coming here. I've never seen his heart so set on one thing. It's like he is possessed by some force that drives him ever onwards to his fate and blinds him to the needs of his family."

"Oh stop blubbering, you two," said Aesc, tossing his apple core onto the fire. "Father knows what he is doing and all he does is for the good of this family."

"You don't really believe that," Hronwena said.

"Of course I do," he replied. "This treaty is a gateway to our family's rule over the Britons in Cantium. Once this war is over then we shall have a land of our own – big enough to rival any eorl in Juteland!"

"You are just repeating what you have heard father say!"

"What if I am? It's all true. And besides, what's all this talk of us not coming back from the war? Don't you think we can handle a few wild tribesmen? Father's built up an enormous cavalry force. And Uncle Horsa commands three keels of our warriors. Allied with the Britons, there isn't an army in the world that could stop us!"

"Well, I am most surprised by your uncle's sudden change of tune," said Halfritha. "A few days ago he seemed all set never to speak to your father again. They haven't been getting on very well lately at all. I always thought uncle Horsa was happy enough with his ships and didn't have a care for all this high society and politics. Now he is only too keen to go and fight somebody else's war. An Aelf must have shot a charmed arrow at him to make him change his mind so drastically."

"I wouldn't say that," said Aesc. "He's been moping around a lot since we got back. I've seen him go off on his own and not come back for hours. He may have pledged his support to father's cause in words, but I think he's got something else on his mind entirely."

"And while you men are fighting wars in the north," said Hronwena, "and I am playing housewife to an old fool in some awful British town somewhere, who will remain at home to protect mother?"

"Well, there will be Octa I expect," replied Aesc. "He has become something of father's retainer."

"Ah, our good friend Octa!" said Hronwena in a withering tone. "How kind of father to leave a half-drunk Saxon to protect his wife."

"I am quite capable of taking care of myself, thank you," said her mother.

"But they might be away all season, or even a year or more," protested Hronwena. "And who knows how long I shall be away before old Verti-whatshisname gives up the ghost?"

"All right, that's enough!" snapped her mother. "I know that the coming days will be hard on all of us, but we cannot help things by arguing and sulking. Now

Aesc, haven't you got things to do in preparation for the feast?"

"Hardly," replied the youth. "Father has so many theows these days that our lot are sitting on their backsides and playing dice."

"Well go and join them or something. I want to have a moment alone with Hronwena."

Aesc shrugged and slunk out of the room.

"What is it, mother?" asked Hronwena.

Her mother removed a golden ring from her finger. It was the ring her father had given her upon their wedding night; a simple band of gold etched with runes. She pulled a silver chain from her belt and hung the ring on it before hanging it over Hronwena's head.

"The ring father gave you..." protested Hronwena.

"I want you to have it. That way you will always have a connection to me no matter where you are or how much land stands between us." Her voice was cracking and a tear spilled down her cheek.

"But won't father notice that it is gone?"

Her mother shrugged. "He will be off to war as soon as you are married. And at present, he has too much to distract his mind to notice something so small."

Hronwena felt like weeping. After all her strong words of loyalty for her father, her mother seemed to be giving up on him and Hronwena came to realise the truth. Her mother's words were only a sham. As always she had some hidden purpose which lay hidden beneath. For the good of her family she was prepared to speak in support of her husband, but deep down, she had abandoned him. The thought of her all alone on

Thanet while they all deserted her filled Hronwena with sorrow and she hugged her mother tight. How many more hugs had they left to share? How many days?

# Horsa

The atmosphere in the hall that night was something that none of the people present had experienced since departing their homelands on the continent. It was a glorious return to the Germanic way of life; transplanted here in a Celtic land haunted by the ghosts of its Roman past.

Boars sizzled and spat over the two monstrous fire pits, serving girls poured out mead and the lights of the fires made the shadows of the dancers leaping giants on the walls and beams. The outside world and its troubles were entirely forgotten and the revellers may as well have been back in Jute-land or Frisia for all they knew.

Horsa sat on the dais with Hengest and his family, picking at the food that was laid out on the great table before them. Behind them the dual horse banner hung; resting in its new home before it would be carried off to war once more.

A scop read a poem he had composed about Horsa's victory over the Wane-worshippers and their evil troll-mother. It was all very exaggerated. Horsa watched with a sour face as the audience lapped up the scop's every word that boomed out bloody thunder and daring heroism. He sighed.

When the scop was done, a young warrior who had clearly drunk his fill clambered onto a table and raised his horn to the dais. "May the Ese bless our leaders and our coming war in the north! We are led by Hengest; the hero of the Fight at Finnesburg and Horsa; slayer of the troll-mother! We cannot fail!"

There was a cheer at this and Horsa scowled as he saw his brother lift his own horn in appreciation of the drunken arse-licker. As the man stumbled down from the table and staggered off into a corner to piss, he passed the dais. Horsa leaned out and said to him; "Let me tell you something, warrior. The fight at Finnesburg was nothing more than a slaughter. And there was no troll-mother down in that wet cavern, only the greed of men."

The man looked confused but his bladder wouldn't let him stay to contest the point and he hurried off, fumbling at his breeches.

Hengest leaned over to Horsa. "What's wrong, brother?"

"I apologise. I'm just not in the spirit of merrymaking. And these exaggerations of our deeds irritate me. It's bad enough that they bring that golden statue to life as a living, breathing troll-woman, but they also say that I tore off a troll's arm and nailed it to the door of the Wane-worshippers' hall!"

"Let them have their stories and their imaginations. The gods know there's precious little else left to us in this world. So they exaggerate. Where's the harm in it?"

"I just don't like being made out to be something I'm not."

He hadn't meant this to be a barbed criticism of his brother, but clearly Hengest saw it this way. "Look around you, Horsa," he said. "What do you see? Women, children, families. We are not just a band of warriors in a foreign land. We are a people. I brought them here and as their leader I am charged with their safety. They look to me to see them through the winter and to defend their doors. Am I wrong to want to carve out a home for them in this hostile land? This land can be ours, we only have to fight for it!"

Horsa slid out of his chair. "I need some air," he said.

As he passed through the antechamber he spotted a guard he recognised leaning on his spear, looking bored at missing the festivities. He handed the guard his mead horn. "Briac, isn't it?"

The guard drank from the horn gratefully and nodded as he swallowed. "Yes, lord."

"You're a Briton aren't you? By birth?"

"I am."

"Christian?"

The man hesitated, and then nodded slowly as if wondering if this was some sort of test. There were plenty of Christians in the ranks. Many native-born Britons had joined Hengest's army for the booty and regular meals. On nights such as these, when the Germanic gods held sway, the Britons tended to be placed on guard duty where they nervously touched the crucifixes round their necks and no doubt contemplated their god's judgement on them.

"I don't suppose you're familiar with the old British tales. The ones from before the coming of the Christ-messiah?"

"I know of them, lord," the man replied. "We may worship the Heavenly Father now, but we still know the old tales, even though they are mostly children's nonsense."

"How about the one about Culhuch and Olwen?"

"Oh, that's a well known one, lord."

"Tell me it."

Briac looked about, clearly feeling a little foolish. He cleared his throat. "Well, Culhuch was the son of a British nobleman. His mother died giving birth to him and his father married a wicked witch of a woman who already had a daughter. This witch wanted Culhuch to marry her daughter and when he refused she was so angry that she placed a curse on him. She made it so that he would never love another woman except Olwen; a woman so beautiful that white flowers grew in her footsteps wherever she went.

"Olwen was the daughter of the giant Ysbathaden; a cruel and evil tyrant. Culhuch set out for Ysbathaden's lair and, after slaying his guards and hounds, went before the giant and demanded Olwen as his bride. Ysbathaden set Culhuch a task; to shave him. The only razor sharp enough to cut the bristles on Ysbathaden's chin was the tusk of the great boar Turch Trwyd."

"The great boar?" put in Horsa.

"Yes, Turch Trwyd was the mightiest of all boars who had gored to death many a man who had hunted him. Ysbathaden promised to give Culhuch his daughter in marriage if he brought back Turch Trwyd's tusk and used it to shave him.

"Culhuch hunted the boar across the whole of Albion and eventually slew him. He cut off his tusk and brought it back to the lair of Ysbathaden where he began to shave the giant's beard. He cut so deep that he shaved all the flesh from the bone and sliced through Ysbathaden's neck, beheading him. Culhuch and Olwen married and lived out their days together in happiness."

Horsa blinked, taking in the Briton's words. It wasn't much of a story, it had to be admitted. Aureliana had put it in such better words, conjuring up feelings of eternal, forbidden love and the triumph of two lovers over all odds, not some horny young warrior stealing a bride after beheading her father with a boar's tusk. But he at least understood the story a little better now. And he had learned what Turch Trwyd was. *A boar? Well, well...*

"Thank you, Briac," he said.

"My pleasure, my lord."

Horsa left the hall and stepped out into the night air where the stars glimmered down on Britta, the history of that land and the secrets of its people forever remembered in their constellations. He wondered if Turch Trwyd was up there too. And he wondered if Aureliana was looking at those very same stars at that moment.

# Hengest

The war council was held in the great hall of the palace in Londinium. Hengest stared at the Britons on the other side of the table. He didn't recognise any of them and assumed that they were minor commanders in Vertigernus's army. A map of Britta was spread out between them. Lines and Latin words were written on it denoting tribes, territories and roads. It was much more detailed than Hengest's own map and he wondered how long it would take for an army to cross the island from one tip to the other.

"Where's this Lord Vertigernus, then?" Beorn said to him. "He called this meeting and yet he's late."

"As is my brother," Hengest replied. "Have you seen him?"

"He said something about taking a ride in the woods outside Londinium."

"Alone?"

"He's been sneaking around ever since we returned," said Ebusa. "Is it some girl he's got?"

"I've never known him to spend much energy on any kind of relationship that lasts more than one night," Hengest replied.

As if on cue, Horsa entered through the large doors and made his way up to them.

"Where have you been?" Hengest asked him.

"Out and about. The woods outside the town are beautiful."

"I swear, Horsa, you are getting softer with age. The Horsa I knew would have spat on the idea of taking rides in the countryside."

"Maybe I just wanted to take my fill of life before we find ourselves up to our arses in blood, mud and shit with Pictish warriors swinging axes at us. I saw a group of our men down by the river on my way into the town. They were wading about in the water and that Bishop Calvinus was dipping their heads down into the river, one by one."

"They are joining the Christian religion," Hengest explained. "It's some sort of cleansing rite they must undergo before taking up their god."

"Our own men becoming Christian?"

"Yes. Bishop Calvinus has been taking them down to the river in groups every few days or so. It's only a small number."

"What kind of people abandon their gods on the eve of war?" Beorn grumbled.

"Christianity is nothing new amongst our people here," said Ebusa. "You fellows are new to Britta so of course you cling more strongly to the customs of our homelands. Many of us who have lived here longer have taken up worship of the Christ-messiah."

"Not you, surely?" Horsa asked him.

"I was born here," the Saxon replied. "I was baptised at a very young age – so young that I cannot remember it."

"And do you worship the crucified god?" asked Horsa.

Ebusa shrugged. "He is a very silent god. Offending him seems to raise more ire from his followers than from he himself. So I make a show of it, but in all honesty, I try to keep out of the shadow of any god just to be on the safe side."

"But these mass baptisms," said Beorn. "Surely these will offend our own gods? Can't we put a stop to it seeing as we're about to march off to war where the blessings of Woden, Thunor and Tiw and all the others may be needed to see us through?"

"Ah, what's one more god anyway?" said Hengest. "Besides, most of our men could do with a good wash."

A delegation of Britons walked in led by Vertigernus and Ambrosius Aurelianus.

"Greetings, Sais brothers," Vertigernus said. He looked down at the map on the table. "How do you like our island?"

"Very nice," said Hengest. "But you will have to show us where these Picts live or else we shall never find them."

Vertigernus laughed at this. "Never fear, Hengest. I wouldn't dream of sending you north all on your own. Aurelianus here commands a very great army of which you shall be a part. You shall become great friends I think, on the long, hard road north."

Hengest glanced at Aurelianus and the general looked like he was sucking on a lemon slice.

"Time is of the essence," Vertigernus continued. "I had hoped for the army to set out the day after my wedding to your daughter. What say you?"

"So soon?" Hengest replied. "I will need time to rally my men and send for my horses from Cantium."

"By all means. But the season is not getting any younger. If you set out as soon as possible, the war should be over before the first snowflakes are dancing in the air. All the sooner for you to return and enjoy your new estate. Now, let us turn to tactics. Aurelianus, you have something to say as to that."

"I shall take my army along the northern road with half of Hengest's men," Aurelianus said. "The other half of the Saeson shall proceed north in their ships along the coast, ready to reinforce us if we need it. We shall keep in constant contact by the use of messengers. This way, if any Pictish army attacks us, we can trap them between our two forces as between a hammer and an anvil."

"Not a bad plan," said Hengest, rubbing his chin. "My brother, Horsa shall lead our fleet as he is the better seaman of the two of us. But what is our ultimate goal and where?"

"We are to rendezvous with Prince Talorc and his army here, beyond the wall," Aurelianus said, indicating a part of the map where the island narrowed before widening out into a bulbous head. "It is in the land of the Votadini; a tribe once loyal to the Romans, despite living beyond the wall. They were originally a buffer state between the wall and the Picts, along with the Selgovae and the Novantae, but their lands have been overrun in recent years."

"Does Talorc command many men?"

"A fair sized army. Not as large as ours, but enough to be of use to us."

"And his sister?"

"That we are less sure of. She resides in Din Eidyn; the old royal seat of the Votadini. Even Talorc does not know how many warriors she commands. She may be reinforced from other tribes north of Din Eidyn. There may be some sort of Pictish confederation lending her support. If so it must be smashed. Prince Talorc must be placed in charge of the lowland Pictish territories. He will be our new buffer against the barbarians."

"So the plan is to unite the two armies along with whatever forces Talorc commands north of the wall and then march on this Din Eidyn together," said Hengest.

"In effect, yes," replied Aurelianus. "But we can't allow Galana to escape. I may decide to send your brother's ships up this inlet here, north of Din Eidyn to cut her off should she flee. But there will be time to plan our attack in greater detail later. For now I want your ships to be ready at this point here. The greater part of the army shall camp nearby and rendezvous with Talorc. Then we shall discuss our next move."

"It would be wise for you to take a guide with you who knows the coastline," Vertigernus said to Horsa. "It gets very treacherous the further north you go; marred by rocks and jagged inlets. I shall provide you with a suitable man."

"Then we have much to prepare," said Hengest, turning to his brother. "I shall begin marshalling our troops and equipping them with horses. Horsa, you start outfitting the *Bloodkeel* with supplies and weapons. I want her ready to leave for Rutupiae the morning after the wedding. You are to take Halfritha back with you and see that she is safe in the town before taking the rest of the fleet north."

Talk turned to munitions and supplies until the light of day that shone in through the tall windows gradually turned to orange haze.

# Hronwena

The day of the wedding came all too quick for Hronwena and she found herself frightened and awestruck by the way the whole of Londinium got carried away in the preparations. Streets were swept and scrubbed clean, flowers were arranged on balconies and the beggars and prostitutes were rounded up by soldiers and sent to the outskirts for the day.

The wedding took place in the church within the ruined basilica. She had never seen a building so massive and intimidating. Its cavernous interior and sweeping mosaics were grander than anything she had seen in the palace where she and her family had spent the previous few days in preparation. The whole building was filled to bursting with people. Noblemen and their families from across Britta had been invited upon Vertigernus's request and they formed a great sea of faces and expensive silks that stood before the altar. At the forefront of them stood her family dressed in their finest clothes.

Bishop Calvinus married them under the gaze of their crucified God. Hronwena felt the Latin words that she had spent so long memorising flowing out of her mouth without any effort. The whole ceremony went by as if in a dream. A dream? No. It was more like a horrible nightmare from which she could not wake. When the Bishop's words were over the crowd burst into a thundering applause. It was done. She was married.

They walked in a column from the forum to the palace along clean streets lined with jubilant townsfolk.

Rose petals were thrown from balconies and they filled the air like dancing snowflakes. Trumpets blared as if a new king had been crowned and the cheering was deafening.

But not all the townsfolk were happy about the union and as they rounded a corner somebody shouted; "Go home, pagan bitch!" Hronwena's face burned crimson as she comprehended the British words hurled at her and she saw a couple of Aurelianus's soldiers push their way through the crowds and grab the loudmouth. She craned her head but could not see what happened to the man for the procession had moved too far along.

The many halls of the palace had been set out for a feast and every table in the building had been put to use in bearing food and drink. Candles flickered in every corner and the scent of the many vases of rose blossoms was as strong as the smell of roasted meat, fresh shellfish and baked bread. Wine was dispensed liberally to the guests by the palace servants who were outfitted in wreaths and crowns of spring flowers.

Hronwena found herself sitting on a couch alongside her new husband, who she could not bring herself to look at just yet, accepting the congratulations of a never ending line of noblemen and their wives, none of whom she recognised. They went past her in a blur as she held out her hand to be kissed over and over, nodding politely and thanking them in her best British for coming.

Gifts piled up behind them. A mirror of copper with a solid gold handle set with gems from Lord Elafius. A sword of Caledonian iron from Lord

Vortimer to his father and a small box made from sweet woods containing incense for his new stepmother. A codex of Tacitus's Germania from Lord Marcellinus brought out smiles and discreet titters from several other guests and made Hronwena feel like she was missing out on a joke at her expense. Jewellery, silk, jars of spices, amber trinkets and other valuable items soon littered the couch and side tables. One guest, clearly trying to impress his lord, presented them with a bizarre creature in a cage. It was somewhat man-like in its shape but was covered in bushy hair and had a pinkish face and backside which was extremely prominent. It elicited much interest and amusement from the guests but began to screech like a demon and hammer at the bars of its cage. It made such a racket that Vertigernus had his servants carry it out into the gardens where it could be left to rant and seethe without further disrupting the feast.

Tired though she was, Hronwena felt like grasping at the departing evening as if it were a lifeline trailing in the wake of a rapidly departing vessel. For when all was said and done, the most terrifying part of the whole ordeal would be upon her. Somewhere, in the upper chambers of the palace, she would have to lie down on silk sheets and part her legs for her new husband.

## Vortimer

The light of dusk played on the trickling waters of the garden's fountains while the noise of the feast played out through the open arches beyond. Vortimer heard two pairs of feet approaching him.

"Not enjoying the festivities, Lord Vortimer?"

He turned and extended his arm in greeting to Lord Elafius and then to Lord Marcellinus. "Good of you both to come," he said. "It is a long journey for you both."

Elafius smiled. "Appearances must be upheld, Lord Vortimer. Your father is a powerful man as you were so keen to remind me when we last met."

"I apologise for my manners that day," said Vortimer. "I was out of sorts and your comments sparked off some strange sense of family loyalty in me. Have you expressed your congratulations to my father and new stepmother yet?"

"Oh, yes," Marcellinus replied. "But I must congratulate you on your organisation of this wedding reception. A most grand affair. The oysters are particularly good. From Rutupiae, I expect?"

Vortimer searched Marcellinus's face for his meaning but couldn't find it. "I warn you both now, that this is neither the time nor place to brooch certain matters."

"What matters might they be?"

"A certain thing Lord Elafius mentioned to me the last time we met."

"Ah," said Elafius. "Well, there have been further developments since then as I am sure you know."

"What developments?"

Elafius lowered his voice and a fire came into his eyes. "This sham of a marriage for a start. Your father, the leading member of the Council marrying a pagan? It has swayed even more to the opinion that he has gone too far. Pagans for Pascha is one thing but marriage to the daughter of one of them in the holy basilica, but a few feet from where Bishop Lentilus fell to his death? It sits very ill with the Council and the people. Very ill indeed."

"I am not in disagreement with you," Vortimer replied, looking over Elafius's shoulder to make sure that nobody was in earshot. "You must understand that for me, this is a personal insult as well as a political one. My mother's memory has been shamed by my father's infatuations before, and I have several younger siblings to show for it, but this Saxon witch..."

"Infatuations?" murmured Marcellinus. "I was under the impression that this marriage was purely a political one out of necessity for a union in the sight of God."

"Do not joke on the matter, Marcellinus. You know as well as I that my father has an ungodly lust for young women in his bedchamber."

"He might have any woman in Britannia for his consort," said Elafius. "Why pick this Saxon's daughter if not for political gain?"

"My father's ambition is matched only by his lust. And once has set his heart on something he will suffer nothing to stand in his way."

"You can't deny the political gain of the union though," said Marcellinus. "To have this Saxon horde at his beck and call, forever subservient to him, will make him more powerful than any Briton has been before. Dangerously powerful."

Vortimer was silent. He knew he was being manipulated. Elafius had tried before and now he was back in greater numbers. These two old snakes possessed four times the wit he did not to mention the experience in navigating dangerous political waters.

"Are you with us then?" Marcellinus asked.

"No!" The word was a hissed pleading. "I cannot discuss this! Whatever it is that you are planning, I want no part of it!"

"And yet we cannot proceed without your compliance," Elafius said. "You are the only candidate for your father's chair. Nobody else has the support of the Council."

"You must understand that bloodshed is something we wish to avoid at all costs," said Marcellinus. "The good Lord knows that this island has seen enough of that in recent years. The current opinion is that by requesting the intervention of Aetius of Gaul, the rule of your father could be ended peacefully and legally allowing you to take his place with the minimum of upset."

"Legally?" said Vortimer bitterly. "I'm afraid that term has lost all meaning in these times."

"Quite," said Elafius. "But we must conform to some idea of the word else what are we? Barbarians?"

"There is one other matter that must be addressed before our request is put to the mighty Aetius," Marcellinus went on. "In a word; Aurelianus."

"He has been loyal to your father ever since his own was defeated at the Battle of Wallop," said Elafius. "He commands every drop of military strength on the island. We need his support if we are to attempt anything with Aetius. The last thing Britannia needs is another civil war."

"Would Aurelianus really go against Aetius if he came here?" Vortimer asked.

"Hard to believe, I know, but there is no telling how deep his loyalty to your father runs. If we are to bring Aetius here, then Aurelianus must be with us."

Vortimer let out a snort of mirth. It was more a sound of relief and he knew that the other two heard it as such. "Well, then there, my lords, you have a problem. Aurelianus has been my father's man since I was a boy. He will not turn. And if Aurelianus is not with you, then neither am I."

The sour expressions on their faces were laughable. "I must leave you now, dear friends, and play my part of the proud host. I bid you both an enjoyable evening."

Elafius seized his arm. "Have you no self respect?" he demanded. "Have you no honour or courage? Do you not love this island?" The mask of friendly persuasion had slipped to reveal anger born out of desperation.

"I love this island more than any man," Vortimer replied. "But I love life also. I may lack courage but I do not lack the wit to stay on the winning side." He shook himself free of Elafius's grip and headed back indoors.

# Horsa

Horsa watched his niece from the corner of the room, a cup of wine in his hand and a sour expression on his face. She seemed helplessly miserable, sitting there alongside that old man with whom she must lie down tonight, speaking a language that was not her own. He thought back to the damaged, pale girl he had helped rescue two years ago from the slave market in Daneland. She had been frightened and meek but he had seen a fire in his niece's eyes that burned fro freedom and happiness. He had grown fond of her, just as he had grown fond of Aesc, and it pained him to see that fire crushed by this marriage nobody but his brother and the groom wanted.

He scowled at Hengest who was on the opposite side of the room with the ever loyal Halfritha by his side as he revelled in his role as father of the bride, thanking the various guests who came to shake his hand. The bile rose in Horsa's throat but he forced it down, desperately trying to keep himself in high spirits. Today was not the day for bitter family squabbles, and besides, he had pledged his loyalty to Hengest and his war in the north.

Aurelianus was over there, looking equally peeved. He still found it hard to believe that this was the father of the beautiful woman he had met in the forests outside Londinium. The black hair and dark eyes were the same but Aurelianus possessed a cold, hard face where his daughter's was a soft. He wondered what her mother must have been like.

*Aureliana.* He had thought of little else since they had returned home and now he was back in the same room with her. There she was, looking like a goddess beneath the light of a brazier, talking with some other nobleman's daughter. How he wanted to go over and speak with her!

*But not yet.* Not with her father so close.

He watched as Aurelianus was called over by two men he did not recognise. He sauntered over to Aureliana. The girl at her side saw him approaching and slunk off, clearly having no desire to make small talk with a Saxon. But Aureliana remained, a small smile touching her mouth as she cradled her wine cup in both hands. They stepped into the shadows together.

"I was confident we would see each other again, Horsa the Jute," she said.

"I've been looking all over for you," he said. "Have you not been out riding?"

"There was too much to prepare for this wedding," she replied. "I am sorry that you missed me."

"I brought you a present."

"Oh?"

He reached into a pouch at his belt and drew out a small, gold object and placed it into her palm. She inspected it. It was a comb fashioned into the shape of a boar with a tall ridge of straight bristles and two pairs of stumpy legs. On its surface had been engraved swirling patterns in the Celtic style and its eye was a small red gemstone that caught the candlelight. It was old, very old; harkening back to a time before Romans and Saxons when Britta was a land of tribal chiefs and pagan gods.

"This is beautiful, Horsa," she murmured as she stroked the curving Celtic lines engraved on the boar.

"I took it from a British trader that was trying to sneak away to Gaul, laden with treasures last year."

"It is a boar," she said. "I take it that this means you found out who Turch Trwyd is."

"I have. It is my way of thanking you for that song for it remains with me night and day, as does the voice that sang it."

"You are quite the flatterer, Horsa," Aureliana replied with a sly wink. "I expect you have many women at your beck and call."

"None," Horsa lied. But it didn't feel like a lie for he saw Aureliana in a completely different light than the various wenches and doting girls he knew in Rutupiae. To him she represented perfection and purity; the one good and bright thing in his otherwise bloody and sordid life. He wanted her, that was true enough, but he also wanted to preserve her, to shield her from life so that she would not become stained and corrupted like him. And perhaps, even a little part of him secretly hoped that if he bathed in her presence enough, part of her goodness would reflect back on him and drive away at least a part of the darkness he felt within.

"I too have been thinking of you," she said. "I stay up late some nights just so I can see the light of Earendel rising above the rim of the world. When I see that, I know that another dawn has broken on a world we both share and that gives me great comfort."

Horsa's heart soared. She had as good as admitted that she loved him as he loved her.

"I know that that star will continue to reassure me when you are gone from here. When you are far in the north with my father, I can look to the morning of each day and each day that Earendel rises I will know that he is guiding you both and that you are safe."

Horsa looked down.

"Are you sad too?" she asked him. "Does it hurt your heart as much as it does mine, to know that we will not see each other again for a very long time?"

"More than you know," he said. "I have never met anyone like you, Aureliana. I never thought that women could be so good and pure outside of the songs. Whatever happens in the north, I will always be glad that I had the chance to know you."

"I wish that we could know each other a little better," she said. "We have so much to learn about each other."

"I know, but we leave upon the morrow. Our time is short."

"Then we must make the most of tonight," she said and at that moment Horsa would have cut his own throat if he could only hold her and kiss her there in the shadows.

# Hronwena

The celebrations drew to their eventual, inevitable conclusion. Hronwena would have given anything to halt time in its tracks and had been afforded a brief moment of hope when her new husband, roaring drunk, had fallen off his bench and had to be helped to his feet. Perhaps he would be too drunk to do anything but snore? But this hope was snatched away from her as he showed no intention of failing in his husbandly duties and hauled her to her feet amidst cheers and lewd remarks. Now she was alone with her new husband in an upstairs room of the palace.

She held the sheets tightly to her, covering her naked body as Vertigernus disrobed. By the flickering candlelight she could make out slack flesh scattered with greying hairs and networked with purple veins. She shuddered. He mounted the bed and began to pull the covers away from her. She resisted, holding tightly to the cloth.

"Don't play the prude with me, girl," he said through a grin. "I don't expect my women to be virgins, particularly the pagan ones. What have you got to hide?"

"I agreed to be your wife for the sake of my father's alliance with you, but do not touch me," she said through gritted teeth.

He seemed surprised but quickly overcame it. With a sudden jerk, he ripped the covers away from her. Angered, she lashed out with her foot, striking him in the jaw. He gasped and pounced on her, seizing her arms and pinning her down, pressing with all his weight.

His tongue slithered out of his mouth and tried to lick her cheek. She bit at him and he withdrew like a startled snake.

"By God, but you've got some fight in you, Sais," he said with a smile. "But I'll tame you, as I've tamed others before you. And I shall enjoy the exercise."

She wriggled and he loosened his grasp, allowing her to squirm free. She tried to scramble off the bed and make for the door but he caught her ankles and dragged her back onto the bed like a cat toying with a mouse. She found herself beneath him with one of his hands in her tangled hair, pulling, forcing her head backwards as if he were reigning in a horse. It hurt like searing fire, but she clenched her teeth. She'd be damned if she let him get any pleasure out of her suffering.

He was cold, icy cold against her trembling flesh and she almost retched when she felt the bony fingers of his right hand run over her breasts and down to dig into her hip. She closed her eyes and tried to think of Thrydwulf. She tried to remember his perfect skin and fair hair and was distraught to discover how hard she found it. He was the man she had wanted to give herself to, not this beast who licked at her in the darkness. As he pushed himself inside her she squeezed her eyes tight, cursing herself for allowing a single tear to trickle out and hoped that he couldn't see it.

# Aureliana

In another room of the palace Aureliana lay awake in bed thinking sinful thoughts. In a corner of the room Seren dozed in her chair, her gentle snores filling the room. The moonlight that shone in through the window was suddenly blocked and Aureliana sat up in bed, a cry of fright escaping her lips as a dark figure clambered up onto her windowsill. He swung his legs down into the room and as the moonlight fell upon his face, Aureliana sighed with relief and excitement.

"Are you mad, Horsa?" she demanded in a whisper. "To come here under cover of darkness whilst my father sleeps on the other side of this wall!"

"Perhaps I am a little mad," he admitted. "But only through love of you. I had to see you one last time for we set out to war tomorrow morning."

Seren awoke with a start and nearly let out a cry at the sight of a man in the room but Aureliana hushed her. "Quiet, Seren! Do you want my father to come storming in here? It's only Horsa."

"Well, I must say, my lady!" the old woman hissed. "This is most improper!"

"Then leave us!" Aureliana said.

"Certainly not!"

"Get out, Seren! I am old enough to do what I want!"

"My lady, I beg you! Your father would feed me to his dogs if he knew I let you alone with this man!"

"He would do that anyway if he found out you were with us in the forest and did not tell him. Now get out!"

The poor woman muttered under her breath as she reluctantly obeyed. Taking her blanket with her, she left the room to find somewhere in the hallway to sleep, looking thoroughly miserable as she did so. When she had gone, Aureliana leaped out of bed and flung her arms around Horsa, kissing his bearded cheek.

He grasped her tightly and together they fell down onto the bed. He kissed her neck and chest again and again, leaving no area of her pale, soft skin untouched by his lips. He ran his hands up her naked thighs beneath her nightclothes and she writhed beneath him with pent up longing for more.

She had wanted this for many nights, but had never dared admit it to herself for surely it was a sin so evil that she would be bound for Hell. But in that moment, with his hot breath on her skin, she did not care about the priests and bishops, not even about God Almighty himself. If something was so forbidden, then why on God's good earth did it feel so right? The priests would quote some scripture at her about the forbidden fruit tasting the sweetest for it was laced with the Devil's temptation, but again, she cared not.

She felt him fumbling with the buckle on his breeches and then she felt him enter her and she gasped with pain. But it was not a discomfort so terrible that she wished him to stop for there was a pleasure there too, a secret, hidden pleasure that she had dreamed of many times but had never dared to dwell on in her waking hours. All her feelings for him seemed amplified suddenly through this vulgar, primal act and her insides burned with a pleasure that was surely sent from Heaven.

Her nails raked his skin beneath his shirt and she drew him to her, arching her back as he moved slowly in and out, steadily increasing in speed. She tried to stop herself from crying out in ecstasy, but failed. He moaned also and suddenly his whole body shuddered and the sweat stood out on his skin.

He collapsed on top of her and then rolled to one side, this powerful barbarian warrior; drained of all his strength to the point of paralysis by the company of a woman.

"How many women have you loved?" she asked him once her breathing had slowed down.

"Many," he said. As he saw her face fall he added; "But none have stirred such feelings in me as you have."

"What feelings?" she asked through a smile.

"I've... done bad things, Aureliana," he said. "I'm not what your priests would call a good man."

"Few are, though they pretend to be," she replied. "But what terrible things have you done to convince you so?"

"I will not go into them here," he said. "But it is enough for me to say that whatever you Britons have heard about my people is true. I come from a dark land where there is much evil of which I am a part. For many years I have journeyed throughout the north, raiding, fighting and killing; doing things that would make you hate me if I told you. Bloodshed and battle used to thrill me but now my soul feels black and alone and I am tired, so tired of death and butchery. When I am with you, somehow I feel as if there may be some good in me after all, trying to get out. With you I feel human again." He kissed her lips and she caressed his neck.

"I don't know what it is about you," Aureliana said. "But I can't believe that you are as bad as all that. Ever since I was a little girl, I have heard tales about the savagery of the Saeson and their barbaric ways. Terrible stories that kept me awake at night in fear. But then I met you and you were nothing like I imagined a Sais to be. You are kind and gentle and human. True, you have your rough ways and coarse manners and your religion is a far cry from what we consider good and holy in this land, but I am drawn to you all the same. You excite me, Horsa. I love everything about you. And I don't want you to leave tomorrow."

"But I must," he said. "My brother is a cold-hearted brute, worse than I ever imagined he could be, but ultimately he is right. Through this alliance between Sais and Briton we can ensure a peaceful future. Without it there will be only war between our two peoples."

"Promise me you'll come back, Horsa. Promise me you'll survive whatever is waiting for you in the north."

"I cannot do that. Even my love for you cannot bring me back here if my *wyrd* follows a different thread."

"Do you mean fate?"

"Yes. Some things are far stronger than us mortals. There are dark forces at work in this world that have a pull on me. I have done things in my life that I may never escape from and perhaps I have no right to expect to."

"Oh, don't talk like that! What things? What possible forces could defy the power of God? He knows that we love each another. I shall pray to him everyday to keep you safe and I believe that he will answer. I must believe..."

"What I am afraid of is that no god can save me. For it is a goddess I have angered."

"A goddess?"

"Back in the lands across the sea, I destroyed her image and did much evil to her people. Later I met a witch who told me that my *wyrd* was under the sway of this goddess. As I had offended the fair sex of woman, it would be a woman who would bring about my downfall. And tomorrow I march to war against a northern queen who has untold forces at her command. Now do you see why I am afraid that I will not return?"

Aureliana was silent. There was so much she didn't understand. All she knew was that it wasn't fair. It wasn't fair that the one man she had fallen in love with was the one man she could never have. Even if he returned to her alive, father would kill him if he knew... It was all so dreadful that she could have wept there and then. But she was determined not to. This may be the last night she had with him; her last night of happiness. And even if it meant she would be bound for fiery damnation, she was bloody well going to enjoy it.

# PART IV

*(Tir) Tir biþ tacna sum, healdeð trywa wel*
*wiþ æþelingas; a biþ on færylde*
*ofer nihta geniþu, næfre swiceþ.*

(Tir) Tir is a star, it keeps faith well
with athelings, always on its course
over the mists of night it never fails.

# Hengest

"Sorry we're late," Hengest said to Aurelianus as he rode up to the head of the column, flanked by Ordlaf with his banner on one side and Ebusa and Aesc on the other.

The British war-leader barely acknowledged him, his iron-hard face facing the front where the road led north from Londinium. Behind them stood the walls of the town where a great many nobles and their families had gathered to bid goodbye and good luck to the brave men who stood on the cusp of war.

Hengest shielded his eyes against the sun and could make out Hronwena standing at the side of her new husband. It was good to know that one member of his family was there to see them off. That morning he had kissed his wife and hugged his brother goodbye before watching the *Bloodkeel* row downstream, back towards the coast. Back to the home he was fighting for.

"Get into formation," Aurelianus said to him. "We march."

Hengest led his thegns to where his three-hundred odd horsemen were clustered behind Aurelianus's vanguard. A bellowing peal rolled out from a bronze horn and as one, the army moved forward. Hengest saw Aurelianus turn in his saddle to gaze briefly at the town walls behind them. He followed his gaze and saw Aurelianus's daughter waving. Hengest waved to his own daughter. She did not wave back and soon she was consumed as the walls of Londinium receded and became obscured by the dust of hundreds of tramping feet.

Hengest had to marvel at the organisation of the Britons. It was a massive gathering of troops that set out. Banners and standards fluttered above tidy formations of archers, infantry and cavalry. At the rear creaked the carts piled up with equipment, armour and provisions and beyond those trailed the mass of cooks, blacksmiths, stable boys, whores and all the other followers of any army.

The Britons sang songs. They were the last army on their island, travelling the road of their fathers to fight an enemy that had been old before the Romans had left. But for Hengest, that first leg of the journey quickly became tedious. The countryside changed little and consisted primarily of rolling green hills and wooded valleys.

He was annoyed to find that Ebusa got on with Aurelianus much better than he did and could only watch as his thegn and their war-leader spent much of the journey in discussion about tactics and the customs of Roman commanders of fame and notoriety. Hengest tried to follow the conversations which, mercifully, were in British, but the constant reference to Latin terms like '*turmae*', '*alae*' and '*cohortes equitatae*' left him utterly befuddled.

They had not travelled far the following day when Hengest noticed two groups of his riders heading away from the group in opposite directions. Both groups were of about thirty men each and they left a trail of dust as they disappeared into the countryside. Infuriated, Hengest drew his sword and bellowed after them; "Stop! Cowards! You dare desert when we have not marched for two full days?"

Ebusa wheeled his horse away from Aurelianus's side and galloped along the line to Hengest's position. "My, lord? Is there something wrong?"

"You're damned right there's something wrong! Those cravens have deserted us! And without the slightest whiff of a fight in the air!"

"They haven't deserted us, my lord! I sent them out."

"You sent them?"

"Yes, my lord. Two *turmae*."

"Don't give me that Latin shit! What's a *turmae*?"

"A turma is a group of thirty riders. Aurelianus thought it best if we sent out scouting patrols.

Hengest had the feeling that he had made a fool of himself in front of his men. He sheathed his sword as discretely as he could. "Oh, he did, did he? And do you take orders from Aurelianus?"

"I... I'm sorry, my lord," Ebusa said. "I should have notified you."

Hengest exploded. "Notified me! You should have taken the order from me and not Aurelianus! Or have you swapped sides again?"

Ebusa lowered his head in respectful shame, but kept his teeth gritted and his eyes narrowed. "I was not aware that there was more than one side in this army, my lord."

Hengest had half a mind to make an example of his thegn, but checked his anger. "Sending out scouting patrols is not a bad idea, Ebusa," he said. "But the order should have come from me. In future, if Aurelianus has any more bright notions, please run them by me first. These are my men, not his."

"Of course, my lord. My apologies."

Hengest watched him trot off. His face burned partly with embarrassment and partly with rage at Aurelianus. *Scouting patrols?* They were barely out of bowshot from Londinium. Where was the need for scouting patrols? He had the feeling that he was being tested. Aurelianus clearly saw him as a stupid savage and intended to keep him in his place. Well, he would find that he was no biddable Briton to be bullied into compliance. They had asked him for help on this expedition and if Aurelianus thought that he could treat him like some common soldier, he was in for a sore lesson.

It took them several more days to reach what was considered 'the north'. It seemed to Hengest that the further they went, the more desolate the rural scenery became. Villages seemed blighted as if by an invisible menace. Buildings became shabbier and farms poorly kept. It was as if Londinium was some sort of candle radiating light and the further towns were from it, the colder and darker they were.

They passed the town of Lindum. At this point, Aurelianus said to Hengest; "We shall soon be entering Britannia Secunda; the realm of Lord Elafius."

"The man with the crippled son?"

Aurelianus seemed surprised that he would remember this. "Yes. Elafius's stronghold of Eboracum is another two day's march."

Settlements grew fewer and worse in appearance. Some were wholly deserted and were little more than mouldering thatch and burned out shells of buildings. The people seemed melancholy, grey and withdrawn, tending to their meagre crops and noting the passing army with a kind of grim acceptance. By the time they got to Eboracum, there was little in the surrounding countryside that suggested life.

"Pictish raids have been a menace to this region ever since the last years of Roman rule," explained Aurelianus. "The towns are no longer safe and many have taken to the hills and forests to scratch out a living. This is why we are here; to ensure that life in the north can return to some sort of acceptable level, free from barbarian incursions. Eboracum is the only safe place left in the north. Lord Elafius is holed up within its walls, holding the torch of civilisation against our barbarian foes."

This was the most Aurelianus had said to Hengest throughout the whole journey. He could see in his eyes that these words were words of hope and deep desire. He was a strange man, this Briton, Hengest decided. He had a love for his people and country but it was almost wholly masked by his melancholy.

The town was situated where the River Fossa met the River Usa. Between the two rivers lay the Roman fort with its high walls and towers. The old *colonia* - the walled town that had grown up alongside the fortress – sat on the western side of the River Usa and from what Hengest could see, was utterly devoid of humanity.

"The rivers regularly break their banks," explained Aurelianus. "The town gets flooded often and the walls are in such a poor state of repair that the locals that are left have taken to living in the fort for safety."

"Why doesn't Elafius repair the walls, then?" Hengest asked. "Or redirect the river to stop it from flooding the town?"

"Where would the money for that come from? Not to mention the manpower. Elafius, like the rest of the rulers on this island, is forced to make do with what he has and that isn't very much."

Lord Elafius himself came to meet them as the army entered the fort and began finding barracks to accommodate them.

"My lord," said Aurelianus, dismounting and extending his arm to greet the Lord of the North.

"Greetings, Aurelianus," said Elafius. "It pleases me to see our fort filled up with soldiers once more. It is as if the Caesars still paid us a care." He glanced at Hengest and then at the furs and leather garments of his men. His smile curled somewhat in distaste and Hengest got the impression that his pleasure in seeing the army extended only to the British portion of it.

They conversed in Latin and Hengest got Ceretic to translate.

"How is your son?" Aurelianus asked Elafius.

The older man sighed. "Living, that much God can be thanked for. But such a life is not one I wished for him. He lies in bed most of the time and cries at night for the pain in his leg is a great torment. I do not think the bone has knitted well. Nothing can be done for him."

"I have physicians with the army. Perhaps they could take a look with your permission."

"Thank you, Aurelianus, but I have had the help and advice of the very best healers in Britannia. I don't think a military saw-bones could do more help than harm at this point. Will you be staying long?"

"Just one night. I hope to reach the wall in two more days. Have you many men you can lend the army?"

"I have two-thousand men, all told, counting cavalry and infantry. They are all yours should you wish to take them."

Aurelianus shook his head. "You have too few already. The wall is broken in many points where the Picts can bypass us. We cannot leave the capital of the north undefended."

"You are doing a sterling job of protecting us, Aurelianus," said Elafius. "It is tragic that Lord Vertigernus is so opposed to sending to Gaul for aid. We former provinces of the Empire should help each other, do you not agree?"

Ceretic did not catch Aurelianus's reply as the two men walked away, leaving the army to get settled in.

Aurelianus and his highest officers attended a welcoming feast in Elafius's villa that night. Hengest was not invited. He instead spent most of the evening ensuring that no fights broke out between his men and the Britons regarding sleeping arrangements.

Many of his warriors would not bed down in a room with Britons for fear of a knife in their gullet in the dead of night. And he supposed that many of the Britons felt the same. It was a poor state of affairs when two sides of an army had to be kept separated to avoid violence and he was reminded of that fateful night in Finnesburg when Jute and Dane were given separate halls. He hoped that the sun would not dawn on a similar tragedy.

# Hronwena

Hronwena gazed out at the grim, grey landscape. Every step of the arduous journey from Londinium to the hills of the west had been one step further from everything she knew and loved. She had held back the tears when her mother had kissed her goodbye before joining Uncle Horsa on board the *Bloodkeel*. She had watched bitterly as they had set off down the Tamesis, leaving her to be consumed by loneliness and misery and in the company of her dreadful new husband.

They journeyed in a *carpentium*; a four wheeled vehicle drawn by two horses. It had a cloth covering which reverberated like a war-drum whenever it rained and had hangings of red silk on the sides that could be drawn for reasons of privacy or warmth. Hronwena gladly sacrificed warmth for not being curtained off from the world with that letch beside her.

"You will be more than comfortable at Din Neidr, if a little wanting of my company," Vitalinus told her. "Most of my time is taken up at Corinium Dobunnorum."

They had stopped for the night at Corinium Dobunnorum before they had crossed the River Sabrina so Hronwena had seen something of her husband's capital town. All she had seen was a smaller version of Londinium; lower walls, shorter streets and fewer foreigners. One thing it did have was a substantially larger amphitheatre on the outskirts of the town.

They had then passed through Glevum or 'Cair Gloui' as her husband called it in British; an even smaller town which petered out into thick forests that seemed to consume them for the best part of a day. After that the ground began to rise up into hilly country and deep valleys.

"I have always preferred to keep my main residence at Din Neidr," he went on. "The Roman towns are a constant reminder to those who too often let their hearts yearn for the Empire and her dwindling influence. My son likes the stone corridors and marble busts of the Caesars and he is welcome to them. That is why I gave him Maxima Caesariensis to rule so he can strut about Londinium to his heart's content. As head of the Council it was really for me to rule the lion's share of the island, but I grow so tired of politics. I fear that if I spend too long away from my roots in the west, I may become like all the others; Britons playing at Roman theatrics.

"No, it is for the next generation of Britons to rule this island. With Vortimer already in position, I await my other sons to reach manhood so that they may be given territories of their own to rule. You'll meet Cadeyrn and Pasgen when we reach Din Neidr. In time, there won't be a single acre of land in Albion not ruled by one of my bloodline."

He didn't seem to notice or care that Hronwena wasn't paying him much attention. She focused on the rolling hills and moors that slid past. Vitalinus talked incessantly and she found it extremely tiring to try to comprehend the British language hour after hour.

"Din Neidr is a monument to our heritage as Britons," he went on. "My ancestors ruled it when Albion was a collection of tribes at the coming of the

Romans. Now that the Romans have gone I fully intend for my blood to continue to rule it for generations and generations."

Hronwena shuddered. The continuation of his 'blood' was something of an obsession for him. He spoke relentlessly of 'heritage' and 'ancestry' and had forced himself on her more than a few times, once even in the confines of the carpentium but a wheel had hit a hole in the road causing him to slip out of her and land sprawling on the floor between the seats. After he had finished cursing the driver to all the torments of the Christian Hell, the vigour had gone out of him and he desisted in his efforts.

It was clear that he hoped to sire children on her as soon as possible and, as a precaution, she took crushed fennel seeds every morning and chanted a rune spell before every draught. All her hopes for the future rested on her new husband dying an early death and she had no intention of remaining in this godforsaken land to raise his rotten spawn. As soon as she could she would return to her family in the east.

It had occurred to her to hurry things along a little. She knew that hemleac would kill instantly and leave no traces. There were other plants that would slowly aid his passing from life but what if she was caught? It would mean death for her. Or what if the poison didn't work properly? He would be very ill indeed and very keen to exact vengeance on her for her treachery. She did not dare try. She would wait and let nature take its course and pray that it wouldn't be too long about it.

"Aha! Do you see?" he asked her as a monolithic blot against the sky appeared on the horizon. "Welcome home!"

The ancestral home of Vitalinus lay some eighty miles west of Londinium in the valley of the Afon. Standing proud and tall over the village that lay nestled beneath it upon the bend of the river, the fortress seemed intent on remaining a statement to British authority. Its walls were of high, sharpened timbers and everything about it shouted 'danger' to Hronwena.

*Home?* To her the place could only ever be a prison. As the great iron-bound gates creaked shut behind the small train of carts and soldiers she felt as if a thunder-filled cloud had passed over her heart. The booming of them closing was a toll of doom for all hope of happiness.

The servants and other inhabitants of the fortress had assembled in the courtyard to welcome their ruler and his new bride. Applause greeted them as Vitalinus led her around the yard, showing off his new acquisition as if she were a prize horse. Although his subjects dutifully congratulated him, there were few genuine smiles and Hronwena could hear the mutters of disapproval rippling through the crowd. Few of these Britons were happy to welcome a pagan as their new lady of the house.

Two youths stood expectantly as Vitalinus approached them. "I present to you my sons," he said. "Greet your new mother, boys. This is Cadeyrn and Pasgen."

They both came forward and dutifully kissed Hronwena's hand. Cadeyrn was of a similar age to

Hronwena but Pasgen was younger. They seemed polite enough but showed no great enthusiasm at their father's return.

"They're good lads on the whole," Vitalinus said to her as they entered the main holding. "Soft as runny pigshit but that's due to their mother. She was a wet Briton from a noble family with no backbone. Nothing like you Germanic women, eh?"

She kept her eyes focused ahead and did not answer him.

"You'll soon get settled in. Which reminds me - Deilwen!" he turned his head and bellowed the name again; "Deilwen! Where is that ill-tempered harpy?"

"Here, my lord!" said a small, pretty woman who scurried over to them. She was a little older than Hronwena and had black hair which she kept tied back in a simple bun.

"This is your handmaid, my dear. She's a vicious tart but she knows the household inside out and will serve you well. Take my new wife to her quarters, you hear?"

"Yes, my lord."

Deilwen led Hronwena down a stone flagged corridor and up a wooden staircase. "Speak much British?" she asked her once they were out of earshot.

Hronwena was pretty sure that there should have been a 'my lady' in there somewhere but decided not to press the matter. "Enough, I think," she replied.

"Latin?"

Hronwena shook her head. She didn't like her new handmaid's manners but did not trust her command of the language to chastise her for it.

"Well there's not much call for it in this household. I don't speak a word of it and my lord is as British as they come or at least he tries to be. You will notice that there is a bath house within the fortress walls. Lord Vitalinus can't abide the Romans but can't abide to live without some of their comforts either." She laughed at her jest and they entered Hronwena's chamber.

It was bigger than anything she was used to. A window looked out onto the courtyard and rich hangings fluttered in the breeze. The bed was big and there were other items of furniture dotted around the room; a chair, a tall wardrobe for keeping clothes and a stand with a basin and jug. All were good quality wood with carvings.

"There's to be a feast tonight to welcome his lordship home," Deilwen said, going over to the wardrobe. She opened it and pulled out a long stola of yellow silk. "This should do for the occasion."

Hronwena gaped at the contents of the wardrobe. There were nearly a dozen gowns and stolas in there of varying colours and materials that were dazzling to the eye. "These must have cost a fortune!" she said.

"There's jewellery too," said Deilwen. She opened a box containing gold, silver and amber enough to make a queen of any woman. Hronwena's hand went to her mother's simple ring where it hung against her breastbone beneath her stola.

"Did he lavish clothes and jewels on his previous wife?" she asked Deilwen.

"Wives," corrected the handmaid. "All of them. He sees himself as a king therefore his wives must be queens."

"How many wives has he had? I thought there had only been one; the one who died last year."

"Heavens, you really have been thrown into deep water, haven't you?" Deilwen said. "You are his fourth. Cordula was his first, but that was before my time. She gave him Vortimer, Cadeyrn and Senovara."

"Senovara died as a child?"

"No she saw at least thirteen summers. She fell pregnant by a stable boy who worked here in the fortress. You can imagine that didn't please his lordship and he sent her away to have the baby in seclusion. She was in disgrace, you see. The stable boy was hanged of course. I had all this from the cook; she's dead too now."

"And what happened to Senovara and her child?"

"The curse of the line of Vitalis."

Hronwena blinked in confusion.

"Big heads or so they say. Senovara died forcing the babe out and the child died soon after without its mother to care for it. It might have been different had she given birth here in Din Neidr and not some hovel in the hills."

"When was all this?"

"Just before Cadeyrn was born. In fact Cordula was pregnant the same time as her daughter. All a bit embarrassing really."

"And Cordula...?"

"Died during childbirth, same as Senovara. Big heads is what they say about the males of this family. Tragic, but God has a plan for us all. That's another thing they say."

"What of Pasgen?"

"Son of his lordship's second wife. Adelphia was her name. She had twins. Pasgen and Enys. She fell into a depression and flung herself off the high tower."

"She killed herself?" Hronwena was astounded. None of this had reached her ears in Londinium. "But where is Enys?"

"She died two years ago at the age of twelve. It was a fever. Then his lordship married Brina – the one you've heard of – but she was taken from us last year. A tragic accident. She was crossing the river and the current swept her away. The worst of it was that she was pregnant."

"Gods be good..." murmured Hronwena. So much death in one family. Women splitting open and dying giving birth to babies with abnormally large heads. Accidents, fevers, suicides... It was a wonder any woman went near this fortress. It made her all the more determined never to conceive a child of Vitalinus.

"What everybody is wondering now," said Deilwen, eying her gnomishly, "is what kind of a wife you are going to make."

"I beg your pardon?"

"Cordula was a bit of a shrinking violet by all accounts. Not up to being Vitalinus's 'queen' by any measure. Adelphia clearly didn't have what it took to be a mother to her twins, let alone head of the household and saw death as the only way out. Brina, well, who knows what Brina would have been like in the years to come if the good Lord had had a different plan for her.

"I liked her. She had spirit and wasn't afraid to put his lordship in his place. She took the occasional beating for it but what's a few knocks for a bit of respect from everybody else, eh? Yes, Brina was a fiery one alright. Young, but she knew what was what. So you see, each time his lordship takes a new wife, the household gets to asking itself; will she be made of stern stuff or will she be a frail flower that gets trodden on?"

Hronwena looked sharply at Deilwen. There was an insolence there as she looked her up and down and Hronwena began to understand. She had been testing her. "Tell me something, Deilwen. When you spoke to Brina, how did you address her?"

Deilwen looked surprised at the question. "I suppose I called her 'my lady',"

"I may have married your lord under protest, Deilwen, and I may be a pagan foreigner in your land, ignorant of your customs and manners, but do not forget that I am your lady and you will address me as such. I am sure my husband would not be pleased to hear of any insolence on the part of his staff."

Deilwen looked at her for a moment. Then a smile split across her face. "There's hope for you yet, *my lady*."

The feast that night was similar to what she had experienced in Londinium when the Christians celebrated the resurrection of their crucified god, although the speech by the local bishop was mercifully shorter.

"I must congratulate you on your sons, my lord," said a bald-headed nobleman, raising his cup. "They have grown to be fine lads to do you proud. And how is the Lord Vortimer? It was many years ago that he rode out with us on his first Beltan hunt."

"He is as he always is," replied Vitalinus. "Indecisive, cowardly and lacking in the qualities it takes to truly rule a province. Fortunately I am able to spend much of my time in Londinium to steer Maxima Caesariensis away from total ruin."

The bald nobleman frowned. "But in Cadeyrn, surely, you have a son truly your equal in quality. He is the finest warrior in Din Neidr, I hear."

Cadeyrn's face glowed at the compliment but his father merely snorted. "It doesn't take swordplay to rule," he said. "If it did I would have found a more suitable heir from my guards. One who has the guts to do what is necessary instead of weeping for common sluts when they are taken from him."

Cadeyrn's smile suddenly vanished and for a brief moment, Hronwena thought he was going to weep right there and then, but the young man steeled his face and said; "I am not the only man in Din Neidr who has a passion for common sluts, father."

"Careful, boy," Vitalinus said with narrowed eyes. "You are in the presence of my wife; your stepmother. And any noble-born man knows the difference between fucking a farmer's daughter and falling in love with one."

Hronwena had, for a moment, thought that Cadeyrn's barbed comment had been directed at her and her sympathy for her stepson had almost vanished, but she realised that he had been broaching another matter; a previous dramatic episode in the life of the fortress which she had not been privy to.

The atmosphere at the high table had soured and many were suddenly interested in the contents of their goblets. Hronwena merely seethed on the part of Cadeyrn, despite having only just met him. He seemed a good sort, despite his family, and it pained her to see him humiliated by her husband in front of the guests. Before she knew what she was doing, she spoke out, feeling acutely self-conscious of her accent.

"I would have thought that nobility was something a father passed on to his sons, husband. Perhaps the absences of qualities in a man stem from the lack of a role model."

The silence that followed could have been cut up and served on a platter like the meat from the hearths. The noblemen stared at her opened mouthed and she even saw a touch of surprised gratitude on Cadeyrn's face.

"Another woman who insults me by poisoning every word without having the guts to speak her mind openly," snapped Vitalinus, before pouring a mouthful of wine down his throat. "Lord have mercy! Why must all women be this way? And if that wasn't bad enough, they pass on these damnable female traits to my sons! Even Pasgen there who is on the cusp of manhood shows nothing worthy of the name in his actions. He should be ravishing peasant girls and sporting wounds won in the training yard as I did at his age. But he would rather wallow in the memory of his lost twin. God knows, I have buried enough wives and daughters in my years to come to terms with death. It is time you did, boy."

Pasgen did not possess the self-control of his older brother and tears welled up in his eyes. He rose from the table and left.

"Well, damn you all!" Vitalinus roared. "Are we to let my miserable sons ruin my homecoming feast? Eat! Talk! Laugh!"

The hall nervously obeyed, tucking into their food and quickly raising trivial topics to usher out the poor mood. Cadeyrn stared sullenly into his goblet. Hronwena, still feeling sorry for him but wanting more than anything to engage in conversation with somebody who was not her husband, spoke to him. "Tell me, Cadeyrn, what is this 'Beltan' that was mentioned earlier?"

"It is our summer festival," he replied, meeting her eyes somewhat reluctantly. "It symbolises warmth and light. It used to be a pagan tradition. Something to do with the sun god and fertility, but we still honour it. Every year my father holds a feast and afterwards the men ride out to hunt by moonlight."

As the evening wore on, Vitalinus got drunk and his hand kept slipping from the table to grope Hronwena beneath her stola. After much squirming, she decided that she could not take any more and rose to leave the table. Most of the nobles were too drunk to see her leave but as she passed into the corridor, Vitalinus caught up with her and forced her against the stone wall. A nearby torch illuminated his drink-addled face as he pressed in close to kiss her. She struggled and managed to wriggle free, setting him off balance to stumble clumsily against the wall.

"Christ, woman!" he bellowed. "You are the most frigid sow I've ever tried to fuck! Get out of my sight! I'll attend to you later!"

He stormed off leaving Hronwena gulping in air to offset the sobs that were rising in her throat.

"Has he struck you yet?" said a voice from further down the hall that made her jump.

She turned to see a guardsman place his spear against the wall and approach her. He was young with black stubble and a knotted brow. "He struck his last wife, you see, whenever she refused him. Not that it did much good. She was a strong one. She held out against him even if she took a black eye for it."

"He has not struck me, not that it's any business of yours." She was on the defensive now, and wondered at the guard's insolence.

"He will. The question is, will that make you give in to him?"

"You're very forward for a guard," she snapped.

"I haven't always been a guard."

"What's your name?"

"Berwen."

"Is every servant in this fortress so bloody rude? How should you be addressing me?"

His eyes hardened a little. "My apologies, *my lady*. You must understand that certain changes are difficult for some of us here to accept. Shall I escort you to your chambers?"

"I think I can manage that," said Deilwen emerging from the great hall. "Don't you have a post to be guarding?"

"Is an army attacking?" Berwen said insolently.

"Well if there was then we wouldn't bloody well know of it with lackwits like you protecting us! Go away and let me tend to my lady."

The guard slunk back into the shadows and Deilwen took Hronwena protectively by the elbow.

"That guard," said Hronwena once they had rounded the corner, "How long has he been here?"

"Oh he's harmless enough," Deilwen replied. "Bit of a mouth on him but they say the same of me. Must have been a year ago when he joined his lordship's guard. Not long before the lady Brina died." She saw the look in Hronwena's eyes. "Oh, don't you go jumping at conclusions, my lady. If there was any foul play, then it wasn't on the part of Berwen. He adored the lady Brina, though he tried to hide it. It might make him a little prickly to you, seeing as you are taking her place."

"Is there any reason to suspect foul play in Brina's death?" asked Hronwena.

Deilwen sighed. "She and his lordship were often at odds and there was little love lost between them in the months before her death. But no, I can't say that there was anything but a tragic accident that did for her."

"Were Brina and Berwen secretly lovers?"

"Lord bless you, my lady, no! In Berwen's dreams perchance, but the lady Brina was a noblewoman through and through. They were thick as thieves and I had a job keeping up with all the gossip that passed between them. But she would never carry on with his sort. I knew her well enough to say that with certainty. She may have hated her husband but she was a faithful God-fearing woman, which is more than I can say for his lordship. Oh, I apologise my lady, I did not mean to speak ill of your husband."

"Never mind that. Tell me, Deilwen, is he unfaithful?"

They stopped walking and Deilwen peered down the gloomy corridor to make sure that nobody was about. "He's a savage animal, begging your pardon. But then you must know that by now."

Hronwena was silent.

"He has appetites that range from noble to commoner, merchant's daughter to handmaid."

"Oh, gods, Deilwen, not you?"

"No, my lady, I never have, and that's a promise. Though he did try it on with me several times in the early days. I fought back and nearly ended up out in the mud or worse. But he leaves me alone now. He doesn't like it when anybody stands up to him and he's careful enough to avoid scandal."

"He'll come for me tonight, won't he?"

Deilwen nodded. "He's worse when he's in his cups. Look, my lady, I want to make a gift of something for you. I know it's not my place and I've only known you for a day, but it's my job to protect you as much as it is Berwen's so here it is." From beneath the folds of her dress she produced a slim dagger in a squirrel-skin sheath and gave it to Hronwena. "Remember what I said about his previous wives? How the ones who stood up to him fared better?"

Hronwena took the dagger and drew it slowly. The blade was wickedly thin and caught the light of the sconces like the wink in a serpent's eye. She didn't know what Deilwen expected her to do with it. Kill him? The temptation almost outweighed the consequences, but a better plan began to form in her mind. "Thank you, Deilwen. At least I have one friend in this place."

Deilwen curtseyed and left her to prepare for bed.

It was several hours before Vitalinus reeled in stinking of wine. Hronwena had not slept. She had been waiting for him with the covers pulled up to her chin. Her heart hammered in her breast as she wondered if she could go through with her plan. It was risk all now or submit to him forever. He stumbled about for a bit, tugging at his breeches before yanking the covers away and scrambling up onto her.

"Now then, my little Sais slut, let's see if we can't make you sing a different tune to your regular one." He froze as he felt the cold blade press against the side of his testicles.

"One move and they're gone," whispered Hronwena.

His eyes were wide and filled with fear in the darkness of the room.

Hronwena smiled. "Now then, let's see if you can listen as well as you can bluster, you British swine. You may have married me and dragged me away from my family to this sorry shit-smeared place. You may fuck other women behind my back and you may call me all the names you can think of to my face but if you ever force yourself on me again, I will sever those things you hold most dear and throw them out of the window for the dogs in the courtyard to snack on."

He goggled at her and managed to find some courage in his voice. "I could have you executed for this you fucking pagan whore!"

"On what grounds? Will you let your whole household know the truth; that your pagan whore nearly lopped off your manhood while you had your breeches around your ankles?"

He visibly simmered with rage but his silence told Hronwena that she had him beat. She withdrew the knife and he hopped off her as if he were a quarter his age. Fumbling for his clothes he made for the door. "I should have known better than to marry a yellow-haired heathen witch!"

Once the door had slammed shut, Hronwena slid the little knife back into the sheath that was strapped to her thigh and breathed out slowly. She allowed herself a small smile. She may not have won the war yet but she had just won the most important battle of her life.

# Hengest

Hengest's eyes widened to take in the sight as it grew steadily larger with each plodding step of the army. Winding snake-like across the hills like some gigantic wyrm, its back notched with battlements, the wall stood proud, defying the harsh landscape that surrounded it. It was a sight that instilled a silent awe in each and every member of the army. Even the Britons who may have seen it before showed a subdued respect for this relic of their ancestors.

"Surely, only giants could build such a thing," said Hengest.

"Wrong, pagan," said Aurelianus with a proud smile. "This was built by Roman and British hands. Set up by the Emperor Hadrian, this was the frontier between Britannia and the barbaric lands to the north. The end of the Empire. The end of the world."

As they approached the wall the years of neglect became apparent. Birds nested in the nooks and crannies in the rock face. Ivy crawled up the sides as if the land itself was trying to tear down this monolithic creation of man that scarred its surface. Forts and farms lay derelict along the roadside that ran parallel to the wall; rotten structures of wood encrusted with moss that had once housed and fed the proud soldiers of Rome.

They camped early by the ruins of one of the forts that guarded a gate in the wall. The massive iron-bound doors stood shut to the wilds of the land beyond; a gateway that would be tackled tomorrow after hot meals and sleep for all. None complained about this delay. The army was quiet that night as if in silent trepidation of what the morrow might bring.

Morning came soon enough and Aurelianus directed men to open the gate. The hinges were caked with rust and it took several men a long time to heave the massive doors open wide enough for the army to pass through.

"If these gates have remained closed for so long," asked Hengest, "How is it the Picts get in?"

"There are whole sections of the wall that are naught but rubble," replied Aurelianus. "They swarm through those. But we are civilised enough to use the roads and the gates."

The mood of the army changed drastically once they were on the other side of the wall. There was little singing and laughter and all the Britons seemed on edge. It was as if, in their minds at least, the great wall, despite being unmanned for a generation, still worked as some sort of protective barrier against all that was un-civilised and barbaric.

The rolling moorlands were thick with heather and scrub and there was no sign of any people or villages. The road that had carried them safely from Londinium quickly became broken and overgrown before vanishing completely. The sky seemed as if it was about to fall down on them for want of anything to keep it up and Hengest was reminded of Jute-land where it felt as if the plains and fens were all there was to the world and nothing more.

Eventually they passed some wooded areas and these grew into forests where shadows lurked and the endless tramping feet of the soldiers became stifled.

"Send out two *turmae*," Aurelianus said to Hengest. It was an order he had given several times during the journey north and had irritated Hengest no end. He was no lowly centurion to take orders without question. This time he would lead a *turma* himself.

"Is that wise?" Aurelianus asked him. "We are in potentially hostile territory. You may only be an auxiliary commander, but I don't want to lose you at this early stage."

Hengest scowled at him. "This is where we differ, Briton. I am not afraid to share whatever danger I put my men in. And neither is any thegn under my command. Ebusa, you lead the second. Aesc, follow me close."

With his son and twenty-eight riders following him, Hengest galloped ahead, ignoring Aurelianus's words of caution. A river ran nearby beneath the shelter of the trees and he made for it. They dismounted and let their horses drink, glad to stretch their aching legs.

Hengest looked around with distaste at the thick forest that grew on all sides. Behind him, through the trees, he could hear the advancing army; faint despite their close distance. These forests were as thick as blood and twice as dark. His men were not used to them. They had come from the wide open moors of Jute-land to the urban towns of Britta and now to this shrouded world of pines, oaks and beeches where every sound was muffled and every footfall soft.

There was a slight hint of movement in the dense undergrowth and Hengest spun around, squinting into the darkness. Aesc had seen it too; the rustle of branches caused by something moving past, slowly and silently. The men loosened their swords in their scabbards and gripped their shield straps tightly. The horses nickered, probably sensing the presence too.

Hengest motioned to his men to follow close in tight formation as he stepped forward to investigate the darkness. Their shields overlapping, they moved forward as one.

They had barely taken more than a few steps before something lean and muscular darted across their path, partly shielded by the trees. They caught the briefest glimpse of a naked body painted with swirling blue designs and a shaggy mop of coppery hair before it vanished into the undergrowth.

"Fall back!" Hengest called. "Back to the horses! It's a trap!"

Without turning their backs on their elusive enemies, Hengest's men retraced their steps back to the river where their mounts were tethered.

"These forests are infested with Picts, father," Aesc told him, mounting his mare. "If we venture much further we'll be slaughtered by invisible arrows. Gods, I hate all this skulking about in the trees! Give me an open battle any day."

"Agreed," said Hengest. "Let's fall back to the column and tell Aurelianus that the road is no longer safe unless we scour the woods with more men."

They began their trip back through the trees towards the road but were cut suddenly short as three arrows sang between the branches and embedded themselves in the earth a few feet from them. The horses, startled, reared up and whinnied in fright.

"Warning shots!" shouted Hengest. "They must be all around us! Make for the road with all haste"

"We can't," Aesc replied.

"Why not?"

"Because they stand between us and the rest of the army."

Hengest looked at the tree line in confusion and then, as if they had suddenly appeared by magic, he noticed the Picts. There were arrayed in two lines, each holding a spear or a bow aimed at them. Dark eyes peered from painted faces and naked limbs tensed, clearly waiting for the order to kill.

# Horsa

High cliffs swept down to meet the crashing waves where puffins flapped about on the rocks, ruffling their feathers with their brightly striped beaks. They occasionally looked up to pay the passing ships the most casual of glances.

Horsa watched the birds from the *Bloodkeel* and listened to the creaking of the mast and ruffle of the sail. The winds had been good since they had left Thanet with very little need to drop oars at all during the journey north. They should make their destination before nightfall and he tried to share the eager exuberance of his crew.

If the weather was unusually trustworthy, then the shoreline was treacherously changeable. It rose up and down like the waves itself; sometimes flat fenlands, other times high cliff tops where long grass wavered and danced against the sky. At other times thick forest grew down to the water's edge and it was into one of these shadowed realms that they passed now.

Horsa gazed at Gwynfor - the guide Vertigernus had lent him - for any sign in the Briton's eyes that he sensed danger. He had proven his worth so far by pointing out dangerous sandbanks and sharp reefs. For years Gwynfor had been an emissary to the Pictish tribes, travelling mostly by road, but occasionally by sea, carrying gifts and correspondence from the Britons to their northern neighbours.

"It is not advisable to pass so close to the shore in such areas," said Gwynfor. "The Picts are masters of concealment and will no doubt have been following your ships for days. They will have arrows notched to their bowstrings in anticipation of a passing target."

"Very well," said Horsa. "Beorn! Head out a little."

They drifted away from the shore and out of bowshot from any hidden danger lurking in the trees.

"Gwynfor, do you have no sense of loyalty to your people?" Horsa asked his guide out of interest.

"The Picts have not been my people since I was a mere boy," he replied. "I may have been born to a Pictish fishwife with bones in her hair but it was the Britons who truly raised me. It was amongst them that I heard the word of Christ and was born again into a different life. Now I am only too happy to aid the war against the northern savages if only in hope that my mother's people may come to accept the word of the True Lord."

Beorn hawked up a gob of phlegm and spat it over the bulwark as if to counter Gwynfor's words. He considered it extremely bad luck to have a Christian on board, especially as they were sailing off to war. Horsa had noticed his sour face whenever the Briton had knelt down in prayer on the deck, muttering Latin words to his god but had forbidden his first mate to say anything to their guide. There was no point in bickering about religion. They may need all the divine intervention they could get in the days ahead.

As the day began to sink over the cliffs in the west they grew closer to their destination. A river flowed out into the sea and sandy beaches frosted its mouth. The neck of the river was narrow with trees growing down to its banks.

"Thunor's cock, that's not very wide," said Horsa. "We'll have to stick to the middle and hope those Pictish bows don't have much range. Strike the sail and drop oars!"

As the sea behind them vanished beyond a bend in the river and the forests grew thicker and darker all around them, Horsa's heart sank. He hated sailing inland. He preferred the endless open stretches of the ocean where a vessel could pursue or be pursued for days and still have plenty of room to run. Battles between vessels in such narrow waters never lasted long.

He peered into the darkness between the trees for any sign of their elusive enemy. The light was dimming and he dreaded the thought of paddling down this unknown river at night. He dared not light torches for they would be a beacon to all around and yet he had no desire to drop anchor and sleep on deck with darkness pressing in on all sides.

"Captain, boats!" the fore lookout called.

Horsa ran down between the oar benches to the bow and peered into the gloom. Setting out from the left shore several meters ahead were fifteen to twenty small vessels. They appeared to be made of leather stretched over wicker frames and carried two men apiece, each with a paddle. Even in the fading light he could make out bare chests and blue paint.

"Picts!" he bellowed. "Ship oars! Draw weapons!"

"Captain, are we sure that they are not Talorc's men?" asked Gwynfor. "He is camped somewhere further down river and may have sent a delegation to meet us."

"Can we afford to take that chance? Or do you recognise what tribe these warriors belong to? One Pict looks like another to us. Anything in their war paint to suggest their allegiance?"

"Too far off to tell that much," Gwynfor replied.

"Then if I were you I'd get under cover and let us handle the situation until we can find out if these are friend or foe."

As if in answer, a stone from a slingshot whistled through the air and cracked into a shield with a nasty splintering sound. The boats were closer now and the warriors they carried had stowed their paddles and were preparing for battle. Most had slings and a few had bows.

Missiles and yelping war cries were sent towards the ships with a devastating ferocity. Arrows thudded into shields and the bulwarks and stones bounced and cracked all around them. Horsa saw one of his men take one full in the face which sunk deep, shattering bone and cartilage and sending him tumbling down between the benches.

As the boats drifted alongside the *Bloodkeel* the Picts set down their bows and slings and scrambled up onto its bulwarks, daggers between teeth and axes and garrottes in their belts.

"For the sake of all the gods, don't let them get on board!" cried Horsa, drawing his saex and lifting a buckler to protect his flank. A painted face poked up a few feet from him and he slashed at the neck that supported it and rammed the buckler into its jaw to send it back down to the waters from which it came.

The rest of the crew was doing much of the same, stabbing, slashing and kicking at anything that emerged from below. A few weren't quick enough and were claimed by these nightmarish creatures from the darkness that seized them and slipped garrottes over their heads and then leaped back off the ship dragging their prey viciously down by the neck.

The tide of invaders seemed to subside and many empty leather boats rolled and bounced in the wake of the *Bloodkeel*. But already Horsa could see a second wave putting out from the shore. He looked back at the rest of his fleet. Several boats had assailed the *Fafnir* and the *Raven* too but had been dispatched with relative ease. The *Bloodkeel* had taken the brunt of the assault.

"Get the other ships closer!" Horsa told Beorn. "We have a better chance of fending them off if we can protect each other's flanks."

Beorn sent the signal and the vessels edged steadily closer. The second wave of Picts was almost upon them and the men aboard the *Bloodkeel* tensed for the fight. The war cries reached them first and then came the dreaded hail of arrows and slingshots. When that had subsided Horsa's men emerged from behind their shields and let loose their fury at the first of the savages to make it up onto the bulwarks.

There were more of them this time and the fight was hard. But the *Fafnir* and the *Raven* soon drifted alongside and their respective crews lashed out with spears at the men in the boats below, skewering many of them like spitted birds ready for the roasting.

Caught between vessels, the Picts were trapped and the fight soon turned against them. Horsa's ships drifted even closer so that the warriors aboard could nearly reach out and touch the strakes of the opposite vessel and the leather boats below were crushed between the drifting hulks.

No further waves of men set out from the banks and Horsa thought he could see the shadows of men retreating into the forest.

"Run, you cowards," he said quietly. "We are here now and the first victory is ours." He did not scream this as a challenge as he knew that there would be many more battles to come and their enemy was clearly a fearless and cunning one.

Darkness had fallen fully now and Horsa gave the order to beach the ships in a likely spot and make camp. He ordered a shield wall to surround the camp with watches relieved every few hours until the dawn came. Fires were lit in defiance of the darkness that surrounded them. Fuelled by their recent victory the men sang and laughed all the louder as if daring their enemies to try again. But Horsa could hear the nervousness in their voices.

When dawn finally came it was shrouded and wet. Mist hung low as if rising up from the rotting forest floor and everything was wet with dew. Taking a company of forty men and leaving the rest with the boats, Horsa set out in search of Talorc's camp.

They followed the river until noon when Gwynfor said that they should cut south through the trees. They held close formation and kept their eyes and ears open for any sign of movement.

A voice called out to them through the trees. The men halted and stood firm, ready for an ambush.

Gwynfor called out in reply to the Pictish voice that hailed them.

"It's Talorc's men," he said to Horsa.

They all breathed a sigh of relief. Through the trees lay a clearing where a cluster of warriors stood waiting for them. Several of their highest rank sat astride horses. When the customary greetings and translations had been carried out, the Picts led Horsa's men to the camp of their leader.

It was a huge, sprawling collection of hide tents and brushwood constructions, campfires, forges, horse corrals, livestock pens and workshops. The forest grew in and around it and the camp was so large that no end to it could be seen through the trees. They were led up to the largest tent of all which Horsa assumed must belong to Talorc himself.

The tent was open on one side and a table and row of chairs occupied it. In the highest chair sat the prince, flanked by his captains. Some sort of court seemed to be in progress as an elderly warrior put his case to their chief. None of the Pictish babblings made any sense to Horsa and he looked about at the various warriors who were milling around.

One Pict was very much like another to his eyes They wore coarse woollen garments, furs and skins and bared much more skin than Jutes and Saxons. But here and there, in small clusters, he saw the polished segmented armour and plumed helms of British soldiers. Was Aurelianus's army here already? He looked about for Hengest or any other man he might recognise but his search was cut short as voices called for him to approach the prince.

Talorc rose and gripped Horsa's arm, in friendship. "Welcome, Horsa mab Wictgils. We are pleased and honoured to have you here."

He spoke in British which, Horsa was given to understand was not so very different from Pictish but his grasp of the language was nowhere near strong enough for him to understand the northern dialects of these men. "I thank you, Prince Talorc," Horsa replied. "We had a fun journey of it, but here we are at last."

"Yes, Gwynfor here tells me that you were attacked by my sister's warriors. I hope you did not lose too many men. Parties are known to hunt far from Din Eidyn but we did not know that they would dare come so far south as this. Her confidence must be growing. We must act fast. Go now. Rest and eat. In the morning we shall discuss our plan of attack."

Talorc returned to his chair and Horsa led his men away to find a fire and some food.

"I wondered if you'd ever find your way here, sea rat," called a voice to him, "or if you'd paddled off down the wrong river!"

"Brother!" Horsa exclaimed, striding forward to embrace Hengest. "I saw some Britons milling around and assumed Aurelianus got here before us, but I thought they must have had enough of your pompous noises and ditched you on the way! Been here long?"

"A day. We had a stiff march north and made it past the great wall. Gods, Horsa, you must see this thing! You won't believe the tales until you set your eyes on its stones! After that it was mostly tramping through forests and we thought we were done for when a pack of these Pictish wolves crept up on us. They turned out to be Talorc's own men. They'd been following us for over a day. Apparently we make enough noise to raise the dead. But what of your adventures? You encountered Galana's warriors I heard."

"We did and we showed them how Jutish warships repel borders. There'll be many Pictish bodies floating out to sea by now!"

"Ha! Isn't this wonderful, Horsa? Here we are on the cusp of battle like the old days. No greasy coastal towns to govern or their endless streams of paperwork and politics to deal with."

"Ready to fight so soon, are we?" asked a man in Roman style armour as he emerged from a nearby tent.

Horsa's grin faded as he saw Aurelianus and remembered with a sudden pang Aureliana back in Londinium.

"I'd get some rest if I were you," the gruff Briton said without a word of greeting for Horsa. "Talorc wants to march on the morrow. You haven't left your ships too unprotected I hope?"

"My men can handle anything these forests can throw at them," Horsa replied testily.

"I hope so. We shall need those ships of yours."

Horsa scowled as Aurelianus walked off.

"Pay him no heed," Hengest told him. "He's been insufferable on the journey. He thinks our lot are a bunch of thick-headed savages who can't tie their own boots. I've been wanting to prove our mettle to him but haven't had the chance yet. But there'll be more than enough opportunity in the battle to come for us both to show these Britons what we're made of. And the Picts for that matter. Come, now, let us eat and drink to our women back home."

# Hronwena

Hronwena stared at the piles of yellowed documents that lay strewn across the table in front of her. She'd had no idea there could be so much paperwork involved in the running of an estate and this was just for the fortress and the surrounding farms. Presumably there were further clerks and offices filled with paperwork in Corinium Dobunnorum.

Hronwena didn't read a word of Latin but since her husband had left her more or less in charge of running the household in his absence, she had invited herself to watch Treven the clerk go through accounts in the small library. More out of boredom than anything else, she badgered him for lessons in Latin and hoped she could pick up enough of the Roman language to comprehend the ins and outs of the household.

Treven was a curmudgeonly, elderly man who gave Hronwena the impression that he had survived the many years of her husband's rule by quietly doing what he was told and keeping his nose buried in paperwork. Even so, he showed a certain amount of irritation at her constant presence in his little cell of solitude.

"Just when I think I am getting a handle on this blasted Roman language," she told him, "I come across a group of words that make absolutely no sense to me."

Treven glanced up, exasperation showing on his face at this most recent tug on his concentration. He had explained over and over the forms, tenses and prepositions of Latin and had spent hours helping her to untangle the sentences of a hundred records he had in his office, but she constantly called on him for assistance in deciphering some new text.

"Here, for instance," she said, handing him a roll of paper. "What does this say?"

Treven peered at the paper. "Hmm. That's an old record pertaining to an iron mine over on the other side of the river. The current state of the land meant that no workers could be found to maintain it and it fell into disrepair. That was many years ago. I'm surprised that this document hasn't been burned."

"If it is abandoned," said Hronwena, studying the figures, "why is it still supplied by Din Neidr? Sacks are sent to it from our granaries every month."

Treven, quickly reached out to take the scroll from Hronwena. "Doesn't my lady have more important things to occupy her time with?"

Hronwena was surprised by his sudden abruptness. "What's so special about that old mine? Who is there that receives grain for nothing in return?"

Treven sighed. "Look, my lady, the running of your husband's land is a complex operation. I have no say in how he sees fit to organise it and you have little understanding of the things involved. It would be best for both of us not to ask too many questions."

Hronwena stared at him. He was hiding something. Or at least he was too frightened to look beyond the menial tasks of accounting and recording. Perhaps that was why he had lived to such an old age in this nest of vipers.

Bored by the dusty little room and its endless reams of records and irritated by Treven's patronising, Hronwena went out into the courtyard. Some of the younger guards were honing their sword work. Berwen was lounging against the fence to the pig run, his spear propped up next to him. He certainly was a slovenly specimen and Hronwena's irritation made her feel like goading him.

"Are you any good with a blade?" she asked him.

He shrugged. "When I need to be."

"My brother is a good swordsman. He certainly taught you Britons some tricks back in Cantium."

"A Sais besting Britons?" he answered. "That I must see. All we hear of your people is how your blood runs freely into the sea courtesy of British blades."

"Blood rusts blades, or so I hear. Perhaps your people have wetted their iron all too often and now their swords are dulled and flaky. My father seemed to have no problem in taking his slice of British land back east."

Berwen smiled. "My lady jests with her servant. What is on her mind?"

"Nothing," Hronwena said, lapsing into sullen silence. Their contest of words had not given her the entertainment she had hoped for.

"Do you come from a big family?" he asked.

She shook her head. "I have only my brother."

"I have one brother also. Do you miss yours?"

"Yes. And my mother." She didn't know why she was opening up to this man she barely knew, but, other than Deilwen, there was nobody else in the fortress who seemed inclined to talk to her. "Do you miss your brother?"

"No, not him. But I do miss somebody."

"The lady Brina?"

He jerked his head to glare at her. She smiled. "I'm not stupid, Berwen," she said. "I have ears."

"Deilwen told you?"

She nodded.

"She had no right. She's just a handmaid."

"And you're just a guard. What were you playing at? Did you really think the lady Brina had feelings for you?"

His face turned sour at her words. "We had planned to run away together. I was going to help her. She trusted me with her life and now she is dead. You know nothing of it."

"You were in love with her, weren't you?"

Berwen looked at her through eyes that had suddenly become moist. "I loved her more than anything, but I was not *in* love with her." He glanced around to make sure that they were not overheard. "She was my sister."

"Your sister?" Hronwena whispered. "But... I don't..."

"Don't understand how she could be as she was a lady and I am a mere spearman? I have not always been such. I am the second son of a minor lord in Dyfed. My father is dead and my older brother is lord now. Brina and I were close in both age and friendship. When my father married her off to Lord Vitalinus I fought and rallied against the idea, not only because I feared to lose her, but I had heard tales of Vitalinus that turned my blood cold.

"Brina was not married to him more than two months before bad tidings began to reach my ears. It was said that he often struck her. Others said that he took her against her will in her chamber. I vowed then that I would protect her if nobody else would. I disguised myself as a common spear for hire and took service in this fortress. That way I could be close to Brina and help her and, if needed, kill her husband for her."

"What happened?"

He shrugged. "All I know is that my sister was too good a rider to cross a river at its widest part during the spring melt. Either she was being chased by somebody or something else killed her and threw her into that river."

"But why? Who would want to kill her?"

Berwen raised his eyebrows and said nothing.

"Not Vitalinus, surely? What reason could he have?"

"Brina was outspoken and rebellious. Even as children she was the more forward of the two of us; always getting me into scrapes. And she had a fearsome temper too. Quick to mouth off. Your husband had his hands full with her. A few black eyes never dampened her spirit. She hated him even more than I do. Maybe he grew sick of her and needed her out of the way before he found another bride. This was only last year, you see. Whatever the reason, it was he who killed her, I've no doubt as to that."

"It doesn't make any sense," said Hronwena. "He's obsessed with siring more sons. The way he goes on, you'd think he wanted to infest all of Britta with his spawn. Your sister was pregnant. I can't believe that he would murder a woman carrying his seed inside her, no matter how mouthy she was."

"Then perhaps you do not know your husband as well as we do, my lady."

"So why are you still here? Why not return to your father's lands?"

"Because I failed her. I vowed to protect her and now she is dead. I have no desire to return home in shame. It is my punishment from God that I remain here in the service of the man who murdered my sister. I await only the chance to take my revenge on him. When he is dead, then perhaps, I shall return home."

Hronwena returned to her chambers, cursing Din Neidr and its ruler. *So many secrets! So much hidden hate!* Berwen was a coward, of that she was sure. He must have had a hundred opportunities to kill Vitalinus but he had never acted. She paused. Was she really any different? She could have poisoned her husband any number of times over the past weeks and got away with it. What did she really fear?

The next day, Hronwena told Deilwen to change into her riding clothes and to fetch warm cloaks for them both.

"Are we going somewhere, my lady?" she asked.

"These walls stifle me. And now that my husband is gone, I have a mind to venture into the countryside."

Her handmaid did not argue, something which could not be said of Marchudd; captain of the guard. He stood at the gate, blocking their way with three spearmen at his back.

"Going somewhere, ladies?"

"Stand aside," said Hronwena. "I have a mind to find a secluded grove to pray in."

"To your pagan gods?" sneered Marchudd. "Not on my watch."

Hronwena injected as much fire into her gaze as she could. "Do you dare to stand in your lady's way? Perhaps my lord husband will see fit to teach you some manners upon his return."

Marchudd looked ready to contest this when Cadeyrn appeared. "I suggest you let my stepmother pass, Marchudd," he said. "You're in no position to lay down the law to her."

Hronwena gave Cadeyrn a grateful look. She hadn't expected help from anyone, especially not her stepson.

"I am under orders to protect you, my lady," said Marchudd. "If you insist on leaving the safety of Din Neidr then I insist on sending a patrol with you."

"You will insist nothing, captain," said Hronwena. "I am ruler of this fortress in my husband's absence and you will do as I say. Now stand aside."

Marchudd scowled and turned to Cadeyrn.

"You may well look to me, Marchudd," said Cadeyrn, "For I am lord of Din Neidr in my father's absence. I care not where the lady Hronwena goes nor what she does. But I will not have the likes of you rising above their stations."

Reluctance slowing his every step, Marchudd gave the order for the gates to be opened and Hronwena kicked her mount forward, spattering him with mud as she passed.

It felt wonderful to gallop across the open, empty wild lands after so many days cooped up in the grim chambers of Din Neidr. As she had been taught by her father, she rode astride her mount, her skirts bunched up and flailing behind her while Deilwen struggled to keep up riding side saddle after the fashion of British women.

"Are you going to tell me where we are going now, my lady?" she asked when Hronwena slowed as she crested a rise. "I've seen you pray to your gods in your chamber many times without the need of a grove."

Hronwena smiled. Of all the people in the fortress, she counted her handmaid as the cleverest. "I want to visit an old iron mine on the other side of the river."

"Why on earth do you want to see a dirty old iron mine?"

"I found something in Treven's papers about it. It used to be owned by my husband but fell into ruin years ago. And yet he still sends it grain every month. Treven knew nothing about it, or at least he pretended he didn't. And after what Berwen told me about his sister, I trust nothing that goes on in this land."

"I'll never forgive that lad for lying to me all this time," said Deilwen, her rage at the revelation still boiling inside her. "Fancy not letting on that he was my lady's brother. Not even once! And as for her, if she were alive I would give her a piece of my mind! I never gave her a reason not to trust me. She should have confided. I could have helped her!"

"Don't be hurt by it, Deilwen," Hronwena said. "I'm sure she did trust you. But she had her reasons. Think if it became known that Berwen was her brother. He would have been strung up for his dishonesty."

"Well she could have said *something*."

"Maybe she wanted you to have no part in it. Maybe she feared for your safety. After all, look what happened to her. As for myself I would never want to put you in that kind of danger."

They could hear the rushing of the river and the eerie realisation that they were about to cross the very waters in which Brina had perished hung over them and they fell into silence as the hooves of their horses splashed into the ford.

The river had lost some of its swell during the early months of summer and was not too deep. Foaming torrents rose up above their mounts' fetlocks but they managed to get to the other side without getting their feet wet. They stood for a while on the bank looking at the rushing water that possessed such an unpredictable power that it could sweep away all in its path; trees, soil, love and memory.

"Do you think she was murdered?" Hronwena asked.

Deilwen did not take her eyes from the foaming river. "Yes. At least, she was ushered in the direction of death."

"Why?"

"That I don't know. She was lost to me during the last few weeks of her life. She became tight-lipped, almost frightened, like a little girl lost in the world."

Hronwena nodded slowly. "I know how that feels."

"Something changed between her and his lordship towards the end of her life. Their relationship had always been turbulent, but at the end she really showed her hatred of him. She got beaten black and blue for it of course, but by then she didn't care. And then she was gone. I wish I knew why."

"That's what I want to find out too."

"Look at those dark clouds coming in!"

It was true; the northern sky boiled with black thunderclouds and they seemed to be steadily creeping towards them, swallowing the patches of blue sky. Hronwena smiled. "Those clouds might aid my plan perfectly."

By the time they reached the old iron mine the heavens had opened and rain lashed down. Thunder roared like an awoken lion and the ground beneath them was a slippery confusion of mud and water.

The old iron mine was a collection of dismal huts, falling apart with rot. The only building that looked like it might be habitable was the water mill. It was a towering stone construction that had been built by the Romans with little windows suggesting at least three floors. A roof of wooden shingles slimy with moss sagged over the great wheel which still turned in the river despite having lost half of its paddles.

Their hoods up against the pouring rain and their cloaks soaked through to their dresses, they trotted up to the front door. Hronwena hammered on it, desperately hoping that somebody would answer. They waited. She hammered again. Presently it opened and the thin, suspicious face of a woman peered out.

"My good woman," Hronwena began, knowing that her accent instantly marked her out as a foreigner and wishing that she had prepared a cover story in advance, "My friend and I have got lost in the storm and are wet to the bone. Would it be possible to presume on your hospitality for the night?"

"We're not a lodging house," snapped the woman.

"I can see that, but if we do not find somewhere warm to bed down for the night, we shall surely perish from the cold and rain."

The old woman seemed to consider this and then turned her head to call to somebody within. Presently a young lad came scampering around the corner to take their mounts to the old shack that passed as a stable and Hronwena and Deilwen were admitted.

"This is most good of you," Hronwena said as they were led through into a room that contained a hearth and a table. "We were out riding and got separated from our husbands. I don't know what we would have done if we hadn't found this old mill."

"They will be looking for us all night, poor dears," commented Deilwen, playing the part Hronwena had thrust upon her admirably. "This is really most Christian of you."

"We don't have much food to spare," said an old man as he entered the room. "But you are welcome to share what we have."

A stew bubbled over the fire and was ladled out into wooden bowls. A basket of loaves was placed on the table and they were joined by a younger girl whom Hronwena took to be a servant. The old man gave thanks to the Lord in Latin before they tucked in.

There was a hammering on the door and the old lady rose to admit two burly men. She doled out some stew for them and gave them a loaf each. They peered at Hronwena and Deilwen curiously before the old woman hurried them back out into the rain. She resumed her seat at the table and carried on eating without giving any explanation.

"One of you is a Briton and the other has an accent I can't place," said the old man as he dipped his bread in his bowl.

"I am from Hibernia'" said Hronwena, quickly thinking of some land that was distant enough. "I came to Albion when I was a little girl but I never lost my accent. My husband teases me for it."

"Interesting," said the man. "I have met several people from Hibernia and they do not look nor sound as you do."

Hronwena cursed herself for not saying Gaul or Frankia.

"But then, Hibernia is a large island. There must be many different accents and looks to the people there," the old man added thoughtfully.

"But what of you?" asked Deilwen, clearly trying to steer the conversation away from her lady. "What do four people in a dilapidated old mine as this?"

"Surviving," said the old man simply. "My wife and I used to run this place but since the workers deserted us, we have been unable to continue to mine here. We have only the stable boy, who is a local lad, as our servant. Those two men who came in just now are blacksmiths who used to work for the mine. They're brothers. They're from this valley and refused to leave it when the workers left. They work a small farm now and we feed them in return for small services; mending things and suchlike. And it's good to have a pair of strapping young lads about in such times as these. The girl here is my niece. Since her father died I asked her to live here with us. It's not much but there is hot food and a warm bed every night. We get by."

"It's almost a little family," said the woman.

Once dinner was finished they retired to bed. Hronwena and Deilwen slept on furs by the glowing embers of the fire and listened to the rain hammering against the hide window coverings and the wind creaking in the rafters.

"What do you think my husband's interest is here?" Hronwena asked Deilwen in a whisper.

"Couldn't say, my lady."

"If this mine is no longer in operation, why does he supply it? They seem simple enough folk. What are they to him?"

"Begging your pardon, my lady, is it not possible that that young girl has taken his fancy? Perhaps he drops by here for a bit of whoring on his way to Corinium Dobunnorum?"

"Perhaps. But it seems an expensive whore that demands several sacks of grain every month for her guardians."

Deilwen had no more to say on the matter and they lay in silence, each thinking their own thoughts until sleep came.

Hronwena awoke sometime in the small hours and looked about her. It was pitch black apart from a faint glow from the hearth. Somewhere, in a chamber above them she could hear a child crying. It could not have been any older than a babe, but it bawled for attention and then was suddenly silent as if a hand had been clamped over its mouth.

*So that was it.*

A child. A bastard child that Vitalinus kept here in this forsaken old mill with a handful of servants and a few sacks of grain every month. *That bastard!* Those two so-called blacksmiths were evidently guards. Vitalinus didn't want anybody poking around here.

Morning came and they gave their thanks once more to the old couple and the girl for their hospitality. Hronwena wondered how young she had been when she became her husband's lover, no, *victim*, she corrected herself.

The sun was shining and the storm was gone without a trace. Their horses had been fed and brushed and as they trotted out of the yard, Hronwena turned for a final glance at the old mill. In the uppermost window she saw a face looking down at them.

"Look! Up there!" she said.

"Where, my lady?" Deilwen asked, following her gaze.

But the face had gone. The window was just a black rectangle, the same as the others.

"I saw somebody. Somebody we did not meet last night."

"What did they look like?"

"A girl. Young. Our age. She had black hair. The small part of her clothing that I saw was of a rich, colourful fabric. Not the coarse garments of peasants."

"Perhaps that was our mysterious mistress, then, not the servant girl."

"I think so. There is a child too. I heard it last night."

"Lord have mercy. The poor girl."

"Tell me something, Deilwen. Did you ever see Brina's body?"

"My lady, that is an odd question to ask!"

"Did you?"

"No, I can't say that I did."

"Did anyone?"

Deilwen thought for a moment. "I can't say. I mean, guards came back to Din Neidr bringing the news. They found her cloak downriver and her horse wandering nearby."

"But Brina's body was never brought back to the fortress?"

"No, it was assumed she was washed away by the river. What exactly are you thinking, my lady?"

"Brina had black hair didn't she? And she was no more than a year older than me?"

"Yes."

"I think that might have been her in the window. I think Brina is being kept here with her child."

"Now, my lady, this is all a bit much..."

"Think about it, Deilwen! Her relationship with her... *my* husband had soured. She was volatile. *Dangerous.* And I know that Vitalinus is desperate for more children. He wouldn't have killed his pregnant wife. But he might have hidden her away here and said that she had been killed."

"But why raise the child in seclusion? How can he ever acknowledge the babe if everybody thinks that the mother has been dead for over a year?"

"I don't know. But I think we should tell Berwen. He has a right to know."

Marchudd was visibly fuming when they returned. "Is my lady aware that I have had patrols out all night scouring the countryside for her?" he raged as they trotted in through the gates. Thank the Lord that your husband is not currently here or my head would be on a pike for this! Where in God's name have you been?"

"Mind your tongue, soldier," snapped Hronwena as she dismounted and handed her reigns to a stable boy. "We got lost in the storm and spent the night with a shepherd and his family."

"A shepherd, by God!" bellowed Marchudd. "And my men out catching their deaths in the wind and rain!"

"I am sure they will live. They drink enough mead to keep warm at any rate. Now, out of my way, captain, I am tired, hungry and am in no mood for your insolence."

Hronwena saw Deilwen stifling a grin as Marchudd's face turned from pink to beetroot.

They found Berwen on the northern palisade. When Hronwena told him of their findings, his face turned ashen. "Are you sure it was her?" he asked.

"Well, I never knew your sister so I can't be sure. But it seems possible."

"Then she has been alive all along. A prisoner. And I have been wasting time here..."

"Now listen to me, Berwen," Hronwena told him sternly. "Don't do anything rash until I have had time to plan my next move. I will get your sister out of there and return her to you, I promise. But you must give me time."

He did not answer her. He stood with his hands on the spiked palisade, staring at some point in the distant hills. She left him there, seeing that he needed his own time to be alone with his thoughts.

Hronwena cast the runes that night in her chamber. Four of the carven wooden chips landed face up in a vague cross pattern. The left rune of a cross always represented the past and this time it was *Ac* – oak – and the rune that stood for the truth, knowledge and wisdom. That was good. It was the truth of the past she sought.

The rune at the centre of the cross stood for the present and it was *Peorth*; game or gamble. Usually it heralded secrets uncovered or mysteries solved but the rune was inverted which might be a warning against taking risks.

The top rune represented a force that worked in one's favour. It was *elk*; symbolising victory as well as the hunt itself. *Not at all bad.*

The bottom rune was all that worked against one and it was *Pynn* – joy – inverted. That could mean misery or loneliness.

The rune to the right stood for the future and it was *Lagu*, representing water. It was inverted symbolizing the ebb tide and the waning of power. *Whose power? Vitalinus's?*

It was when Deilwen brought her her evening meal of lamb roasted with wild garlic that she told her that Berwen had vanished.

"Damn him!" said Hronwena. "I told him not to do anything until I said so! He's gone storming over to that iron mine, hasn't he?"

"I imagine so, my lady. I can't say that I blame him."

"No, I can't either. Perhaps it was my fault for telling him. Maybe I should have waited. But those two brutes will kill him if he tries to force his way in."

"It can't be helped my lady. I don't want anything to happen to him either, but if we go over there now, we'll only put ourselves in danger too."

"I hate feeling helpless, Deilwen. I've felt helpless all my life and I can't stand it."

"Neither can I, but it can't be helped. Try and eat a little."

Hronwena picked at her lamb but she felt too sick with guilt to eat much. What on earth was she doing? Her plan had been to bide her time until Vitalinus died and she could return to her family. Somehow she had got mixed up in the intrigues of the past – things that had nothing to do with her - and she had stirred up something dangerous.

# Maelona

Maelona the Whore ran her slim fingers down the young man's chest, lingering over the downy patches of youthful fuzz above each nipple as he hoisted her up and down with his hips, straining to reach as deeply inside her as he possibly could. The oil lamps illuminated his pale, thin body which was a stark contrast to her womanly form with its full curves.

Despite her nickname, she had never really been a whore. In fact, Maelona was not even the name she had been given in the land of her birth. She didn't remember where that was. Some men said she had the look of a Greek about her, others Egyptian. She remembered that her father had been a trader and she remembered the storm that had wrecked them on the Dumnonian cliffs.

She had been nine. Water had swamped the little vessel as the sharp rocks splintered its hull. She had been swept overboard and dashed on the rocks, her shoulder torn open by their sharp teeth. Her father had been killed but she had survived and was taken in by a local family. They stitched her up with fish gut and nursed her back to health but they were poor fisher folk and could not keep another mouth to feed. They handed her over to a potter who was passing through on his way to Londinium to sell his wares and required an apprentice.

The potter was kind to her and taught her British as well as his trade. He gave her a British name and she grew to womanhood by his side. She was not ungrateful to the potter, but her heart yearned for something more. She saw the ladies of nobility being carried through the streets in their litters and the sight of those rich silks and dyed cloths reminded her of something. Had her father traded in those things? The bright colours taunted her in her clay-smeared apron and she knew that she was destined for something far greater than a potter's apprentice.

But what other prospects did a girl of uncommon beauty and nothing but common status have in a town like Londinium? There were no Bishoprics or Lordships or civic offices for women, and without a noble family, marriage to a man who held such power was not written in the stars for her. No, with her beauty the only gift God had given her, there was only one name the men of this world would ever call her by.

And she *was* beautiful.

The youth exploded inside her and gasped in ecstasy. She leant forward and kissed his sweating brow as a reward for his efforts. It was not their first time together but she was the first woman he had experienced intimately. The indulgence of the flesh was a new pleasure for him. The lofty heights of power that he had so recently found himself swimming in meant that doors previously barred to a man of his profession were suddenly opened.

Her master had arranged their meeting with the insistence that he deserved better than any common whore of the town. 'We politicians have our own pools to wet our beaks in' he had said. The youth had been hesitant at first. She knew he considered himself to be a pious man, but the insistence of her master had convinced him that men of their status were not as answerable to the laws of God as the lowly plebs who had simpler concerns in life. It was well enough for those who lived in monasteries on wind-swept moors to live lives of celibacy, but here in the great town of sin where temptation crawled the corridors of power like the very snake from Eden, none but a true saint could stick to the vows mumbled in one's youth.

Maelona's master did not always use her for sex. She had other skills, honed throughout her years. Eavesdropping for one. With a dirty cloak to conceal her slender body and a hood to cover her remarkable face, she could pass for a seller of dried fish in the street and hover by a curtained litter or pass down the corridors of the palace bearing a sack of laundry to listen at a closed door. She was a thief too, stealing seals, signet rings and dispatches for her master's perusal. He called her his little sparrow. What he did with the information she twittered into his ear mattered little to her. She enjoyed the game. She was good at what she did and enjoyed a challenge. Sex was no different.

"You are getting better and better, my beautiful boy," Maelona purred in his ear. "I am positively wet through and through."

"You... you really enjoyed it?"

"Oh, yes. Who would have thought that a meek man of the cloth could be such a passionate tiger in his own bedchamber? Any more of this treatment and I shall wake the dead on the outskirts of the town with my screams of pleasure."

He stifled a giggle. "That would not do. No one must know of us. I can trust you?"

She sighed. After the sex the worrying always set in. "Do you trust my master?"

"Well, yes. He has been good to me."

At this she affected a sigh. "I wish he were as good to me."

He blinked at her. "He treats you ill?"

"He uses me. He sends me to fuck his friends. I am just his slave."

"I... I thought you liked it..."

"Oh, you I like. You are so gentle and kind. Some of the others... They treat me badly. Sometimes they make me do things... Sometimes they beat me. Sometimes my master beats me. Do you see this scar?" She bent her shoulder to him to show off the semicircular line that marred her perfect flesh.

He rolled up onto his side and gazed at it with wide, pity-filled eyes. "Oh, my poor child. I had no idea."

It sounded absurd. She was at least five years older than him, but his profession demanded that he be a good listener and treat all God's children as his own after a fashion, regardless of their age. All priests, deacons and bishops were like this, or at least they should be. And as the new Bishop of Londinium, young Calvinus was clearly striving to be better than any peer. Well he had proved to her that he was a good listener. Now she needed him to be a good talker.

## Aureliana

With her father engaged in the war in the north, Aureliana found the weekly trips to the forum to hear mass a lonely and tedious affair. Seren came with her and two guards from the villa accompanied them to the town's outskirts, but without the mighty Ambrosius Aurelianus to introduce his daughter to the noble families gathering on the steps of the building, she missed out on a great deal of gossip.

Oh, she recognised many of the congregation and even considered some of the girls her age friends, but for the most part, she was ignored as she and Seren made their way up the steps. She knew that not everybody in Londinium was happy with the alliance with the Saxons and maybe even some blamed her father for the arrangement. Couldn't they see that it was all Lord Vertigernus's plan? Her father wanted nothing to do with the Saxons. She knew that, but to everybody else, he was Vertigernus's man and therefore shared Vertigernus's ideas.

Everybody seemed so helpless these days. Even her father, whom she had always considered a mighty pillar of strength and control, had no say in this awful war. She lay awake at nights praying for his safety as a good Christian girl should, but she constantly found her mind wandering to the face of another man who shared the very same danger as her father.

She could not shake his savagely handsome features from her mind and her dreams were filled with his long brown locks, bristly face and bulging, scarred forearms. Increasingly she had dreamed of being crushed by those powerful arms and feeling the damp, hot skin of his bare chest pressing down on her breasts.

The service began and she tried to concentrate on the words that echoed out across the nave. She had decided that she liked the new Bishop Calvinus after all. His services were not as dry and tedious as the lectern-thumping rants of Lentilus. He was a youthful, energetic man unsullied by the greying and dulling of time. His service that day was in praise of her father's campaign against the Picts. At the mention of his name, Aureliana felt some eyes upon her, but afterwards, as they all filed out of the nave, none came to talk to her.

Beggars gathered on the steps to ask for alms from the nobles and although many swept past them without a shred of sympathy, Aureliana always spared a few coins for the wretches. God knew, there were enough of them in this town.

"Here's some coin, Seren," she said as she handed her a small purse. See that it is distributed to those who seem to be most needy."

"Of course, my lady. But where are you going?"

"I have a mind to talk with Bishop Calvinus."

"Bishop Calvinus? What is wrong with Bishop Tomwyn? He stopped by the villa only yesterday."

"I just need to speak with somebody who is not a friend of the family. I won't be long."

Seren gave her a suspicious look. Her nurse knew that she had been somewhat confused in her faith of late. She probably couldn't understand why she would want a private talk with a stranger. But the truth was, Aureliana didn't trust Bishop Tomwyn. Oh, he was a good enough man, that was true, but he had been a close friend to her grandfather and had known her father since he had been a boy. The sins that weighed on her conscience must never reach her father's ears, under any circumstances.

She had to wait as Bishop Calvinus was already engaged in conversation with somebody else. The footsteps of the last of the congregation leaving the church echoed around the chamber. She sat in the nave and gazed upon the holy image of Christ painted on the far wall. He was beardless and dressed in common robes, holding the staff of a shepherd. His pale face with its golden halo radiated love and compassion.

She knew that the only way to find forgiveness for your sins was to talk directly to God. But Aureliana had always found the heavenly father to be disquietingly unresponsive. She knew that sometimes, priests and bishops would hear the sins of a member of their flock and advise them how best to repent. This might involve extended periods of prayer or fasting. For very serious sins the act of exmologesis might be called for. This would mean that the sin would be confessed in front of the congregation and penance would be carried out in public.

She shuddered at the thought. She remembered, as a young girl, seeing a middle aged man crawling on his belly across the nave to kiss the steps of the altar as punishment for coveting his wife's sister. There were also tales of people being excommunicated for ten, fifteen, sometimes twenty years and they would undergo such ordeals as joining the 'weepers'; wretches who stood outside the church with ash rubbed into their skin, wailing and rending their sackcloth garments.

She knew that what she had done might not be considered one of the mortal sins, but it had been a grossly unchaste act nonetheless. As she gazed on the flat, painted face of God's son, she silently prayed to him to forgive her and spare her the more serious penances she had heard about. Could God be so cruel as to utterly destroy her for falling in love with the wrong man? She would do anything to save her father from the shame of her crime being made public.

"Yes, my child?" said Bishop Calvinus. He had finished with his previous business and was waiting patiently behind her.

"I would speak with you, Father," she said. She was frightened by how loud her voice sounded in the nave and lowered it. "It is on the matter of sin and penance. Is there somewhere private we might go?"

"Over here," said the bishop, leading her to the corner of the room where a small seat had been set up. "I sometimes hear the sins of my flock here while they kneel at my feet."

She knelt down, feeling the hard floor of the ancient basilica through her stola, cold and unyielding. She hoped that her penance would not involve too much of this.

"Now, my child, what is it that you have done. Do not fear overmuch, I am sure that a creature so young and fair cannot have committed much wickedness in her short life."

"Father," she began, "I have fallen in love with a man not of our faith."

# Hronwena

Several days had passed since Berwen's disappearance before word reached Deilwen that he had been seen drinking in one of the taverns in the village. Hronwena immediately set out to meet with him, brushing aside Marchudd's protestations once more and promising him that she would return before nightfall. She said nothing of Berwen.

Marchudd had been so incensed by Berwen's desertion that he had put out a call for him to be immediately brought in should he be seen. Guards who left their posts without leave were treated with the utmost severity and Marchudd promised to have the hide flogged off him as an example. But few liked Marchudd and no reports reached his ears.

They found Berwen sitting alone at a table, nursing a mug of beer. His face was a bruised, purplish mess.

"What did they do to you?" said Hronwena as they sat down by him. The barkeep eyed them suspiciously and Deilwen ordered two mugs of beer.

"What does it look like?" he slurred. "They wouldn't let me see her."

"Did you think they would, you idiot?" snapped Hronwena. "Did you think you could just dance right in there and take her away? She's guarded for a reason."

"She's my sister. Don't expect me to sit here while she's locked up somewhere. I had to try."

Hronwena saw his point. Would she have done any differently if it had been Aesc kept prisoner? "We will rescue her, I promise you," she told him. "But we need to use our heads. We are only three. We need to even the odds."

"What do you have in mind, my lady?" asked Deilwen.

Hronwena looked around at the colourful characters in the tavern. "Berwen, you must know some tough bastards."

His puffy, bloodshot eyes swivelled to meet hers. "Blades for hire you mean?"

"Men who are willing to do a little work but can be trusted to keep their mouths shut."

"I know of a few. I can get them for you."

"But, my lady," said Deilwen, "if we do take Brina by force, what is your next step? We can't just march her back to Din Neidr, you would be usurping yourself as his lordship's true wife."

"Believe me, Deilwen," said Hronwena in a tired voice, "I would love nothing more than to be relieved of that position for ever. But you are right; caution must be followed. If my husband were to find out that we even know of his crime then all of our lives will be in danger. If we are to expose him as a bigamist, then we must confront him with the evidence before the whole of his kingdom."

"Beltan!" said Deilwen in admiration.

Hronwena nodded. She had thought much on the runes she had cast. Perhaps the Elk rune that was to work in her favour had something to do with the hunt that was coming up.

"'Isn't every nobleman who owes my husband allegiance invited to a feast in the great hall the night of the hunt?" Hronwena said. "What better time or place? And in front of the clergy too."

They did their best to sober Berwen up and when they arrived back at Din Neidr Marchudd gave orders for him to be immediately put in irons.

"Stay your hand!" said Hronwena. "This man is under my protection!"

"He's a filthy little deserter, my lady!" cried Marchudd. "He must be made an example of!"

"From now on this man will be acting under my personal orders," insisted Hronwena. "If anything happens to him, I will hold you personally responsible, captain."

That shut Marchudd up and his eyes spat fire at Berwen as they passed under the gate. When they dismounted Hronwena turned to Berwen. "Get some sleep," she said. "In the morning I want you to set out and round up three good fighters. Here's some coin. If Marchudd gives you any trouble, you let me know and I'll have him mucking out the kennels for the rest of the year."

# Vortimer

Vortimer could smell her perfumed hair. She was certainly something to look at, and smell and, he was fairly sure, he could almost taste her presence in the air whenever she had vacated a room; that potent, sexual energy that always seemed to linger long after he had sent her away. But in all the years he had employed her, he had never touched her.

She had tried her tricks on him in the early days and he would not deny that he had never been tempted. But he was a married man and, he hoped, an honourable one. His father might have made a hobby of collecting whores (and wives) but if there was one thing Vortimer did not strive to be then it was his father.

"What news from our most holy of men?" he asked her.

"He has not had word from your father since he departed for the west," replied Maelona as she lounged on a couch with a cup of wine in her hand. Her tunica was very slim fitting and one bare arm rested on her travelling cloak which she had discarded when she had entered his chambers. Her knees were curled up beneath her. Bare, smooth and creamy as butter.

His father had his spies, his agents and his assassins, but it gave Vortimer great pleasure knowing that Maelona was unequivocally his. His father knew nothing of her and probably didn't think his son had it in him to employ spies, let alone ones with such heavenly tits. But there were many things his father did not know about him. He had always been a fool in his eyes. Well, this was one thing that would never be his.

She had come into his service after he had caught her stealing papers from him. Some petty nobleman had put her up to it but it was of no consequence. He had considered having her executed but it had seemed a shame to let such a beautiful creature go to waste. She had talent and he offered to double whatever her employer was paying her to switch sides. Once she agreed, her first job was to quietly dispatch the snooping nobleman. Since that day he had used Maelona for many tasks and he trusted her as much as anybody could trust a hired assassin, thief and spy.

Her most recent task had been to seduce Bishop Calvinus and worm information from him. Ever since his father had installed that ludicrous deacon as his personal lackey in the clergy, Vortimer had made it his business to find out all that passed between them. So far it had all been pretty mundane stuff about the appointing of bishops and deacons and the accompanying bribes as well as the ongoing fight against Pelagianism, the threat of which, as far as Vortimer could make out, had been greatly exaggerated.

There had also been some mildly interesting gossip she had winkled out of him concerning the sins of his congregation. Gallo the butcher for example had been terrified that his perverted relationship with his pig carcasses was a ticket to hell and damnation. Such titbits were good for a laugh but not terribly useful.

"There is one other thing you may find amusing," said Maelona, after she had run by him all the inconsequential goings on in the life of the bishop.

"Yes?"

"It seems that Aureliana Aurelianus has been a very naughty girl."

"Oh? How so?"

"Fucking, put simply."

Vortimer leaned forward, a grin emerging on his lips. "Fucking who?"

"Horsa. The Saxon."

Vortimer's grin widened. "Are you telling me that the daughter of our ferocious *Comes Britanniarum* is fucking one of those yellow-haired heathens?"

She mirrored his grin and sipped at her wine. Vortimer guffawed.

"If ever that stone-faced arse licker finds out I only hope I am around to see his face! But amusing as this knowledge is, it is not the sort of information that I can use. Is there anything else?"

"Nothing of note."

"Well, I'll trust your definition as to what is 'of note', but I do hope that you will bring anything further to my attention."

She left and he sat back and allowed himself another smile when he thought of Aurelianus's daughter. Lord God, but that was funny!

# Hronwena

It only took a couple of days for Berwen to find three suitably tough types to carry out Hronwena's plan and when he returned to Din Neidr to inform her that they awaited her orders down in the village, she prepared to set out.

"Must we go too, my lady?" asked Deilwen. "This is a job for rogues, not women."

"I trust Berwen's associates only so far," Hronwena replied. "This is a delicate matter and I want to oversee every part of it."

"But it might be dangerous."

"I'm sure it will be. You gave me a dagger once, Deilwen. I wonder, do you have the courage to use such a weapon yourself?"

Deilwen seemed affronted by this, but a little thoughtful too. "I suppose I would if my life was put in danger."

"That's all I ask," Hronwena replied. "I imagine that you carry a similar dagger with you."

"Well... these are dangerous times, my lady..."

"Good."

"But what of you? Could you kill a man?"

Hronwena considered this. "I don't know. My mother killed her uncle when she was my age. He had kidnapped her and tried to marry her by force. She gutted him with a spike."

Deilwen stared at her open mouthed. "You truly come from another world, my lady."

They met Berwen's associates in the yard behind the tavern. They did not disappoint. The three of them were tall, scarred and brutish and even Deilwen seemed a little cowed in their presence. Once Hronwena had explained the plan to them they set out for the old iron mine.

Hronwena and Deilwen did not speak on the way. The three sell-swords knew each other from previous jobs and laughed and joked as if the whole thing were nothing more than a jolly outing. Afternoon faded into early evening and the dragonflies hovered in the long shadows of the meadows. They must have been seen a mile off for the old man came stumbling out of the mill, his face red with indignation.

"What is the meaning of bringing these armed men on to our grounds?" he demanded. He then recognised Hronwena and Deilwen, for his face turned even redder. "You! We gave you sanctuary! We fed and housed you! Why have you returned with these men?"

"We are here to free the woman and child you hold prisoner!" said Hronwena, trying to make her voice carry as much authority as possible.

"I knew there was something odd about you!" said the man and Hronwena saw his eyes flit to something or somebody behind her.

She turned and saw the two men who had posed as blacksmiths jogging towards them, swords drawn. Berwen and his mercenaries needed no order from her and they dismounted and drew their own weapons, ready to meet the oncoming pair. "We want no bloodshed!" Hronwena cautioned, but it was too late. The two guards had honour enough not to desert their post or give up their charge without a fight.

Steel clanged and slithered as four met two. It was an unfair fight, but life had not been fair to that poor woman and her babe locked up in that old mill, thought Hronwena and she felt no sympathy when the first of the guards fell, his collarbone splinted by a sword's edge. The other suffered a chop to his shield arm which must have shattered the bone and left him stumbling and reeling with the pain.

The small resistance was over and Hronwena led the advance on the old mill. The man staggered back inside and bolted the door. A few boots from one of the mercenaries caved the entrance in and the men piled inside, filling the room.

Hronwena stepped inside followed by Deilwen. The old man and his wife as well as the serving girl cowered in the far corner; frightened eyes fixed on the red blade one of the mercenaries carried.

"Where are they?" Hronwena demanded. "The girl and the child. Show us to them now!"

"Upstairs!" cried the terrified woman. "They're not harmed!"

Berwen was off, taking the wooden staircase two steps at a time. Hronwena called out after him for caution but was ignored.

The floor directly above was vacant but for some sleeping pallets and odd bits of furniture so they continued to the upper floor. Behind a wicker screen that divided the room into separate sleeping quarters Berwen had halted. Hronwena caught up with him and looked over his shoulder. The dark-haired woman she had seen at the window sat on a bed, cradling a whimpering child of about two. Both looked terrified.

"It's not her," said Berwen in a flat voice. "It's not Brina."

"I'm sorry, Berwen," Hronwena said. She felt terrible for him. There had always been that chance; that the woman might just be some other girl Vitalinus had taken a fancy to. But she had never voiced this thought to Berwen for fear that he would lose interest in the cause. She now felt like she had betrayed him.

"My God!" gasped Deilwen as she joined them, panting from the dash up two flights of stairs. "Heavens preserve us! It's Enys!"

The girl stared at Deilwen, showing some flicker of recognition. Hronwena looked from one to the other. "Enys?" she said. "Pasgen's twin?"

"I thought you were dead, girl!" said Deilwen as she forced her way into the room to embrace Enys, "We all did!" Both of them began to weep. Berwen slunk out of the room.

"What's been going on here?" Hronwena asked, a sick feeling rising in her gut as she considered the only possible answer she could think of.

"Father keeps me here," Enys said. "He keeps me prisoner. They treated me well, the old couple. You haven't harmed them?" Her eyes were wide and hopeful.

"They are not harmed," said Deilwen. "Who is the father of the child?"

Enys gazed down at the bed sheets, shame and humiliation written on her features. Her silence was her admission.

"Lord have mercy..." murmured Deilwen. "When did he start to rape you?"

"Over two years ago. Back when I was living at Din Neidr. Then I fell pregnant."

"Was he angry?" Hronwena asked.

She shook her head. "He was overjoyed. He kept telling me that I had strengthened the family; purified the stock... I don't understand it even now."

"But this is abominable!" said Deilwen. "His own daughter! I can't believe that he would!"

"Then you do not know him as I do," said Hronwena. "It would make sense in his own perverted mind. The thing he wants most in the world is to spread his seed; to continue his bloodline. But women from other families are not good enough. What he really wants is to sire children on his children."

"But he could never get away with it! The clergy would excommunicate him! His children would be declared abominations!"

"That's why there was all this secrecy. When Enys fell pregnant he claimed that she died of a fever. He had her sent here where she was kept under guard while he married somebody else."

"Brina."

"Yes. He planned to sire a child on Brina and when she was good and ripe he would kill her and bring Enys's child here back to Din Neidr. That way he could claim that Brina died in childbirth. But Brina grew too volatile and became a liability. Perhaps she found out a little of the truth. Whatever it was it was enough for him to do away with her and claim that she had died while crossing the river."

"Then he married you..."

"Yes. I was more than a mere peace offering between Briton and Sais. I was to be the mother of his child. This child here."

"But that couldn't work! This babe is at least two! Nobody would ever believe that he was yours."

"I don't know. Perhaps he planned to keep me confined for a few years, claiming that I was ill or something. Everybody seems to have believed his lies so far."

"Does he come here to see you often?" Deilwen asked Enys.

"Every few weeks," the girl replied. "To see Britu here and to... see me."

Hronwena shuddered. Her husband was beyond all definitions of repulsiveness.

"He would have killed her and taken her child from her," Deilwen said on the verge of tears. "That monster..."

"No!" said Enys. "Kill me? Why? The other one lived out her days here, the one before me until she grew sick."

"What other one?" Hronwena asked.

"There was another girl who lived here. She had a child too. This was years ago. The old woman told me. The child was taken away and she lived here until she grew sick and died. They buried her out in the yard. I've seen the grave. It's unmarked."

"My god," said Deilwen. "How many girls has he done this to? What do we do now, my lady?"

"We continue as planned. The fact that he is not a bigamist is irrelevant in the light of all this. Fathering a child on his own daughter? That's enough to ruin his reputation and for the clergy to wash their hands of him."

"My lady, I've never asked, but what are you to gain by all of this? You are putting your life into extreme danger."

Hronwena narrowed her eyes. "I'll never escape Vitalinus's clutches. I could escape from Din Neidr but even if I made it across the hundreds of miles of British territory, I would have shamed my father and destroyed his treaty with the Britons. I came to terms with this long ago. But if I somehow manage to bring Vitalinus's power crashing down around him, I may be able to win my freedom. He may wish to return me to my father voluntarily."

"Or kill you."

"That is a chance I am willing to take."

"So you plan to take Enys back to Din Neidr and expose her at the feast of Beltan?"

"That is up to Enys."

The young girl gazed at her. "You risk much for me and I would be ashamed to fail you. But I am so afraid. My father... you don't know what he is capable of..."

"I do know, Enys," said Hronwena. "And I want to make sure that his reign of terror over all women on this island is halted. Only by confronting him and having the courage to challenge him can we do this. I of all people know that it is hard to stand against one's own father. Perhaps if I had done so, then I would not be here today. But if we work together, we can right some of the wrongs that have been done to us. Are you with me?"

Enys searched Hronwena's eyes. "I do not know you, lady, but Deilwen has always been a good friend to me and if she trusts you then that is enough. I am with you, and may God help us in our endeavours."

"As am I, my lady," Deilwen added. "But one thing concerns me; how do we go about sneaking them into Din Neidr? And surely Britu's cries would be noticed."

"There lies a true problem," said Hronwena, considering the possibilities. "I think I know how to get Enys into the fortress but as for Britu, I think it would be safer and simpler for him to be left out of our plans until later."

"You want to separate me from my boy?" asked Enys, her eyes wide with horror.

"Only if you are willing," Hronwena added. "And it would only be for his own safety. We don't know how your father will react. We must find a safe, secret place where he can be kept for a few days."

"I believe I know of a place, my lady," said Deilwen.

"Where?"

"Where I came from. Or grew up at least. I was an orphan. My parents were taken by a fever when I was but a few months old. A priest came and took me to a good Christian couple who lived nearby. They took in orphans on occasion and raised them and gave them work to do on their farm. I don't think the good Lord ever blessed them with their own children so they made do with unfortunates who had no parents."

"Deilwen, I had no idea..." began Hronwena.

"Oh, it was a good upbringing, my lady. I was not mistreated and they showed me every love and kindness an orphan could hope for. I worked on their farm until I was nearly a woman but one day a passing traveller came by. He was a servant up at Din Neidr and said he was looking for young girls to serve his lordship and wife.

"The couple who raised me were sorry to see me go, but they told me that I was a woman now and should take whatever opportunities God sent my way. I still send them money whenever I can spare it for I know that they still take in the occasional unfortunate once in a while. I am sure that they would not object to minding Britu for a while. If we could somehow see that they were not left out of pocket."

"Do not worry as to that, Deilwen," said Hronwena. "I will reimburse them from my own purse for their troubles. If Enys is willing."

"I am willing," said Enys. "If it is only for a short time. Can we trust these people?"

"I look on them as my own kin," said Deilwen. "And none at Din Neidr know of them. The old servant who took me into employment passed away a year ago."

It was agreed upon. They packed up what little items Enys called her own and went downstairs where the three mercenaries were still holding the old couple and their servant girl at sword point.

"What's to be done with them, lady?" asked one of the sell-swords.

"Leave them," Hronwena replied. "They are villains to keep a woman and her child locked up and away from her family, but I suppose we have all been pawns in my husband's grip to some extent. I want no more bloodshed."

They passed out into the yard where Berwen was waiting with the horses. He gripped the reigns tightly in one fist, his eyes searching the grey hills in the distance. "My sister is truly dead, isn't she?"

"Yes, I believe so, Berwen," she told him. "I am sorry. I had hoped that you would be reunited with her here, but instead we found a much darker secret and more horrible crime. I must ask you now, are you still my man? Will you still help me or will you take off on the wind to find whatever solace this world can give you? The choice is yours; I will not pressure you for you have helped me much already."

"This world can offer me no solace that I deserve," he replied. "I failed my sister in life and have failed to avenge her so far. My only hope for peace lies along the same path as yours. My sword is yours for as long as it takes to bring Vitalinus to his knees and if possible, to bring justice to Brina's memory."

# Aesc

"Do you think your mother will like it?" Aesc's father asked him, holding up a necklace of silver and precious stones to catch the sunlight.

"Very nice," said Aesc. "Where did you get it?"

"Bought it from a merchant on the road. It's Roman or so he says. Fine workmanship. I can't very well return home with nothing for the wife, eh? If only Hronwena were home too. I would have bought her something as well."

"It'll take more than fancy Roman jewellery to convince mother to forgive you," Aesc said.

His father nodded grimly. "You're right about that, son. But what else can I do?"

They looked around at the camp in silence, listening to the constant drone of army life; the clink of hammer on anvil, the whinny of horses, the laughter of men at play. During their time marching with Aurelianus's column, their own men had improved from a rabble to something resembling a professional army, but whatever ordered and disciplined shape the column had taken over the past few weeks had been utterly ruined by the addition of Prince Talorc's four-hundred odd warriors.

The Picts travelled on foot for the most part with only Talorc and his highest lieutenants riding astride sturdy, squat horses native to northern Britta. They did not ride as a single unit nor at any fixed point in the column, but moved through the ranks freely, jostling back and forth, calling out encouragement to their men and generally causing more disorder than was necessary.

Cattle also seemed to be part of the Pictish force they had brought several hundred of the horned beasts with them in a great lowing, stumbling mass. This was something of a mobile kitchen and when they stopped for a meal, several cattle were slaughtered and their meat chopped up and boiled inside their own stomachs with barley. The huge Deerhounds the Picts used for hunting were as poorly disciplined as the men and they ran about the camp, stealing morsels of food and were kept in check by kicks and whacks on their noses with knife hilts.

The Picts themselves wore minimal clothing and armour. A knee-length tunic of rough wool seemed to suffice for the most part while others wore colourful breeches and nothing else. Some wore leather shoes but many went barefoot; the soles of their feet hard and calloused from many years of such tramping over heath and hill. There was the occasional helmet; either Roman or British in style and some of the wealthiest warriors even wore scale armour. Their faces were painted in swirling blue designs that followed the contours of their cheeks and animals and other unknown symbols adorned bare chests and arms.

Aesc noted that their weapons were similar to those of their own men, although the sword blades were bluish, having been left unpolished from the forge. This, his father had explained, was to protect them against rust in the dismal British weather which seemed to switch from sunshine to mist and rain in the blink of an eye, even in summer. They carried small bucklers either circular or oddly square; all painted with animal designs similar to those that adorned their bodies.

In his dreams Aesc felt his hands wet with the blood of the man he had slain in the tavern in Londinium. He relived that moment every night just as he used to relive his butchering of Gwrangon. One vivid nightmare had replaced the other. He tried to tell himself that it had been a necessary killing. If he had not killed that man, his father would be dead. But the very memory of his body toppling over and the blood pumping from the wound when he removed the knife made him sick. He was worried that he was not cut out to be a warrior.

But he had saved his father's life. And so his father had showered him with praise and admiration. That was all Aesc had wanted from life. Why then, could he only think of going home? It wasn't just homesickness. He missed his mother and he even missed Hronwena. He missed the sights and smells of Rutupiae too but it was the sense of impending dread that troubled him the most. He dreaded the bloodshed that was sure to come soon. Battle lay in the north. Every day they marched was a day closer to the inevitable clash of blades, screams of men and horses and stench of blood and opened bowels. This was the moment he had been waiting for since before he could remember; a chance to prove his mettle. And now that he rode on the cusp of it he felt hopelessly inadequate.

The following day they entered the forests south of Din Eidyn. Their destination drew near. A wide path led through the forest and the steadily tramping column of infantry and cavalry seemed oppressed by the gloom of the tall trees on either side. For as far as Aesc could see in front and behind them, the helmeted heads and wavering spears wound away like a silver snake.

Faint cries of alarm drifted through the forest of spear tips up ahead. Aesc squinted and could see formations breaking and men falling as the attackers charged from the trees, slamming into the foremost ranks. Talorc drew his sword and yelled a Pictish war cry.

"Hold!" shouted Aurelianus. "Hold position!"

But it was too late. Led by their prince, the Picts set off, galloping and running in no formation at all to where the action was.

"Damn him!" roared Aurelianus. "It might be a ruse! Now we are weakened at the rear."

Aurelianus's prediction seemed to be true for the attackers were already disappearing back into the forest before Talorc's mad charge. The prince showed no sign of stopping. Pict chased Pict into the shaded gloom of the tree line, leaving the British and Germanic parts of the army in an unsteady column, wavering and vulnerable.

"We are near Din Eidyn now," said Aurelianus to his captains. "We do not stop for anything. If we are attacked I want minimal engagement. We push through at all costs!" His captains galloped off to relay his orders to every part of the army. Aurelianus turned in his saddle to Hengest. "Can I count on you not to show Talorc's stupidity, Sais? Strength in numbers is the key. We must not get drawn into the forests; they would pick us off like hares."

Hengest did not have a chance to reply for the front of the army suddenly came under attack again, this time from a fresh batch of Picts who had been lying in wait further down the line. It was a stronger force this time and the Britons held their shields up against the painted warriors who hurled themselves upon them like mad dogs. The army began to slow.

"No!" cried Aurelianus. "Push through! Push through them! Keep moving!" He drew his sword. "*Britannia! Christus!*" and spurred his steed into a gallop, his guard following close behind.

Aesc, his heart hammering for he knew that the wait was over and battle was truly upon them, followed his father. He could hear the clamour of three-hundred sets of hooves roaring like the sea as they ran the length of the column to where the fighting was. They slammed into the Picts who barely saw them coming.

Swords wheeled down on them and spears pierced naked, painted breasts while hooves trampled those who fell, shattering bones and crushing the life out of them. Aesc was jostled from side to side in the press of horses, his spear arm uselessly cramped.

"Keep the army moving!" he heard Aurelianus reiterate to the captains in the ranks. "Don't stop until you reach Din Eidyn! We'll take care of the ambushers!"

More Picts flooded from the forests and Aesc surmised that they had been placed at regular intervals along the forest route with the intent of wearing the army down with constant abrasion rather than a full on attack. This was a surprising display of strategy considering what they had seen of them so far. The

Picts certainly knew how to tackle invaders who passed through their forests. No wonder the Romans had never fully conquered the north.

Arrows sang through the air and tore through the British ranks. Men screamed and went down with black shafts in their necks, chests and limbs. Those who were quick enough to raise their shields did not stop to remove the arrows that were embedded in them; jogging ever onwards at a frantic pace, fear written on their faces at the thought of the inevitable second volley.

"Over there!" Aurelianus called, pointing to a wooded hill where roughly fifty Pictish bowmen had been arranged.

"Do I have your permission to pursue?" Aesc heard his father ask him.

"Cut every last one of them down!" came the reply.

"Aesc, Ordlaf, with me! Ebusa, remain here with Aurelianus and the rest of the cavalry. Three *turmae* should be enough to handle them." He blew his horn and took off.

Aesc was glad to leave the horrid press of battle in the ranks and feel the rush of cool air flowing past him. They rounded the foot of the hill and even succeeded in drawing the fire of some of the Picts away from the infantry. The arrows fell short, landing in the earth churned up by the horses' hooves. The hill was steep and the climb was painfully slow. The horses stumbled and voiced their protest but they forced them on, hoping that they would not be too worn out before they reach the plateau.

The Picts were too focused on picking out targets in the infantry to realise that the cavalry had made it up the hill at their rear and so the attack came as a total surprise. Hengest roared and swung *Hildeleoma* as they tore through the bowmen. Arrows loosed from interrupted draws went wild as men fell beneath the press of cavalry.

There was nothing hindering Aesc's spear arm now and his first kill found its way onto his spear point almost by accident. He felt the horrible deadweight of the writhing man he had pierced through the neck and wrenched his spear free before the weight could drag him from his saddle.

Blood running down the shaft, he lunged at another target but missed, battering the Pict aside with the flank of his horse only to find another waiting for his quick spear thrust. It was almost too easy; like a game. If he focused on simply finding new targets, he almost forgot that these were living, breathing men.

*So that's the key!*

He knew he would pay the price for it later, when the memories of the screaming, bloody faces came back to haunt him when he lay in the darkness before sleep, but for now, he felt nothing of the sickness and fear he had dreaded. It had been replaced by something else; something primal and comforting. In this moment he had finally become a warrior!

His father swung the charge around in a wide arc before they reached the edge of the hill and followed its contour, turning back on the drastically reduced cluster of Picts. By the time they made it through them again there were none left standing.

From the hilltop they could see the running infantry emerging from the forest, headed for a purple hump in the hazy distance. That, Aesc assumed, must be Din Eidyn. Below, the remainder of the cavalry led by Aurelianus was busy mopping up the rest of the ambushers, but still stopping short of pursuing them beyond the road.

They headed down the hill to join them but by the time they got there it was all over. Talorc and his warriors emerged from the forest behind them, whooping victory cries. Aurelianus visibly seethed but refrained from berating the rash prince in front of his own people. They had won and that was enough.

The Picts were ecstatic. The thrill of battle in their veins and the scent of blood in their nostrils seemed to be the one thing they lived for. "A good fight!" called out Talorc. "You Saeson fight well, it is true. The Dark Lady shall glut herself tonight!"

"The Dark Lady?" Aesc asked him.

"She is the dark part of the Mother Goddess," Talorc explained. "She is raven. She is death."

Aesc could see the corners of Aurelianus's mouth curling with distaste and some of the Britons showed some confusion, but he thought he understood. This Dark Lady was the Pictish notion of the Waelcyrie; those women who swept down on the battlefield and chose those who were to join the gods in Waelheall. The raven was their animal also.

"Well, that seems to be that," his father said to Aurelianus. "Although I am somewhat disappointed. I had expected a larger host to meet us. Perhaps the strength of Galana's forces has been exaggerated."

"Makes no sense," grumbled Aurelianus. "If that was all she had then she would have kept them holed up in Din Eidyn. It wouldn't take much to hold that fortress against a siege for many days. Why send out this ambush?"

"Perhaps she has a larger host at Din Eidyn," suggested Hengest. "This was just the welcoming committee designed to wear us down and break our morale."

"Then it's a shocking waste. Why sacrifice so many men in a nuisance raid? She would have knowingly sent these men to their deaths. No, she is planning something else. There is something hidden here that I cannot see and I don't like it."

Aesc gazed at the dead that littered the forest path and met his father's eyes doing the same. He knew what he was thinking for he was thinking the same thing. They had thought that these warriors were pitching a last ditch defence of their home; desperate men each fighting with the spirit of a trapped bear. But if they had willingly sacrificed themselves for some scheme on the part of their queen, well, that made them a people far more fearsome and dangerous than they had previously thought.

# Hronwena

Preparations for Beltan were underway. Herdsmen drove their cattle out into summer pastures and large mounds of kindling were prepared on hilltops. When darkness fell they would be lit and the cattle driven between their purifying light and warmth. The truly pagan portion of the populace prepared sacrifices to Belen the sun god, whose summer fire gave the ancient festival its name. This was much to the ire of the Christians, but there was little to be done about it. The heathen beliefs of those whose livelihoods depended on good harvests and fat, healthy calves were not to be swayed by those who grew plump on their grain, milk and meat in the towns.

It was an ongoing battle of beliefs that had lasted generations and would last many more, but the Christians were not stupid. Rather than wage an all-out war on the ancient Celtic festivals, they had begun to embrace them while downplaying some of their more intolerable pagan aspects. Thus the doorways of Din Neidr were decorated with garlands of yellow summer flowers while its halls rang with hymns to the Christian god sung vigorously to drown out the muttered superstitions of a populace who, while Christian in name, were still ruled by ancient custom.

Hronwena found herself biting her nails nervously in the days approaching the festival. All the pieces of her game were in play and there was nothing else she could do but wait. Vitalinus was due back from Corinium Dobunnorum any day.

Enys was in the fortress, kept hidden in Hronwena's chamber. Cartloads of ale, wine and mead had been ordered for the feast along with various other supplies and at least twice a day the gates would be opened for the latest delivery to lumber into the courtyard on creaking axels. Once again, Hronwena used Berwen as her contact without the fortress walls and he arranged for Enys to be smuggled in in an empty barrel.

Berwen made sure that he helped with the offloading of the barrels and had the one containing Enys set to one side by the entrance to the kitchens. When darkness had fallen and the bustle of cooks and potboys had vacated the cooling kitchens, Hronwena helped Enys out of her cramped barrel and ushered her through the lower portion of the fortress, disguised in the cloak of a maid, up to her chamber where she fed her and let her rest in her bed after her jolting and nerve-wracking journey.

The night of the feast was one of almost unbearable tension for Hronwena. The noblemen and their wives flocked into the great hall in their colourful tunics and cloaks, their arms and necks dripping with gold, where the tables had been laid out with all the food the kitchens had been furiously churning out over the last few days.

Hronwena took her seat next to her husband at the highest table. Cadeyrn sat opposite her with Pasgen a little further down, just as at the previous feast. That was good. She wanted them close enough so that there would be no doubt in their minds when the moment finally came.

She had dressed Enys in the old maid's cloak once more and taken her down to the hall before the nobles had entered. There must have been twenty such hooded females bustling around, filling horns and goblets and scuttling back and forth from the kitchens so Enys blended in perfectly. When the appropriate moment came, Hronwena would rise and reveal Enys to all with the appropriate dramatic flourish. Exactly what sort of moment that would be and when it would come, Hronwena had no idea.

She listened to the Latin and British tongues chattering around her, hoping that conversation would turn to some matter that may give her an opportunity to speak. Her eyes kept flitting to Enys who was holding up admirably; carrying jugs of wine and mead with the best of them, her face well shaded by the deep hood. It would not do for her to be recognised too early but there was little chance of that; almost everybody in the hall thought she was dead and in her grave.

It was sometime after the second course that Hronwena lost track of Enys. She had been distracted by an irritating nobleman who insisted on making conversation with her and when she was done pretending to laugh at his jest, she could not see Enys anywhere. Her eyes flitted from maid to maid, searching every face. Vitalinus leaned in close and spoke so soft and near that she could smell the stewed onions on his breath.

"I imagine you are looking for my daughter."

Hronwena's heart rose from a canter into a gallop.

"Did you think I wouldn't notice? Did you think that pair of old fools at the mine wouldn't tell me who came barging in with her own private army to kidnap my daughter and grandson?"

Hronwena realised the flaw in her plan too late. Of course he would have found out! He probably stopped at the old iron mine on his way back from Corinium Dobunnorum. He would have wanted to see his perverted hope for the future of his precious bloodline.

His hand gripped her thigh under the table; his fingers digging in painfully. "It really was a bold scheme, my pretty. To bring a girl back from the dead is strong magic indeed. I underestimated you, I admit, but it has been rectified. She has been removed and your plan has failed. Of course, I want to know where my grandson is, but that is a topic we shall discuss later as well as the matter of your betrayal. For now, enjoy the rest of the feast and play your part as a good wife and it may not go so ill with you."

Panic gripped Hronwena. Not for her own safety but for those she had drawn into her scheme; Enys, Deilwen, Berwen, even little Britu. There was no telling what Vitalinus would do to those who threatened to upset his plans and she dared put no cruelty or villainy past him. What had she done? The only thing for it was to get word to Deilwen who stood but a few feet away, supervising a group of maids. But Vitalinus's hand still gripped her thigh and he showed no intention of relinquishing it.

A maid passed and Hronwena, in a moment of desperation, called to her; "Woman! Do you intend to let my husband die of thirst?" His cup was only half full, but if she could only get him drunk...

"Sorry, my lady," stammered the maid as she brought the wine jug over. She filled his cup up to the brim.

Vitalinus stared at Hronwena, seeing right through her plan, she was sure of it. He slowly released her thigh and lifted his hand to take his wine cup. He drank slowly, keeping his eyes on her.

None at the table noticed the exchange between man and wife and the wine and conversation continued to flow. Vitalinus, unable to keep his attention away from his guests for too long, began to return to them, partaking in the debates. When she was sure that he was fully distracted, Hronwena called Deilwen over to her.

"My lady?"

"He knows!" Hronwena whispered into her handmaid's ear. "He's had Enys removed from the hall right under our noses!"

"I know!" Deilwen replied. "I saw Marchudd take her away. I wanted to tell you, but I dared not in front of your husband."

"Do you know where he took her?"

"No. But I sent for Berwen and told him to find out. I also told him to hide her somewhere safe."

"Good, Deilwen. The feast is almost over. People are tiring. We must secure Enys before they ride out on the hunt and make our move. We are running out of time."

The feast was near its close. The noblemen were reluctant to abandon the good food, drink and cheer, but none wanted to ride out too drunk and eyes turned to Vitalinus in anticipation. He satisfied them by standing and raising his arms for quiet.

"Now, my good friends!" he said, his voice reaching even the furthest tables. "We ride out to hunt by moonlight in honour of God, his son the Christ and the promise of summer!"

There was a cheer and the sound of scraping chair legs as all rose to finish whatever was left in their cups. The women filed out of a separate door and the men set out for the stables. Hronwena, free at last from Vitalinus's eyes, found Deilwen amid the press of bodies.

"Where is Berwen? Has he returned?"

"Not yet, my lady."

"Then go and find him! Search the upper floors. Marchudd will most likely have taken Enys to some chamber upstairs."

Hronwena filed out with the other women who were assembling in the courtyard to see their men off. The moon was high in the clear night air and reflected off the wet mud in the yard. The men blew horns from their saddles and wheeled around as if they were setting off for war. Dogs barked and capered between the stamping hooves. Hronwena saw Marchudd assembling a group of guardsmen by the gate. His tunic was stained and his right hand seemed darker than his left as if it were stained with... *blood*? She jumped as Deilwen grasped her sleeve.

"My lady! It's Berwen! He's... God help us!"

"What happened?"

"I found him lying in the corridor outside your chamber. He'd been run through by a blade. He was still alive and I asked him where Enys was. He said he didn't know. He fought Marchudd and Enys got away during the scuffle. He died before I could get him help."

"Well where is Enys now?" demanded Hronwena.

"I don't know!"

Hronwena desperately looked around, scanning every woman's face to see if Enys was with them. This had all gone so horribly wrong. Berwen was dead and it was her fault. Enys was missing and Vitalinus and all his noblemen were about to ride out.

A great cheer went up from the mounted men as Marchudd gave the order for the gates to be opened. All eyes were upon the creaking timbers and suddenly somebody gave out a cry; "Look! There's someone on the palisade!"

It was true. A lone figure in a handmaid's cloak stood directly above the gate, the dancing light of the torches failing to illuminate her hooded face.

"Who is that?" demanded one nobleman.

"Get her down from there!" said Cadeyrn. "Is she mad or drunk?"

Suddenly the figure undid the brooch at her breast and let her cloak slide from her body to reveal her pale face and arms.

Hronwena's heart soared. It was more drama than she could ever have hoped for.

There was nothing concealing her appearance now. A sharp intake of breath could be heard from some of the nobles who had known her and now thought that they were looking upon a ghost. Hronwena watched

Cadeyrn, waiting for him to play out his part in this mad summer play.

"It cannot be..." she heard him mutter. "It's not possible."

The woman was now making her way down the steps to the courtyard. Every step she took was a further confirmation in the minds of all who watched her, all who thought she was dead.

"Enys..." said Cadeyrn, dismounting and walking towards her as if in a trance. "My sister..."

They embraced and the crowd rippled with confusion. "What is happening here, my lord?" demanded one of the noblemen.

"It's a lie!" bellowed Vitalinus. "She's an imposter! My daughter is dead!"

"Enys!" cried another voice from the doorway to the great hall. Pasgen pushed his way through the crowd and his older brother stood aside to let the young twins embrace with all the strength in their arms. "You're alive!" wept Pasgen, "you're alive..."

Cadeyrn turned his attention on his father. "You said that she died of a fever," he said. "We all believed you. We never saw her body but we saw her casket buried. What happened?"

Vitalinus, for perhaps the first time in his life, showed true fear. It was written all over his face, the blood draining from it.

"I can provide that explanation," said Hronwena. "If I am permitted."

There were murmurs at this. The whole business stank of witchcraft and Hronwena knew that she was on thin ice with these nobles. Few wanted to hear from the Saxon witch at this point but Cadeyrn raised his hand for silence.

"Speak, Lady Hronwena."

"Outside my chamber lies the body of Berwen, one of Lord Vitalinus's guards," she began. "He was butchered for trying to prove that my husband's own daughter was alive. Here she stands before us. She was abducted over two years ago when a seed was planted inside her belly. A seed planted by none other than her own father!"

There was outrage at this, not least from Vitalinus himself. "This is mere slander and mummery!" he roared. "Are you fools willing to listen to the lies of a Saxon whore who has nothing in her mind but the wish of doing me harm?"

"It is true that I have little proof for my claims," said Hronwena. "But I am sure that you all see the gaps in the history of the past few years that sorely need filling. I cannot fill all those gaps for you but I can give you Enys here, daughter of Vitalinus, and let her tell you her tale from her own mouth. She does indeed have a son who is at present in a safe location. That son was given to her by her own father."

"I demand my wife be arrested and put in irons to await trial!" shouted Vitalinus.

Marchudd and his guards advanced, spears held low to take Hronwena. Rough hands seized her arms and she found herself being lifted almost off her feet.

"Halt!" called Cadeyrn, and the guards froze, looking from father to son, uncertainly. "I am taking command here!"

319

"You dare defy me, boy?" said Vitalinus. "I'll have you flung into the cells also!"

Cadeyrn rounded on his father. "I don't think so. There are too many questions that need answering this night and we will have them before you give any more orders."

"You insolent whore-son!" raged his father. "I'll have you flogged out of this fortress! I'll disown you! You will be banished from my lands for the rest of your life!"

"No." The word was steady and calm, uttered by one who had been pushed to the point where he could be pushed no further. "I am in command of Din Neidr now."

Vitalinus had nothing to say to this. He gaped at his son, his face pale and jaw hanging stupidly slack.

"All of you nobles here owe me allegiance," continued Cadeyrn. "I now rule in my father's stead until he is made to account for the charges against him."

"Why are you just standing there, captain?" Vitalinus demanded of Marchudd. "Arrest him and take him away!"

Marchudd made to obey, but several of the noblemen had dismounted and had drawn swords.

"Let's not have any bloodshed," said the noble who had bored Hronwena during the feast. "I for one stand with Lord Cadeyrn. If you intend to arrest him, you must go through me first."

Marchudd gazed through narrowed eyes at the nobles who faced him and, knowing he was outnumbered, stood down.

"Spineless worms!" Vitalinus raged at the nobles. "I rule this island! I am Albion! You dare stand against your ruler?"

"Take my father to his chambers," directed Cadeyrn. "He is to be kept there under guard until I say otherwise."

Vitalinus was struck dumb by his rage as he was dragged from his horse and taken indoors, his fur cloak trailing sadly in the mud.

He had been defeated.

Later, in an upper chamber, Hronwena's eyes burned with tiredness. It was late and Cadeyrn showed no intention of ceasing his interrogations. He had called her, Deilwen and Enys to his chamber to iron out the truth of the matter. Berwen's absence was sorely noticeable.

"And my father continued to lie with you even after Britu was born?" Cadeyrn asked his little sister.

"Every time he came to visit," said the girl, almost weeping at the memories. "The last time was merely two weeks ago when he left for Corinium Dobunnorum."

Cadeyrn rested his head in his hands.

"I am afraid that is not all," said Hronwena. "There is worse to tell in this story."

"What could possibly be worse than this?" Cadeyrn asked through his fingers.

"If he was willing to rape his youngest daughter," said Hronwena slowly, "then is it not possible that he did the same with his eldest?"

Cadeyrn looked at her. "Senovara?"

"The sister who died the year you were born. Or so your father told everybody. But we have seen how he spins such lies. Enys was told of another girl who lived at that old iron mine; a girl who died before her coming. This girl birthed a child..."

"My God, woman, are you trying to tell me that the babe was..." his voice failed him as the implication hit him. He leaned forward and cupped his face in his hands once more.

"I am stating no facts, Cadeyrn," Hronwena went on, "for there is more unknown in this tale than is known. All I am suggesting is that as your father tried to murder his wife and sire a son on his own daughter, it is possible that he did so previously."

Cadeyrn was silent.

"There is a grave," Hronwena went on. "Over at the old iron mine. An unmarked grave. It may be worth looking at." She got up then, Deilwen with her, and they left the room. Pasgen was loitering eagerly in the corridor. As they left, Cadeyrn called him in. Hronwena shut the door behind him. The siblings had much lost time to catch up on.

# Horsa

Horsa could just make out the grey hump of Din Eidyn on the southern bank as they entered the firth. The waters were wide and thick forests grew on the northern bank. If Galana slipped past them and made it to the trees, she would be lost to them. Gwynfor said that there was no ford until the firth narrowed much further inland. If she would try to cross then it would be on water.

"Keep an eye out for any boats putting out from the harbour over there," Horsa directed his crew.

All eyes turned to the southern bank. There was no sign of any siege underway at the fortress. No smoke, no coloured banners fluttering, nothing. Hengest and Aurelianus had been given plenty of time to make it to Din Eidyn. Perhaps Galana had surrendered the fortress to them without a fight?

"The *Raven* is hailing us, captain," said Beorn.

There were men jumping up and down on her deck and waving their hands frantically.

"They seem to be pointing at the northern shore," Horsa said. "I see nothing. You?"

Beorn shielded his eyes from the glare of the sun. "Nope. Yes! Look! Further inland! There are boats heading our way!"

"Not again," Horsa growled as he saw the little leather vessels paddling towards them. "Why are they coming at us from the north?"

"The could be attempting to reinforce the fortress," said Beorn.

"There aren't enough of them to get through us. Come up alongside the *Raven* and we'll pick them off as we did before."

The little Pictish boats swarmed towards them like angry wasps. Slingshots ricocheted off shields and arrows sang but, having learned their lesson, Horsa's men refused to engage until they were close enough.

But this time the Picts were being wary also and before they got within five spears' lengths, they turned their boats around and made back for the shore.

"Do we pursue, captain?" Beorn asked.

Horsa considered the options. Their mission was to prevent Galana from escaping Din Eidyn, not to engage the enemy on the northern bank. But what was the enemy doing on the other side of the water in the first place? Anybody with a military mind would know that Galana would want every available warrior within the fortress to repel the oncoming siege. So who were these fellows trying to cross the water?

"They must be reinforcements," he concluded aloud. "There can't be many of them - look they're jumping up and down on the shoreline. They can't get through us, but if we leave them be they may follow the firth inland and cross over where it is narrowest. We can't let them join up with Galana or it will go the harder for my brother and the rest of our men."

"Orders, captain?"

"Make landfall. Only the *Bloodkeel* and the *Raven*. Leave the *Fafnir* in the firth just in case Galana appears. Prepare for battle."

The Picts seemed to lose their nerve altogether at the prospect of two raiding ships landing only a few feet from them and took to the forests. Horsa was the first down into the shallows, his shield and blade held up to stop wood and iron from getting wet.

They dragged the ships quickly up onto the seaweed strewn mud and formed a shield wall. As one, they advance into the trees where the last of the Picts was seen to have vanished.

# Hengest

They found Din Eidyn deserted. Even the settlements at the foot of the great mound of volcanic rock upon which the fortress had been built were devoid of humanity. Livestock and stores were gone and all signs of wealth were noticeably absent.

"They must have left days ago," said Hengest.

"This has all the signs of a pre-battle retreat," said Aurelianus with a sour face. "Galana must be a hundred miles away by now."

The great gates to the fortress were barred but it took a matter of moments to force them open. Hengest had never seen one of the British hill-forts before and he was amazed at how primitive they were in comparison to the luxurious villas and palaces that the Britons in the south enjoyed. Din Eidyn was much closer to halls in his homeland; roaring hearths, vaulted ceilings and hanging banners. Although stone was the preferred building material of the Britons as opposed to wood.

This had been the home of the mighty Cunedda, that was what the Britons kept telling him. Cunedda was held in very high esteem and even Aurelianus showed a grudging respect for the man who, as far as Hengest could see, had been more Pict than Briton. But where were he and his descendants now? They had their own new lands in the west, so the Britons said, and this; their homeland and ancient fortress was left for others to hold against northern invasion.

He wondered briefly what was going on in his own homeland, across the sea. His father had died a couple of years ago, that he had learned from a Jutish trader. He wondered if his mother was still alive and he felt guilty for not knowing.

Directing the searching and securing of every building and granary in the fortress, Aurelianus sent Hengest down to the coast to secure a landing point for Horsa's fleet which, they assumed, would be somewhere in the firth awaiting orders to land.

The northern face of Din Eidyn swept down to grasslands which led to a harbour where a few rotten Pictish boats lay on the mud, green with slime.

"There they are," said Ebusa, pointing across the firth.

The *Fafnir* could be seen sitting in the middle of the water and the faint outline of two further prows could be made out on the mud on the opposite bank.

"Why has he landed two ships on the northern bank?" asked Hengest.

Nobody answered. As they watched, the Fafnir dropped oars and began to move to the northern bank to join the two landed vessels.

"Now what? He's landing his entire fleet on the wrong side?"

There was a scuffle from one of the huts that Hengest had sent his men to search. Two warriors emerged bearing a struggling native between them. He cursed and swore at them in Pictish.

"What's he saying?" Hengest asked of Ceretic.

"He says he's the harbourmaster and not to harm him because he's no man of Galana's. His family served the fortress during Cunedda's time."

"We'll not harm him," said Hengest. "Ask him where Galana went."

The man did not seem reassured by Hengest's words but did tell Ceretic what became of the False Queen.

"He says she left three days ago. Commandeered all the boats in the harbour and took all her warriors across the firth. She's rallying reinforcements in the north and will no doubt be back to lay Din Eidyn to siege."

Hengest peered across the water at the boats once more. He frowned. "What say you, Ebusa? Has my blockheaded brother decided to take on Galana without us?"

"I see no other reason why he would land his vessels on the other side," replied the Saxon.

"He wouldn't be so stupid," Hengest murmured. "Perhaps he is attacking an expeditionary force trying to cross the firth. Something has lured him over there."

He mounted his horse and, leaving his men in charge of the harbour, set off at a gallop back to Din Eidyn.

"Absolutely out of the question!" was Aurelianus's reply. "We have not secured the surrounding area yet. I can't allow the majority of my cavalry to go galloping off on some rescue mission."

The great hall was full of Britons in their armour which had been dulled by the dust and blood of the forest battle. Maps were spread out on tables and wine was being passed around to refresh dry throats.

"It is my belief," said Hengest patiently, "that my brother has engaged what he believes to be reinforcements trying to cross the firth. If Galana has massed a fresh army then it is he who needs reinforcing. I can take my cavalry along the firth to where it narrows and cross over. You have more than enough warriors to hold this fortress and we will be back within a day."

"No!" the word was a command. It echoed around the hall. "If Galana has an army in the nearby forests, she will attack soon and I will need all troops available."

"But my brother and his men could be massacred!"

"Then he should not have disobeyed his orders and tried to take on the whole of the northern tribes with a handful of boats!"

Hengest bit down on his anger. He turned on his heel and stormed from the hall. "Ready the men," he said to Ebusa and Ordlaf who jogged to keep up. "Every *turma*. Send to the harbour. We ride as soon as we are prepared."

"What about Aurelianus?" said Aesc.

"May the wyrms of the earth devour him!" Hengest spat. "I am the leader of our men, not him! And I do not leave my brother to die. Ready the horses!"

# Horsa

Horsa had sent Beorn back to call the *Fafnir* to shore as soon as he saw the Picitsh ranks massed on the rise ahead. He knew that if they made a run back to the *Bloodkeel* and the *Raven*, they would be overwhelmed and slaughtered before they reached them. The only way to survive the trap they had blundered into was to hold their ground until the men from the *Fafnir* could be brought in to reinforce them.

But the gods only know how many of the painted devils there were behind that rise.

"Form a shield wall!" he roared to his men. "As one!"

They clustered together, shields overlapping, standing shoulder to shoulder with sword blades and axe heads poking over the top. The Picts had the high ground and began whooping and howling battle cries; each of them provoking single combat by running forward with their arms spread, showing their bare tattooed chest and then running back to their ranks.

"Nobody engage!" shouted Horsa. "We fight as one. They cannot break us!"

And then it came.

He yelled for shields to be raised as arrows, slingshots and throwing javelins thundered down on them. Leather and wood was split as the shield wall was punctured in dozens of places. A few objects had sunk between the gaps and pierced mail and flesh eliciting screams from his men, but none fell from a mortal blow.

The instant they lowered their shields to peer over their rims, the Picts attacked.

"Hold steady!" commanded Horsa, "we are the rocks and they are the waves! Let them break on us!"

And break they did. It was a resounding thunder as they hurled themselves onto the shield wall, backed up by several smaller thuds as their warriors in the rear ranks caught up and added themselves to the fray.

The feet of Horsa's men were driven backwards in the earth, scoring deep as they struggled to keep their ground against the pressing force. A Pictish axe slid off the rim of Horsa's shield and clipped his helmet, making his ears ring. He thrust his sword out at the attacker and was satisfied by a warm burst of blood over his knuckles as the Pict fell back screaming.

All along the line the tale was the same. His men held firm, ducking and dodging blows, occasionally slipping a daring thrust in wherever they could. A Germanic shield wall could hold up for hours against innumerable odds, but it was no way to win a battle. To do that you had to kill the enemy and it was just a matter of time before the inevitable holes in the shield wall began to appear. When that happened it was all over for the defenders.

Horns blew and Horsa could hear the gush of relief from his men under the shields. The *Fafnir* had landed and their men were coming to join their comrades. None dared to turn their heads away from the Picts to greet their saviours but there was a general swell in the ranks as more and more men joined the shield wall, replenishing tired warriors and adding their weight to the press of men.

The Picts seemed to notice this too for their enthusiasm appeared to wane. Some even fell away from the attack and took a few paces back into their own ranks. The confidence of Horsa's men grew and he had to bellow more orders to prevent sections of the shield wall creeping forward. They were not here to conquer; their only concern was to get back to the ships.

He ordered a general retreat and the mass of men began to edge steadily backwards.

And then he saw her.

She stood on the ridge astride a black mare, her warriors clustered around her feet like children at their mother's skirts. Her face was painted with the blue swirls that highlighted her eyes making them appear dark and fierce. Her hair was bound into two mighty tendrils wound with gold wire and stiffened with lime that protruded from her scalp and cascaded down to her shoulders like the meeting of two swan heads. She wore a tunica that was cut so that her breasts were exposed. Both were painted blue. Gold armbands adorned her biceps and forearms and she held a sword high above her head while she roared guttural Pictish sounds, urging her warriors on.

Horsa did not need to be told that this was Galana; the False Queen and ruler of the northern tribes. His skin prickled like gooseflesh and as he watched her eyes scanning his warriors, he wanted to hide from them and he felt ashamed at his cowardice. He forced himself to look on her. This was a woman; a mere woman, flesh and blood, bone and sinew. If he could only reach her...

But this was a retreat. There would be no ending of the False Queen's life this day. In fact he would thank Woden if he managed to get away in one piece. The ships were just through the trees. But even if they got to them, they would have to fight a pitched battle on the mud before they could clamber aboard and row into the firth. The situation looked grim indeed.

Horns bellowed. The ground trembled. The front line of Picts was suddenly swept away in a roaring charge of cavalry. Mail, plumed helmets, flowing manes and tails danced before his eyes as several hundred mounted warriors galloped past. Picts were trampled, skewered on spears and bashed and battered by swords, axes and the bosses of shields.

Horsa's men roared in triumph as they recognised faces in the cavalry. He too began to recognise some. Was that Hengest? Ordlaf was there too, and Ebusa and even little Aesc who looked every bit the warrior now as he thrust his spear tip through the eye of a Pict and out the back of the unfortunate man's skull.

They wheeled around as one and came back for another pass but the Picts weren't hanging around to withstand a second devastating charge. They were in full retreat now, heading back into the trees.

When Horsa looked up he saw that Galana had vanished from the rise.

## Hronwena

A strange feeling of insecurity had fallen over Din Neidr since the night of Beltan. Vitalinus had been confined to his chambers with guards loyal only to Cadeyrn at his door. Hronwena had not set eyes on her husband since he had been hauled away and that suited her just fine.

The nobles who supported Cadeyrn had lent him troops to bolster his position at Din Neidr and Marchudd, clearly feeling uneasy with the change in leadership, had slunk away leaving Cadeyrn to appoint a new Captain of the Guard.

Cadeyrn himself had left Din Neidr for Londinium where, Hronwena assumed, he planned to explain the situation to his older brother. Cadeyrn may have taken command of his father's fortress, but officially Britannia Prima was still under the rule of Vitalinus.

Hronwena had no idea how their meeting would play out. She was aware that little love was lost between the two brothers. Would Cadeyrn convince Vortimer and gain his support? Or would Vortimer call him a traitor and rally to their father's aid? A war between brothers over this province was not something she desired.

As for Enys, Cadeyrn had accompanied her back to Deilwen's childhood home where she was reunited with her son and Cadeyrn was introduced to his nephew. There they remained and other than Deilwen and Hronwena, Cadeyrn was the only person who knew of their location. They would be well provided for and would be safe until the fate of Vitalinus was decided.

Hronwena gritted her teeth and felt her skin crawl when she thought of him. What he had done to his own family made her sick. He would pay, that she would make sure of personally. No matter what the outcome of his sons' meeting was, she would ensure that he would suffer dearly for his crimes. And there, in the dimness of her chamber with the fading light of the afternoon painting the floor through her window, she swore to Frige that one day, when the time was right, she would kill him.

*But not yet.*

She could wait.

# Vortimer

Vortimer held the ring between shaking fingers, his eyes welling up with tears as he gazed upon its tarnished surface. It was gold with a carnelian stone in its clasp. The image of a horse had been etched into the red gem. It was a ring he had never expected to see again.

"I found it in her grave," said Cadeyrn.

"Then there is no doubt that it is she," Vortimer replied. "I gave it to her on her twelfth birthday. I was eleven."

It had not been a very expensive ring but it had been a token of a brother's love for his sister. Senovara had died the following year, or so he had been told, and he had grieved then for he had lost something in her death; something that had never been replaced.

Then his mother had died and he found himself an older brother to a squalling baby whom he had hated from the very first time he had set eyes upon him. Because that baby had killed his mother when he had needed her the most.

He looked up at the man that squalling baby had grown into and tried to see if there was any way he could forgive him, any way he could forgive himself. "Was there a child found with her?"

"No," Cadeyrn replied. "The grave contained only the remains of one."

Vortimer wondered if Cadeyrn fully understood the implications these revelations held for him. In all probability, Senovara had been Cadeyrn's mother and the little brother Vortimer had always despised was in fact his nephew and brother rolled into one.

Had his father murdered his mother? It was an awful question and one that he was not sure he wanted to know the answer to. But it was a question that had to be asked in light of all else that had been revealed to him. His father's obsession with siring heirs that were pure and untainted could very well have taken on these monstrous proportions. He had done the same with Enys; that sweet little sister of his that he had only met a handful of times over the years. Perhaps it was not inconceivable that he had done the same to Senovara.

He had tried to put it all down as lies on the part of his Saxon stepmother, but deep down he knew that there was too much here for it all to be the result of a barbarian slut's lies. Cadeyrn had found Senovara's grave on her instructions. He had spoken to Enys and had seen little Britu; the boy; his brother... his *nephew*. And in spite of all the hatred he had felt for Cadeyrn over the years, he trusted him now.

He rose slowly and walked around the table. He opened his arms. Cadeyrn seemed awkwardly reluctant at first, and then, for perhaps the first time in their lives, the two brothers embraced.

"I have wasted so much time... so much hatred," said Vortimer through clenched teeth. "Forgive me."

"There is nothing to forgive, brother," Cadeyrn replied. "We have both been wronged by our father. Now, will you be my ally in stripping him of his power? His reign of terror has cursed this island for long enough."

"With all my heart, yes," Vortimer replied. "There have been forces plotting against him for longer than you realise. The rulers of the other provinces are with us. They wait only for my word."

"I want you to know that I have no intention of threatening your power," said Cadeyrn. "Any noble with any sense on this island wants you to be head of the Council here in Londinium. I only wish to govern father's territories in the west. I know the land and its nobles and can rule it justly under you."

"That is good. I shall need all the loyal support I can get if we are to oust father and the Saxons."

"The Saxons? Have they not been put to good use fighting the Picts?"

"As long as they are kept occupied, they are not a problem. But what will happen when the war in the north is won and Aurelianus brings those pagan wolves back to our lands? There will only be trouble. We must rid ourselves of them before they bite the hand that feeds."

"I don't see how we can do so without bringing more war upon ourselves."

"We must prove ourselves stronger than they are. Lords Marcellinus and Elafius agree with me that the best course of action is to write to Aetius of Gaul. If he can be brought here with just one of his legions, then we shall be strong enough to oust them forever."

"But what of Aurelianus? What of our plans when he returns? That man will follow none but father."

"Yes, Aurelianus is the only fly in our ointment. I believe that he would stand against even Aetius if father told him to."

"Then we must keep the two of them from meeting. At least for the time being. He must not find out that father no longer heads the Council. I will stop any correspondence between them."

"Not good enough. Aurelianus will tear Britannia apart when he finds out that we have overthrown his master and then it will be civil war. Unless..." Vortimer suddenly remembered something; an important piece of information that he had dismissed as idle gossip when it had been brought to his ears. He smiled. "Cadeyrn, I do believe that I have the perfect lever to turn that stone-headed ox against the Saxons regardless of father's treaty with them."

# Aesc

Aesc had slept well. In fact he had enjoyed peaceful, dreamless sleep for the past four nights. He was no longer tormented by nightmares of blood and the heaviness of corpses. He wasn't even sure how many men he had killed that day and that was strange to him. He had always imagined that he would keep a record; each life a notch on his spear like some of the older warriors did. But in the confusing, dream-like state of battle, he didn't know how anybody could keep count. He had killed many, that was what was important; that and that their deaths did not plague him.

Four days after the rescue of Horsa on the northern bank, everybody had gathered in the great hall of Din Eidyn to witness the coronation of Talorc. The Pict was dressed in his finest cloak and tunic with his scale armour gleaming from meticulous cleaning and polishing. He stood on a rectangular shield which was carried by six of his highest warriors around the hall three times.

Aurelianus stood rigid, his face unreadable, as he politely tolerated these local customs. He had not roared at them for disobeying his orders as Aesc had expected him to do on their return. Not that he particularly cared what Aurelianus thought of them. They were his allies, not his troops to command as his father had pointed out several times over the past weeks.

Aesc thought that Aurelianus was secretly impressed by their daring cavalry charge into enemy territory and their rescue of several hundred warriors who would be invaluable to the army in the months to come. Galana was still alive and had untold numbers of warriors at her call. The war was not over yet.

Prince Talorc stepped up to the dais and seated himself upon the throne. The priest placed a silver diadem on his head and handed him an ancient spear with was covered in the old Celtic runes; strange, simple slashes and strokes of the knife which were totally unlike the Germanic runes. The priest continued his religious monologue; calling the Celtic gods to witness the making of a king.

Aesc watched his father. He could see the envy in his eyes. He had seen several kings rise and fall now and Aesc had thrilled to the stories he had told of King Hnaef of the West Danes and King Finn of Frisia. He knew that his father wanted to rule his lands as a king not simply as a foreign warlord.

As they watched Prince Talorc become King Talorc he wondered if perhaps one day, he might see his father go through a similar ceremony and emerge as King of Cantium, to have his name remembered in legends and poems down the ages for all time.

# Galana

In a forest many miles north of Din Eidyn a very different religious ceremony was taking place. The stones that stood in the clearing had stood there since before the Celtic peoples came to Britain. Raised by a people long since vanished, the Picts had claimed the standing stones as their own and left their own markings on them in the form of snakes, sun-discs, Z-rods and wheels, etched into the moss-covered rock for all time.

In this clearing the delegations of many tribes had gathered, their designation and totem animals marked on their bodies in blue; the ravens, the wolves, the lynxes, the seals and the bears and many more, one time enemies but all united now in a common cause. They clustered in a circle around the centre stone.

By this stone stood Galana ferch Drest; High-Queen of the Pictish confederation. Her priests stood by her side, pounding their staves into the earth for silence. The Queen was about to speak. She raised her arms and gazed up at the night sky where the spirits of the heroes lay forever remembered in the shimmering constellations.

She called on the Mother Goddess to witness this night; a night that had happened once before, several generations ago when Gartnait; the first High King of the Picts had sacrificed to the Great Mother before launching his master plan, the Barbarian Conspiracy, which had brought the hated Britons and their Roman masters to their knees. This night was one such as that, when the heroes gazed down from the Otherworld to witness the beginning of the end for the Britons.

The prisoners were brought forward. There were three of them; two Picts and a Saxon captured in the recent battle with the Queen's half-brother. Stripped naked they stumbled and fell and were dragged into the centre of the circle, wincing from the kicks of the crowd that bayed for their blood. A huge bronze cauldron was also dragged forward, water sloshing up over its rim. The three men were held up to the vessel and ropes were tied around their necks.

A priest took a man each and began to strangle him, tugging on the rope, digging deep into their straining necks. As their faces turned purple the gathering went wild. Prayers were offered up to the Great Mother.

The three prisoners began to sag but before they succumbed to sweet death they were released of their asphyxiating bonds. Water from the cauldron was splashed onto their faces to revive them. Each priest drew a dagger each and held it to the neck of their charge. Galana spoke more words and then the blades were drawn slow and deep across the throbbing jugulars eliciting three simultaneous bursts of blood which squirted out into the dark waters of the cauldron.

The prisoners gurgled and coughed as blood dribbled from their grimacing lips and ran down from their bubbling wounds to soak their bare chests. Before their faces began to pale the priests thrust their heads forward, down into the water. They were too weak to fight and, with their life-blood floating away from them in crimson tendrils, they began to drown.

This was the triple sacrifice; the highest honour that could be paid to the Great Mother. There was no more shouting. All in the glade were silent as the final struggles of the three men subsided. The priests released them and their bodies hung limp, their heads bobbing.

Galana cried out in the stillness for victory in the battle to come. The Great Mother heard! They were all sure of it! She would bless them with victory over the enemies in the south, and then, when the lands up to the wall were theirs, they would march onwards until all of Albion lay in smouldering ruins!

And in the night sky, the heroes of ages past watched, silent, as fate continued to be written on the land below, a land that never really changed, only bearing witness to various people coming and going and passing into legend, to join the ones who came before where they would dwell in the stars forever.

# AUTHOR'S NOTE

A figure of particular interest in this period, as much as Hengest and Horsa and even King Arthur, is Vortigern. Even his name is a matter of debate with sources using spellings as varied as 'Gwrtheyrn', 'Wyrtgeorn' and 'Guothergirn'. We do not even know if this was a personal name or a title but Vortigern seems to have been a figure of considerable power in fifth century Britain.

Gildas wrote his scathing *On the Ruin and Conquest of Britain* sometime in the sixth century and mentions an 'unlucky usurper' who was apparently part of some sort of council that invited a group of Saxons to the eastern shores of Britain.

Bede, writing in the eighth century, gives the name of this man as Vertigernus. It was also Bede who first named the leaders of the Saxons as 'Hengist and Horsa'. As the king of the British people, Vertigernus invites the Saxons to settle in Britain. A condition of this was presumably engagement with the enemy who were "come from the north to give battle" and are later revealed to be the Picts.

This story is elaborated by the Bangor-born monk Nennius in his *History of the British People* written sometime in the ninth century. A mixture of chronicles and colourful local legends, this work is to be treated with caution but it does present a fascinating story.

Receiving Hengist and Horsa as friends, Vortigern (named here as Guorthigirn) hands over the isle of

Thanet in exchange for their service as *foderati* (mercenaries) against the Picts. Hengist later sends for more of his countrymen who bring with them his beautiful daughter. A feast is held and Vortigern, plied with drink, falls so in love with Hengest's daughter that he demands her in exchange for the whole of Kent. This is without the knowledge of Kent's king; Guoyrancgonus (Gwrangon).

The name of Hengest's daughter is never mentioned but Geoffrey of Monmouth's largely fictional twelfth century epic; *The History of the Kings of Britain* presents several possibilities ranging from Ronwen to Renwein to Rowena.

Hengist then sends for his son and brother. Octa and Ebusa arrive with forty ships to wage war on the Picts. It is not explicitly stated that Octa and Ebusa are Hengist's son and brother respectively, but towards the end of the narrative, Nennius mentions that Octa succeeded his father as ruler of Kent. The *Anglo-Saxon Chronicle* fails to mention Octa and instead names the son of Hengist 'Oisc'. Bede further adds to the confusion by variously calling Hengist's son 'Oisc', 'Aesc' and 'Esc' and claims that he was the *father* of Octa! Whatever the real name of Hengist's son, the founding dynasty of Kent has always been known as the 'Oiscingas/Aescingas'.

So who was Vortigern really? Nennius's 'king of the British people' is unlikely as Britain was in the throes of chaos after Rome's withdrawal and the idea of a single king ruling the entire island is implausible. Gildas's mentioning of a council is perhaps more probable and something aping the old Roman administrative system is easy to imagine with governors and tribunes devolving over time, back into chieftains and minor kings.

It is possible that Vortigern is a title rather than a personal name as a literal translation from the Brittonic word appears as 'overlord' or 'high king' ('wor' = over and 'tigerno' = chief, lord or king). But many scholars insist that this doesn't prove anything as 'tigerno' appears in lots of personal names like 'Catigern' and 'Kentigern'

Vortigern's family is outlined by Nennius who states that he had four sons; Vortimer, Catigern, Pascent and Britu (son of his incestuous affair with his unnamed daughter). More information might be gleaned from the Pillar of Eliseg; a ninth century monument erected in Denbighshire, Wales by Cyngen ap Cadell (king of Powys).

The Latin text on the Pillar of Eliseg is now illegible due to weathering, but a transcription was made by the antiquarian Edward Llwyd in 1696. It claims that Guarthi(gern)/Vortigern was married to Severa, the daughter of Magnus Maximus; the usurper who rebelled against Emperor Gratian. The pillar names the sons of this union as; Britu and Pascen(t), the latter of which is the ancestor of the kings of Powys.

If Vortigern really did marry Severa, daughter of Magnus Maximus, it would most likely have been before 388, which was when Maximus was defeated and executed (politically speaking, a marriage after this date would have been worthless). Aside from the bride's age (Severa could not have been younger than seventy by

347

447) this would make the Guarthi(gern) of the pillar too old to be the Vortigern mentioned by Bede and Nennius.

Unless, it referred to his father.

If Vortigern was indeed a title, it may have passed from father to son, making the Vortigern of later texts the son of the union between Guarthi(gern) and Severa.

So what then, was Vortigern's real name? *The History of the Britons* gives Vortigern's genealogy and his grandfather and great grandfather were called Guitaul (Vital) and Guitolion (Vitalin) respectively. This hints at a common family name that may have been something like 'Vitalinus' or 'Vitalis'. Interestingly, Nennius goes on to say that during the reign of Vortigern, there was a battle between Ambrosius and Guitolinus (Vitalinus). Another person, or the given name for Britain's 'overlord'?

We don't know what the battle was about or who won, but Ambrosius is a name well attested elsewhere. Gildas first mentions an Ambrosius Aurelianus who "perhaps alone of the Romans, had survived the shock of this notable storm. Certainly his parents, who had worn the purple, were slain by it."

'Wearing the purple' could refer to the imperial colour, or perhaps the purple band worn by Roman military tribunes, so it seems that we are dealing with a noble of imperial stock or a high-ranking military commander. Gildas makes it clear that he was some sort of military figure to which the Britons flocked. His wars with the Saxons ultimately culminated in the siege of Badon Hill. Later sources like the *History of the Britons* credit 'Arthur' as the victor of this battle, not

Aurelianus. Nevertheless, Ambrosius, whoever he was, is clearly an important figure in the tale of Hengest and Horsa and more will be told of him in the next novel.

The rune poems that accompany each segment of this novel are from a 10th century manuscript from the Cotton library which, unfortunately, was destroyed in a fire in 1731. Luckily, the scholar George Hicks published a facsimile in 1705 and the particular translation I used is from the *Runic and heroic poems of the old Teutonic peoples* (1915, pp. 12-23) by Bruce Dickens.

# A CING'S LEÇACI

## CHRIS
## THORNDYCROFT

*"At length Vortimer, the son of Vortigern, valiantly fought against Hengist, Horsa, and his people; drove them to the isle of Thanet, and thrice enclosed them within it, and beset them on the Western side."* – The History of the Britons, Nennius

# PART I

*(Peorð) "Peorð biþ symble plega and hleahtor, wlancum þar wigan sittaþ on béorsele blíþe ætsamne."*

(Chessman) The chessman is a source of recreation and amusement to the great, where warriors sit blithely together in the banqueting-hall.

North East Britain, Late Summer, 447 A.D.

# Horsa

The grey skies were frozen over the calm sea. No wind scattered them nor drove the breakers to white foam. Summer was ending and the land seemed quietly afraid of the onset of winter when gales and thundering surf would break upon its shores once more.

Time was running out.

Along the beach rode a lone horseman, his fur-trimmed cloak billowing out behind him. His beard was tawny and his hair was long. He carried a spear but wore no sword at his belt, only the long-bladed saex, suggesting that he was no nobleman but a common fighter in the service of a Germanic war band.

Three heads poked up from the seaweed-strewn rocks and startled the rider, causing him to reign in his mount and wheel around, gripping his spear in fear of an ambush.

The three men wore similar attire and all carried spears. "What do you here, warrior?" called out one of them. "I can see that you are no Pict, but what are you? A deserter?"

"I seek the camp of Horsa," said the mounted man. "I carry a message to him from his brother."

"Are we to move inland? Is the final battle at hand?" asked one of the other men eagerly. "I am not the only one in Horsa's camp who is pig sick of this campaign. There isn't a Pictish settlement left that does not lie in smouldering ruins and there is little food to be found elsewhere."

"Hold your whining!" said the leader of the group. "You, messenger, does Hengest call for us? Why did not Aurelianus send one of his own men? Is it not he who leads the army?"

"Would you or anyone else in Horsa's camp trust one sent by that British dog?" asked the messenger. "I come directly from Hengest and my message is for his brother alone."

This seemed good enough for the three warriors and they beckoned the rider to follow them. He dismounted and led his horse by the bridle as they headed towards camp

The smell of that morning's breakfast of roasted herring still hung in the blue smoke over the camp. The waves gently rolled in between the hulks of the beached vessels, nearly reaching the sealskin tents that had been pitched in small clusters around many hearths.

Horsa took the gold scabbard mounting from the messenger and studied it. He recognized it from his brother's scabbard which he had had made for his mighty sword Hildeleoma. There was no doubt that the messenger was genuine.

"And my brother says that they have Galana pinned?" Horsa asked him.

"They await only your coming from the east to crush her army once and for all."

Horsa leaned back in his throne of sealskins and wolf furs and closed his eyes. Finally. He had hated every bit of this campaign. All season he had led his ships up and down the western coast of Pictland, even up to the far north where it broke up into dozens of islands.

Their mission had been to harry the coastal settlements and prevent them from sending troops to the aid of the Pictish queen Galana whose brother – and rival for her throne – was allied to the Britons.

Horsa's men were born raiders and were as suited to the task as fish were to swimming. The stench of burning homesteads hadn't cleared from his nostrils for months. When he tried to sleep his ears rang with the sounds of slaughter, the death cries of warriors, the screaming of butchered families and the wailing of newly made widows and orphans. There had been no honour in this.

While his brother had engaged Galana in open battles, Horsa had been left with the pitiful homesteads and frightened families most of whose men folk had already left. Still, he had done his job. But with every roundhouse burned he felt himself slipping further and further from who he was, further and further… from Aureliana.

He drank heavily most nights, but the more he drank the more he thought of her and the deeper his shame became. She was his hope for a future without bloodshed and the sound of weeping women. She was his white light in a world of black, acrid smoke. And the longer the campaign drew on, the dimmer that light seemed to him. He was terrified that her light might wink out altogether and he would be left in this cold, bleak north to die without ever feeling her soft, pale arms around him again.

But now, now, the end was in sight. This messenger brought with him the news that he had dared to hope for all season. The final battle was drawing close. If they could only smash Galana and her forces once and for all, they could all go home.

"Strike camp," he said, rising. "Beorn, pick out a guard party to hold the ships. You know who to choose."

"Yes, captain," the massive, bald Angle replied, and he strode off to handpick his men.

"We take only weapons, no camp equipment or supplies."

"Is that wise, captain," asked Aelfhere, the captain of the Raven. "No supplies? It may be a long march inland."

"Then we march on empty bellies," Horsa replied. "Hunger for slaughter is the only hunger we shall feel. We march fast and hard and we do not stop until we have crushed our enemy and are free from this gods-cursed war!"

# Hengest

"You have no authority over my men!" Hengest roared.

The tent was crowded and he felt outnumbered by the British officers who had assembled before Aurelianus to see justice done to two of Hengest's warriors. They had been accused of looting. Not a crime during war, Hengest felt, but as usual it seemed that the British portion of the army was intent on making things as hard as possible for the Germanic auxiliary troops.

Hengest's two men stood by with their hands bound and their faces creased with incomprehension. Poor, silly bastards, Hengest thought. They don't even know what's going on.

"Looting may well be an integral part of your culture, Sais," said Aurelianus in a withering tone, "and I dread to think what your brother gets up to in the coastal settlements, but men under my standard do not act like common brigands. These men are to be punished, yours or not."

"That fortress belonged to Galana!" Hengest protested. "It held out against us for three days and took the lives of many of our men during the siege. We, who shed blood for it, have a right to its spoils, do we not?"

"All spoils are to be divided up by myself and my officers. Your men will get their share. We cannot set our soldiers loose upon civilians like scavenging wolves. Those days are over. We are a Christian army in a

Christian land. We do not loot and pillage our brother man."

"And King Talorc's men? My men were not the only ones looting in the aftermath of that battle."

"King Talorc's warriors are allies, not auxiliary troops under my standard. We are here to help him win back his territory. If he wishes to pillage his own people, that is his business."

"You have your customs, Briton, we have ours," replied Hengest.

"But while you march with me, you and your men will adhere to my law."

"Well at least give these men over to me so that I may punish them."

"And have you treat them as leniently as you please, or worse; set them free? No. They must be made an example of. The army must know that there is just one man who is the supreme authority and that insubordination will be punished ruthlessly."

Hengest ground his teeth but he knew he was beaten. The two prisoners were as good as dead and there was nothing he could do. He would like to storm the tent with Aesc, Ordlaf, Ebusa and all the others, kill Aurelianus and release his men, but that would be an unwinnable battle. Without saying another word, he turned and strode out of the tent, ignoring the pathetic gazes of his two doomed men.

"What happened, father?" asked Aesc, who had been waiting outside.

"He refuses to listen to reason," Hengest replied. "I tried."

"And our two warriors?"

"They are to die, most likely."

"But that's not fair!"

"I know it isn't, son. But Aurelianus leads this army. His word is law. For the time being."

The two men were hanged the following morning before the sun was fully up. Most of Hengest's men were still sleeping when it happened. It was clear that Aurelianus had hoped to avoid any kind of disturbance by carrying out the executions before the comrades of the condemned knew what was happening.

There was an uproar when Hengest's men awoke to find the two lifeless corpses dangling from the branch of an oak tree, their faces black and their tongues swollen.

The incident had put the auxiliary troops in a black mood. They didn't like the Britons and liked seeing two of their number executed by them less still. Hengest felt like he had lost a good deal of their respect. They looked to him to protect them and to lead them onwards, but how could they have confidence in him if he couldn't prevent the Britons from stringing them up over something as trivial as looting? The atmosphere was dangerous. If his troops decided to take justice into their own hands, he did not feel confident that he could control them.

"That our men have not already run riot and started stringing up Britons left, right and centre," said Ebusa, "is a testament to their faith in you as a leader. Let them seethe. They still follow only you."

"Thank Woden this war is nearly over," was all Hengest could say.

They nearly had Galana beat. All season they had engaged in small skirmishes with the Picts. Those blue-painted men of the north were the masters of ambush and their hit and run tactics had devastated Aurelianus's lines of supply, but so far they had avoided open battle with the Britons. With Horsa and his raiders hammering the east coast and putting a stranglehold on supplies and reinforcements, Galana had become more and more reckless. Her warriors were hungry, outnumbered and desperate. They only had to force them into a pitched battle to smash them.

Now the chance had come. There was a valley two days march to the north where, Aurelianus's spies confirmed, Galana had set up camp. It was thickly forested on the northern side and would be hard for a large force to retreat through with any haste. The False Queen had got herself snared in a trap. A messenger had been sent to Horsa to call his raiders to the battle. With them approaching from the east and the Britons marching from the south, Galana would be caught between hammer and anvil. The valley would become a killing ground.

Perhaps that was the real reason his men had not mutinied, Hengest thought. They knew the end was in sight and looked forward to returning to their homes just as he did. One final battle by Aurelianus's side and then they were done as his mercenaries. He only hoped the treaty between Briton and Saxon could hold out just a little longer. It wasn't for his own benefit, but in the lands to the south west, his daughter was wife to the most powerful of all British rulers.

# Hronwena

Hronwena watched the returning troops from a high window in Din Neidr. Cadeyrn was at their head. Their banners were torn and frayed, their armour dented and blood-spattered. Defeat was written all over their faces.

At table that night, her husband, Vitalinus, made much mockery of his son's efforts. Despite having been stripped of his power by Cadeyrn, Vitalinus was allowed to attend meals in the great hall.

"Even when I was a young man watching my father forge this island into some sort of unity, I never lost to a petty chieftain," he sneered. "And a Gael at that!"

Cadeyrn's teeth clenched on a mouthful of bread. "Benlli is more than a petty chieftain," he said. "His strength has increased bit by bit over the years. Had you quashed him when he first rose, perhaps I would not be fighting him now. And as for the Gaels, you yourself have never fought them. You would rather employ others to fight your battles for you. Like Cunedda. Like Hengest." He glanced quickly at Hronwena.

"I have managed to keep the peace with Benlli since before you were born," said Vitalinus."Now his riders plunder our borders and steal our cattle. Perhaps your coup over me is not as popular as you had hoped."

"It is popular with all but Benlli," Cadeyrn replied coldly. "All the other lords have joined me in the fight against the Gael."

"And yet he defies you all. His territory has grown to include Cair Guricon, a town which he never would have dared attack whilst I ruled Britannia Prima."

"Perhaps Benlli is frightened of these rumours concerning Cadell for he knows that should the old heir to Din Bengron resurface, I would support his claim."

"An imposter. A rural rabble-rouser."

"Many of the commoners believe in him and support him."

"The old family who ruled Din Bengron died by the sword when Benlli arrived here from Hibernia a generation ago. Once you have defeated Benlli – if you can defeat him - you must deal with this upstart also. And I must sit by whilst you lose every scrap of land I and my father fought so hard for."

"You have no choice!" Cadeyrn snapped. "You think you can worm your way back into power but you will never rule Britannia Prima again! The people praise my name in the hills and herald the end of tyranny. Together with Vortimer, we shall re-forge Albion into a stronger, healthier land."

Vitalinus let out a short bark of laughter. "My two noble sons, what idealists! Every generation it is the same story; bring Albion back into the light, bring back the old days of peace. Why not even bring back the Romans? But what you do not understand is that the Romans were our enemies, boy. Oh, they ruled us for centuries and left their mark on this island in more ways than one, but now that they are gone we can truly start to be Britons again. And any utopian vision of the future you and your foolish brother have will forever be eclipsed by the days that saw me hold all of Albion in the palm of my hand. Whatever you two conspiring traitors do, people will look back to the days of Vertigernus and mourn his defeat by his wretched offspring!"

Cadeyrn drank down the last of his wine as if to quench his anger and slammed his goblet down hard. "Guards! Escort my father to his chambers. I cannot stomach his miserable face over the dinner table. It spoils my appetite."

Hronwena was relieved to see the back of her husband. If she had her way, he would be locked up in the fortress cells, not taking his meals in the great hall or enjoying the luxury of his chamber one door down from her own. It repulsed her to think of him sleeping on the other side of the stone wall, knowing what he was, what he had done to his own family.

She regularly visited Enys and her son Britu in Deilwen's family home in the forest. She brought them food and occasionally coin to ensure that they had all they needed. All she could do was wait until Cadeyrn and his brother Vortimer had decided what to do with their father. Cadeyrn ruled the province of Britannia Prima now and had the backing of the nobility. If it wasn't for the chieftain Benlli – who had sided with Vitalinus – things might move ahead quicker.

There was also the matter of the war in the north which her father and brother were busy fighting with Ambrosius Aurelianus. She knew that Cadeyrn and his brother anxiously awaited the return of the army for they did not know if the mighty Aurelianus would side with them or their father. Civil war hung like a thundercloud over Britta and Hronwena had even heard Cadeyrn talk of sending to Gaul for Roman intervention.

She cared little for the fate of Britta. All she wanted was to sunder her marriage to Vitalinus and return to her family in the east. But it would do no good to simply flee. She wanted to get some sort of legal annulment of her marriage. She had heard that priests could do that. And until Cadeyrn had full control of his province and he and Vortimer had decided what to do about Aurelianus and their contacts in Gaul, Vitalinus's fate could not be decided and she must remain his wife.

Printed in Great Britain
by Amazon